High Ground

FREYA BARKER

High Ground

ISBN: 9781988733760

Cover Design: Freya Barker
Editing: Karen Hrdlicka
Proofing: Joanne Thompson
Cover Image: Jean Woodfin—JW Photography
Cover Model: Alfie Gordillo

Not much has gone according to plan for mechanic, Pippa Freling, recently. With lots of bridges burned behind her, she decides to stick close to her sister and give Montana a try.

Things are looking up when she joins a local group of animal activists, buys an auto shop for a steal, and even tries her luck with the opposite sex. But it doesn't take long before her hopeful new future is derailed once again.

This time permanently.

Maintaining tight control is the stronghold in Sully Eckhart's life. It served him well during his years in special forces and has kept him out of trouble since. But his self-restraint stretches only so far whenever he finds himself faced with the one woman who has the ability to shake his determination. A woman he's tried to avoid for months—since the first time she shook his resolve—but who now finds herself in the middle of a serial murder case.

However, when she not only ends up a person of interest to the FBI, but firmly in the crosshairs of a killer, he has no other option but to stick close.

And give up all control.

One

"I've got something."

I circle the drone around, dipping a little lower to get a better view.

The red ball cap caught my eye on the first flyover. I can't recall one mentioned in the description of missing hunter, John Harper, but that doesn't necessarily mean anything. The bright splash of color in the rock gully below is definitely out of place and warrants closer investigation.

"Where?"

Jonas leans over my shoulder to see the small screen on the drone's controller.

"Give me a sec, I'm about to swing back over the spot. It'll be the left side of the screen, on the rocks, at the edge of the creek."

I maneuver the drone lower between the trees.

"There he is. Fuck," Jonas mumbles.

Now I can make out the figure of a man in hunting

camo, facedown in the water maybe six feet from where I spotted the ball cap.

Looks like it's going to be a recovery instead of a rescue.

The missing man has family back in Wyoming. He's here a few days before the opening of the bear season, in April every year, to get camp ready before his buddies show up. When they arrived two days ago, they found his belongings at camp but Harper was missing.

The start of the spring hunt is always chaotic so the game warden, with his hands full, bounced the call to the sheriff, who contacted us this morning.

High Mountain Trackers—our search and rescue team —often gets called in for missing individuals and we frequently work together with law enforcement. We search on horseback, which is a bonus in these mountains and often hard-to-access terrain. A bit old-style, but we also utilize technology in the form of the Matrice, my drone. Well, not mine technically, but I operate it. It's a great tool to get the lay of the land before we go in with the horses.

Sometimes we get lucky—like today—and find what we're looking for on the drone's video feed.

"Even if we could get a chopper out here, there's no way they'd be able to get him out. Good thing we brought Hazel," Jonas observes.

Hazel is our new mule. She came to us through Hart Horse Rescue, which belongs to my boss Jonas's spouse, Alexandra Hart. The team's mounts are all sturdy quarter drafts, which can handle a bit, but adding an extra body to their load when they already have to carry us through often rough terrain is asking a lot.

The mule comes in handy, and even though she's ornery and doesn't particularly like people, she gets along well with the horses and she doesn't spook. Perfect for transport. The modified saddle Jonas picked up has a fully adjustable back-rest and straps to secure an injured or unconscious individual. Previously we'd have to double up on one of the horses, often slowing us down and sometimes causing more injury.

"I'll catch up with you," I tell the guys.

I still have to bring the drone back and pack it up, which won't take me long but it doesn't make sense for the others to wait. My horse, Cisko, won't have any trouble catching up to Jonas and Bo.

There's only three of us today. My other teammates, James and Fletch, left for Helena this morning with one of our prize studs, Phantom. Aside from High Mountain Trackers, Jonas also owns High Meadow Ranch. It's a fairly small stud and breeding facility where we all work when we're not out on a search.

Up until recently, Fletch and I were neighbors in staff cabins on the ranch, but last fall Fletch bought a neighboring property where he lives with his new wife, Nella. Bo has always lived in Libby, twenty minutes up the highway, and James and his family live just south of here.

I like my cabin so I don't plan on going anywhere. I've got no family of my own, am close to work, and like the convenience of having my meals cooked for me by either Ama—James's wife—or Alex. I occasionally enjoy shooting the shit with Jonas's dad, Thomas, over a glass of good bourbon and a rare Cuban cigar on the porch, and other than that, I don't need much.

Sure-footed Cisko closes the distance to the others before they reach the bottom of the gully. Bo dismounts first and crouches down beside Harper, who is partially submersed.

He reaches out to feel for a pulse but immediately veers back. "What the fuck?"

"What's wrong?" Jonas voices.

"If that's Harper, I'll fucking eat my hat," Bo announces. "Whoever that is has been gone a while longer."

Both Jonas and I get down for a better look.

Now I can see he's definitely been here for some time. From what is left of his head, this guy looks to have cropped gray hair, whereas Harper's was supposed to be dark.

"Doesn't look like he tripped and fell," I point out.

I can't tell for sure, but it looks to me like he was shot. A high-velocity rifle bullet to the back of the head would leave that kind of damage. Doesn't exactly appear accidental either. More like an execution.

"No, it doesn't," Jonas agrees. "Hands off, Bo. We're gonna have to get the sheriff in here."

He gets on the radio right away and relays the information to Ama back at the ranch, who promises to get Sheriff Ewing on the horn.

"I spotted a clear-cut not far south of here," I volunteer. "There's gotta be a trail leading to it. That may be easier access for the sheriff's department. I can go check it out."

"Sounds like a plan. Whatever we can do to cut down waiting time, because we still have a missing hunter to find," Jonas points out.

Good point. This clearly isn't Harper, so he's still out here somewhere. Hopefully, merely lost and not in similar condition to this guy.

I swing back into the saddle and guide Cisko across the shallow creek and up the south end of the gully. I noticed the clearing on the other side of a ridge. We left the vehicles and trailers up where Harper and his friends usually set up base camp, which is north of here, and made our way down on horseback. It took us close to two hours to find the body, so it would be good if I could find a faster alternate route for the sheriff to take.

This side isn't as steep and it takes me less than fifteen minutes to get to the edge of the clearing.

I didn't expect to see the motorhome tucked in under the trees on the opposite side, but I'm completely thrown when a familiar figure steps out of the door.

~

Pippa

Hell, no.

Last person I want to run into up here—or anywhere else for that matter—is heading straight toward me.

"Once wasn't enough?" he says, the customary friendly expression gone from his face.

I know exactly what he's referring to.

"Are you suggesting I should let fear rule me?" I snap back.

Last year, when I first camped near Libby, I'd fallen victim to a family of thieves stealing recreational vehicles. I was hurt in the process and ended up with a brain injury and memory loss, but I survived and came out stronger. It's how I first met Sully, actually. My sister and her now husband were the ones who found me, but he's the one who transported me out of the woods on his horse. I owe them my life, Sully included, but that doesn't mean they get to rule it. I'm not about to let what happened keep me from enjoying what I love to do most; seeking out nature and solitude.

There's something about being entirely on your own and self-sufficient—a simpler way of being—which feels both empowering and humbling at the same time. My experience last year has only made that feeling stronger.

Sully swings out of the saddle and turns his body toward me.

"No, but at least be a bit more cautious. Stick closer to town, to other people."

"That would kinda defeat the purpose now, wouldn't it?"

I know I'm not being very nice, but his sudden concern for me is coming out of left field. A far cry from the cold asshole he turned out to be last time I saw him. That was a huge mistake I unfortunately can add to a long list of them and will definitely not be repeated.

"Pippa—"

"No, Sully. I'm a big girl. I don't need you—of all people—looking out for me. I'm perfectly safe here."

I watch the nostrils of his patrician nose flare as his blue eyes narrow on me. He's annoyed, which is too fucking bad.

But then he takes the wind out of my self-righteous sails.

"There's a dead man with a hole the size of a fist in the back of his head in a gully less than a mile from here. You may want to reconsider that."

My exit wasn't exactly graceful.

Never mind that I was already packing up to head back to town for an appointment, but after he dropped that bombshell, I was in a real hurry to get out of there. Especially after he mentioned law enforcement being on the way. I hustled, I'm not stupid. Aside from the fact I'm seriously freaked-out right now, I know what will happen when the sheriff arrives and I don't want to be stuck here for hours when I have somewhere to be.

Without another word for Sully, I hopped in my rig and carefully worked my way back down the logging trail.

"Hey, you're back," Marcie answers her phone.

"On my way back to town now. I just picked up a signal."

"How was it?"

"Great, I got a few good hikes in. Nothing else to report though."

The last spot I was at was a little farther up the mountain, north from here. It's where I discovered a couple of baiting barrels on one of my hikes. I immediately packed up and left that spot, calling my friend, Marcie, on my way out to alert the group. That was four days ago but I hadn't been ready to head back to civilization yet, which is why I decided to set up camp down here.

Apparently, a stone's throw from a corpse.

I don't know what it is about me that seems to be in the wrong place at the wrong time a lot. Maybe it is true that I attract trouble. It's something my ex used to say. Of course, he was more trouble than anything else.

I wasn't aware baiting for bear was a thing until I bumped into a pair of hunters in November of last year when I was boondocking on the east side of Libby, not far from the Kootenay River. They were hauling buckets of what smelled like rotting fish and bags of stinky garbage down the trail.

Marcie and I met at rehab in the hospital last fall—she'd been in a car accident—and had struck up a friendship. She's a local real estate agent, an avid outdoorswoman, and also an animal activist. Something I can identify with. When I mentioned my encounter with the hunters appearing to carry garbage into the wilderness, she explained about bear baiting, which is apparently legal in other states but not

Montana. A contentious point for many local hunters and guides.

The basic premise is they leave food in a particular spot, starting late winter. Then when the bears wake up from hibernation, half-starved, the stench of rotting food draws them to these spots. They gorge themselves and keep returning for an easy meal. At the start of hunting season, all the hunters have to do is sit in a blind and bide their time. It's like shooting fish in a barrel.

I don't care if it's legal in other states, I find the whole thing reprehensible. I'm not at all against hunting, but let it at least be equal.

Through Marcie I got involved with Fair Game Alliance, a group of passionate individuals who monitor for that kind of illegal activity. All Fair Game does is keep an eye out and when they see anything suspicious, they alert the Lincoln County game warden to intervene. Here in the Libby area, the game warden has his hands full and can't be everywhere this time of year, which is why volunteers like me keep our eyes open.

It gives me a sense of purpose. Something I'm craving after a good year of floundering.

Oh, it was fun at first, going where the wind blew me, making a bit of money here and there putting my mechanic's license to good use with some RV repair services. But I started craving steady roots and was on my way back home when I ran into trouble here in Montana last fall. Since then my sister, Nella, has moved here and is making a life for herself. Married a local guy, started baking for some local businesses, and now even has a little one on the way. She's all the family I have, and there's no way I want to go back to Canada now.

There's nothing left for me there. Any dreams I may

have had for my future have burned to the ground. The marriage, the business I built from scratch, the family we were supposed to have, those are all gone. My ex saw to that. All I ended up with was a whack of money he had to pay me to buy me out of the business that used to be mine. I bought the Jayco motorhome, stuck the rest of the money in mutual funds, and took off to find myself again.

And I did. Right here in Libby, Montana.

I'm trying to put down roots here. Last month I bought the closed-up auto repair shop on the south side of town I passed regularly. Marcie was able to get me a great deal. Unfortunately, as a Canadian, I can buy a business, but I can't actually work in it. Not without a green card or at the very least a work visa, which I already applied for, but even a visa can take months.

In the meantime I wait, I volunteer, and I try to stay out of trouble.

Which is why I need to avoid Sully Eckhart like the plague. The man is like salted caramel; one taste only makes you want more.

I should know.

Two

SULLY

Two bodies in two days.

We found John Harper this afternoon. Shot in the upper right quadrant of his back, the man had clearly not died instantly, judging by the blood trail he left behind. But he was very much dead when we located him barely half a mile west of the gully where we found the other body.

Hunting accidents happen every year, here in Montana as well. Usually during the busier fall season when the hunt opens for all game and the woods and mountains are packed, but even during the much quieter spring bear season things can go wrong.

Two possible incidents this close to each other in time and proximity is a bit much to be chalking up to coincidence.

Which is why the sheriff and game warden are pulling out all the stops to investigate both bodies. Notable is that in both cases no shooting incident was ever reported and neither victim had any weapons or identifying papers on them when we found them.

All this to imply foul play is suspected.

"Carl has his hands full," Bo comments as we watch them load Harper's body in the back of the van.

Carl Pearson is not only the Lincoln County coroner, but also funeral director at Pearson Funeral Home in Libby.

He's not kidding. For a small town and rather thinly populated county of only about twenty thousand, we've seen our share of death this past week. First there was last week's unexpected snowfall causing that nasty pileup out toward Troy, killing a local family of three. Now Carl has these two bodies to take care of.

"Rather him than me," I admit.

Wouldn't be my thing, carving up dead bodies. I've seen enough death and destruction to last me a lifetime or two. I know finding those poor guys yesterday and today is gonna get to me at some point. Probably during the night, while I'm sleeping and my guard is down.

"Let's head out, boys. Our job is done."

Jonas comes walking toward us. He'd been talking with Sheriff Ewing and Woody Moses—the local game warden—while Bo and I were loading up the horses and Hazel. With the body taken care of and the scene left in the hands of authorities, there is no reason for us to stick around.

I get behind the wheel of the ranch truck, a heavy-duty Ford F-350 which has served us well for as long as I can remember, but the engine has been acting up a little recently. Bo climbs in the back as Jonas gets in beside me, and immediately radios Ama to let her know we're on our way back.

The knocking sound starts up as I pass through Libby.

"We need that damn engine looked at," Jonas grumbles beside me.

"Three week waiting time with Jackson's automotive, unless you want to get it in somewhere in Kalispell," I suggest.

"Or..." Bo pipes up in the back seat. "You can ask Pippa to have a look. She got Lucy's old clunker going again. But it'll have to be off the books, she doesn't have her work visa yet."

How much of an asshole am I that part of me hopes she doesn't get it and has to head back to Canada?

A big one, I know.

"Should'a thought of that myself," Jonas mumbles. "Plenty of work on the ranch vehicles to get her started."

Shit, I know she bought Standish Automotive and hopes to breathe some life into that place once her visa comes through, and it's not that I don't wish her well, but does she have to be in my fucking backyard? It's hard enough now, trying to avoid her, but it'll be impossible once she sets up shop. I already know the guys will take their business to her and I'll just look like a fucking tool if I don't.

What a mess. One of my own creation, if I'm honest.

Granted, she seemed as into it as I was, but it definitely was me who was feeling pretty good and laid a wet one on her. It was New Year's Eve, we'd celebrated Fletch and Nella's wedding, and alcohol may have been involved. One thing led to another and when I woke up in the early hours of January first to the soft snoring of the pretty brunette, I knew I'd made a disastrous mistake.

I'd been fighting my attraction to her almost from the moment I first laid eyes on the near skeletal woman back in early fall. I'm not usually attracted to skinny women, I prefer something I can hold on to, but one look at that face with those big brown eyes and my ass was toast.

She'd been traumatized though. Gone through the wringer and then some. Huge chunks of her memory were gone and no one comes back from an experience like that unscathed. It was clear she'd need stability, which is something I don't have in me to give.

So, I decided I'd keep my distance, which worked fine, since she went off in her motorhome and I didn't see her again until right before the wedding. She'd put some weight back on, looked fucking fantastic, and I felt even more drawn to her. Then I let it get away from me.

For a handful of hours, I lost my head and indulged in something I knew I should've steered clear of. Not only for her sake, but my own too. So, when she caught me sneaking out the door at three in the morning, I was on the defensive and acted like an ass.

In hindsight, that worked for me, since Pippa seemed as eager to avoid me as the other way around, but it makes any run-ins with her uncomfortable. Like yesterday. I couldn't stop myself from feeling instantly protective of her.

Fuck, if she's going to be working on the ranch's fleet, I'll be seeing a lot more of her.

I'm going to need to steel myself.

Pippa

"This is a fucking joke, right?"

My heart is beating in my throat as I feel the blood drain from my face.

This was supposed to be a simple six-month follow-up appointment with Dr. Osborne. I wasn't expecting to get this news.

"Sorry, no. Not a joke. I can refer you to an—"

I cut him off when I lift my hands, palms out, silently imploring him to stop. I can't hear this now.

I need to get out of here for some fresh air and time to process.

"Call me when you're ready to talk," he calls after me as I dart out of his office.

An older couple jumps back when I come barreling out of the clinic, almost knocking them over, and tears blind me as I try to locate my wheels in the parking lot.

"Hey, are you okay?"

I wave off the Good Samaritan calling after me and scramble up in the cab of the old Chevy truck I picked up last November. That was when I still thought I could build a new life here. Now I don't know what kind of life is even possible.

This is a fucking nightmare.

My instinct is to go seek out my sister but I don't want to upset her, she's seven and a half months pregnant.

I mop my face with my sleeve before starting the truck. Then I head for Hart's Horse Rescue where I've been renting a room from Lucy Lenoir.

"Christ. I hope to hell it's not contagious," she comments dryly twenty minutes later, after I spilled my guts to her.

We're sitting at the kitchen table at the rescue, Lucy's dogs, Chief and Scout, at our feet. I'm sipping a glass of water because I'm too nauseated to dare attempt anything else.

"Pregnancy doesn't spread, to my knowledge."

She leans forward on her elbows, regarding me closely.

"Didn't even know you were seeing someone," she points out.

Shit.

I guess I shouldn't be surprised paternity is a question that would come up, but there is no way in hell I'm ready to share that. I may know there is only one possible answer, but no one else needs to. That's information I'd prefer to keep to myself, at least until I can wrap my head around getting knocked up.

"I'm not."

Lucy starts to chuckle. "You saw someone at some point, that's for sure."

New Year's Eve to be exact, but I keep that to myself as well.

"You didn't miss a period or anything?" she continues.

"Haven't had one since September. I was told it's not unusual to skip your periods for months at a time as a result of starvation. I never considered it. I mean, I put on weight, but I figured I was just gaining it back."

I'd lost a fair amount of weight after I went missing last fall, and it took me a while before I was able to eat a regular meal again. I ended up with ulcers that still give me trouble occasionally, so getting back anywhere near my original weight is taking time.

In fact, even now I'm still about fifteen pounds from where I'm supposed to be.

I catch Lucy's eyes as they drift down to my stomach where, at some point, my hands seem to have come to rest. Nothing more than a little swell, I easily overlooked before, feels like a substantial bump in my palms now.

A baby.

Oh boy, I can't do this right now.

Abruptly I get to my feet.

"Keep it to yourself," I snap unreasonably.

"I realize you haven't known me that long, but talking is really not my thing."

She gets up as well and I instantly feel bad.

"I'm sorry."

Lucy beams a bright smile my way.

"Oh, honey. Don't apologize. If the roles were reversed, I'd be throwing china at the walls."

Then she walks out of the kitchen and I'm contemplating grabbing a couple of plates, when my phone rings. I startle when I recognize the ranch number. I'm tempted to ignore it but curiosity has me take the call.

"Hello?"

"Pippa, it's Jonas Harvey at High Meadow. I have a proposal for you."

～

Nothing like a little engine grease under my fingernails and a well-built, six-liter V-8, turbo-diesel engine under my hands to distract me.

"There's a few possibilities. Could be this after-market air filter, an exhaust leak, maybe a dirty injector. Could be resolved by a decent tune-up, but it's also possible the torque converter access plug got dislodged, in which case I'd have to drop the transmission to get at it. Best thing to do is get it into the shop so I can do a proper diagnostic on it."

Technically I'm not supposed to be working, but Jonas's

proposal might make it a concern that no longer applies to me. He's offered to use his connections to fast-track my visa if I would take on the ranch vehicles and equipment and keep his engines running.

It wasn't a hard decision. Jonas laughed at my hearty, "Hell, yes."

My first customer.

I force every other thought to the back of my mind and focus on that—my first customer.

"Shit, now that's sexy; a woman who knows her engines."

I hide my grin at Bo's deep baritone by ducking my head a little lower. I know what he's doing. I've seen him in action with my sister and also Alex. He's trying to get a rise out of his buddies, one of whom I've been ignoring since I got here.

"Fuck off, Rivera," I hear Sully grumble.

Yup, I called it.

Interesting thing about Bo though, he's one of those natural charmers who can't help but flirt with the ladies. The only exception is Lucy, he barely cracks a smile around her.

"All right, kids," Jonas intervenes before turning his attention on me. "When can you work on it, Pippa?"

I back out from under the hood and step down from the inverted crate I carry in the back of my pickup. At five four, it's the only way I can get to the engine.

"If you can get it to the shop, I can start on it right away."

The auto repair shop I bought comes fully equipped, but was boarded up since the Department of Homeland Security recovered explosives from the premises. The former owner—Hugh Standish—was involved with a militant group responsible for the bombings in Helena a couple of years ago. The bank eventually foreclosed on the property, which is how I was able to pick it up for a steal.

How much of a steal became clear when Marcie showed me around the place and I saw the equipment left inside. I haven't had much of an opportunity to test any of it out, so I can't wait to finally put it to good use.

My excitement is short-lived, however, when I hear Sully speak up.

"I'll follow you there."

Wonderful.

Suddenly the prospect of getting my hands dirty isn't as appealing. Not if he's going to be in my space the entire time. I don't need the reminder.

He's literally riding my bumper the whole way to the shop, so I'm pretty fired up by the time we get here. Sliding out from behind the wheel, I throw a glare in his direction but he ignores me, pulling the truck up to the first bay door.

I take my sweet time opening the place up and notice it's quite cold in here. I'm sure last time I stopped in, I kept the furnace running, but it's dead silent and I can see my breath. Good thing winter is behind us and, other than the occasional overnight dip, temperatures are above freezing or that could've spelled busted pipes. I'd better make sure anyway.

I hit the button for the overhead door before heading for the furnace room in the back. The first bay is a drive-through with an overhead door at the back of the building as well, but at the rear of bays two and three there is a supply room, a bathroom, and another small room housing the furnace and water heater that both run on propane.

Beside the actual garage, there's a storefront slash office, with a waiting room for clients. It's in dire need of a facelift, but I'm waiting for temperatures to warm up a little so I can leave windows and doors open to get rid of the paint fumes. Or maybe I should say 'I *was* waiting' because by the time the weather is nice enough, I could be big as a house. Hell, I don't even think you're supposed to paint when you're pregnant.

Suddenly the weight of this new reality almost knocks me over and I have to brace myself against the cold furnace, taking a few deep breaths to stave off the surge of panic.

Holy fuck.

I just sank most of what I have into buying this place. I drive an old pickup and rent a room, for crying out loud. The only roof I own is this auto repair shop and the motorhome, neither of which are suitable for a baby. Christ, all I have is some dinky travel insurance for emergencies I don't think will cover pregnancy, let alone childbirth. What the hell am I doing?

I let out a strangled cry when a warm hand lands on my shoulder.

"Are you okay?"

I press my eyes shut and resist turning around to cry into his shirt. I can't make myself that vulnerable again. Instead, I blow out a breath, and another, then one more before I straighten up and turn around.

"Yeah, it's the furnace, it's not working."

His face is too close and those blue eyes are penetrating. A stray thought hits me and I try to remember if blue eyes are a dominant or recessive gene. The mental image of a cute little towheaded toddler with a couple of dimples and clear blue eyes is a little too easy to conjure.

Oh God.

"Pippa?"

"Yeah," I mutter, forcing my attention on Sully.

"I was saying I'll have a look, it's probably the pilot light."

When I don't immediately step out of the way, he takes me by the shoulders and moves me aside. It makes me realize how confined the space is and I quickly dart out of the room.

By the time I hear the furnace fire up, I'm already elbow-deep in the truck's engine. I don't even bother looking up when he announces his ride is here and he's leaving.

Call it self-preservation.

Three

SULLY

"Whoa, pretty girl."

I run a hand over her soft skin before tugging lightly on her nipple. It's slightly distended and filling up. She side-steps restlessly to get away from my touch.

"She's close," I announce to Dan, who is hanging over the stall door. "My guess is before the end of the week."

"Isn't she early?"

"Not by much, couple of weeks."

Technically High Meadow is a stud farm, but we keep a dozen or so breeding mares as well.

Sunny is a pretty little pinto and the foal she's about to drop was sired by Phantom, one of our resident studs. Jonas and James are the ones who run the breeding program. I personally have little interest in genomics or genetics or whatever the hell they call it, and happily leave that to them. I prefer the concrete, hands-on work as opposed to the theories and calculations.

"Should I call Doc Evans?"

I clap Sunny's rear and exit the stall.

"Yeah, give him an update. Tell him two, maybe three days."

Sunny is a first-timer and although she looks like she'll be good breeding material, there's no way to know for sure. That's why the vet likes to keep track of mares like this one.

She'll be the first one to foal in the new barn. Last year the old one burned down and Jonas decided to push forward on an expansion he'd been thinking about. He already had plans drawn up for a larger barn, with a separate foaling section. Three stalls, each of which is outfitted with an electronic monitoring system, but right now Sunny is the only mare in here.

The barn has a tiny bathroom and small bunk room in the back, in case any of the horses need closer attention. I'll grab a few things at my cabin and will probably bed down here tonight. I could use the distraction. My mind has been on Pippa ever since I reluctantly left her at the shop last week.

Hell, who am I kidding? She's been pretty much on my mind for the past few months. I've second-guessed the way I left things that night many times, and again last week when I waited outside the garage for Bo to pick me up.

She can barely bring herself to talk to me, and it's beginning to piss me off. How ironic is that? I'm the last person who has any right to be pissed. I was an asshole to her first but apparently can't hack it when she's less than enthused to see me. Never before have I let myself get twisted up by a woman like this. I even let Dan and Bo pick up the truck when she was done with it because I've become a goddamn coward.

"Sunny's getting close," I tell Jonas and his dad when I walk into the kitchen.

The two are bent over the dining table, studying a large aerial map of Kootenay National Forest.

"I hope she can wait," Jonas comments. "Got a call from the Lincoln County Game Warden's office. Guess they've got Woody Moses busy working with Ewing on those bodies we found, and they need a hand with some aerial surveillance, pinpointing locations, and documenting activity."

"Of what?"

"Baiting bear. It's what Moses was working on before and they don't have enough personnel to allocate someone else to track down every report they get in. The reports come from volunteers in the field, people who see something suspicious will call it in. Normally, Woody will go check it out in person, but he's got his hands full and they just got a new report in."

"And they want us to send up the bird?"

"That's the idea."

Jonas indicates an area on the map near Pulpit Mountain, about an hour and a half north of here.

"I'm gonna have to get closer," I point out. "Do we have coordinates?"

"We do."

I enter them into the map on my phone as Jonas recites them. It's only three in the afternoon, if I head straight up there, I can have the drone in the air in less than two hours. I'll have a couple of hours of daylight left to get a decent visual.

"I can head up now, but someone's gonna have to keep an eye on Sunny."

"I'm on it," Thomas says.

The man is eighty years old, has a serious heart condition, and is fast losing his mobility, but he's also a weathered rancher who doesn't understand the concept of slowing down. Despite all that, he's a father figure to everyone here and none of us have the heart to deny him the opportunity to still feel useful.

"Appreciate it."

I clap him on the shoulder as he shuffles past me. When he's out of earshot, Jonas turns to me.

"I'll let Alex know too. She'll want to be close anyway."

Alex is an intuitive with horses. In fact, she and Jonas met when Phantom was freaked-out after an injury and Doc Evans recommended her. Of course, at the time, Jonas thought the name, Alex, referred to a guy and as a result those two had a bit of a rocky start. It didn't take much time for her to show her mettle; she had Phantom eating out of her hand in no time, when none of us—not even Jonas— were able to approach him.

I don't like to admit it, but I think all of us guys harbored some preconceived reservations about women in this business. With the arrival of first Alex and Lucy, then Nella, Fletch's wife, and later Pippa, I've learned to no longer question any woman's abilities. But it doesn't mean I'm gonna stop looking out for them, that's ingrained in me.

I stop by my cabin to pick up the drone and stuff an extra memory card in my backpack, along with a bottle of water and a few granola bars before heading out.

As I've done each time I pass the rescue these past months, I glance over to see if Pippa's motorhome is parked out front.

It isn't. I see the old clunker of a pickup truck, but the camper is gone and, like the few other times I noticed it missing, I'm instantly wondering where the hell she's off to now. Only last week she was camping within half a fucking mile of not one but, as it turned out, two dead bodies.

I hit Fletch's number on my phone.

"Yeah."

He's as big a fan of phones as I am, which is why I don't waste time beating around the bush.

"Where's your sister-in-law off to?"

"Pippa? How the fuck am I supposed to know? I don't keep track of her schedule. Shit, I can barely keep track of my own wife. She's never where I expect her to be. What's it to you anyway?"

His tone takes on a protective note.

"Nothing. Simply looking out for her because she's your family now."

"Right."

He drags the word out like he doesn't believe me and I don't bother reacting. What's the point? Fletch doesn't interact a whole lot, but there's not much he misses. He notices more than most.

"Listen, I've gotta get up to Pulpit Mountain, but I should be done in a few hours. Let me know if you find out where she's at so I can check in on her on my way back."

He snorts, but then he says, "I'll check with Nella."

Pippa

I really like this backsplash.

The small hexagonal slate tiles look sharp against the granite gray cupboards and butcher block counter. Those cupboards were a bitch to paint and took me the better of

27

three days to finish, but the result is awesome. It gives the entire interior of my camper a clean and fresh look.

I needed some time to myself, and the tedious task of removing and sanding every cupboard door and drawer front in the motorhome gave me a chance to let this new and unexpected turn my life is taking settle in.

No one can see me from the road. I pulled the rig into the first bay through the rear overhead door and I'm hidden in plain sight. Lucy probably thinks I'm off in the mountains again. She was working with Hope when I took off and merely raised her hand when I passed her.

I did call Nella to let her know I'd be gone for a few days, but that I'd make sure to stay within cell phone range should something happen. My sister has about six weeks to go and given that she refuses to slow down a little, it wouldn't surprise me if my little nephew decides to arrive ahead of schedule.

Learning the sex of her baby had made her pregnancy suddenly real. A little boy I could take camping with me, teach how to fish and build fires, and recognize animal tracks. I'd been excited at the prospect.

Not even in my wildest dreams would I have thought I'd have a child of my own to do those things with.

I wonder what the sex of my baby is. Not that it matters —I don't think I have a preference either way—I'm just curious. Curiosity is better than the nauseating state of panic I felt earlier in the week. I've been on the verge of calling Dr. Osborne's office to get that referral from him.

Nella had been outraged when she found out her pregnancy was referred to as 'geriatric' and considered high risk. I'm three years younger than my sister, but I guess my pregnancy would be labeled high risk as well, apparently that's standard for pregnancies at forty or older.

Maybe it is time to make that call. Especially, since by my calculations, I'm now about seventeen weeks and well through the first trimester.

"Dr. Osborne's office, Meghan speaking."

"Hi, it's Pippa Freling. I was in to see Dr. Osborne last week and he told me to get in touch for a referral—"

"Yes, he said to expect your call. I have the number right here."

Ten minutes later, I have an appointment with a Dr. Lindsey Tippen for nine thirty tomorrow morning. My stomach is doing somersaults, or maybe that's the baby. I'd give anything for a stiff drink right about now, but instead I grab my bottle of water. It'll have to do for the foreseeable future.

I glance around my rig, looking at the amount of work I've done in the past four or so days. I'd stopped in at a few places in town, picked up the necessary supplies—I found some non-toxic paint—got a few groceries, and have been here working on it ever since. I guess I needed it. I've been safe, warm, the place is well ventilated, it's got running water, and I've been uninterrupted. I also sleep better in my RV than anywhere else.

One more night—I'll finish installing the new hardware on the doors and drawers—then tomorrow I'll start dealing with my new reality.

∼

"Baby measures at about twenty weeks, which seems about right."

The doctor's comment penetrates the tearful stupor I've been in since getting the first glimpse of what really looks to be a little person moving inside me.

29

"Twenty weeks? That doesn't make sense, I'm pretty sure the only sexual encounter I had was New Year's Eve."

She glances over from the screen and grins at me.

"We calculate forty weeks from the first day of your last period. Since you didn't have a period to go by, we take the date of possible conception and backtrack two weeks, since most women ovulate around the halfway mark between periods."

Wow. Twenty weeks.

Already halfway there and I'm barely even able to get the word 'pregnancy' from my lips.

"I'm so not prepared for this," I blurt out.

I figure she'd be mortified by my outburst, but instead I see empathy in her eyes and a gentle smile on her face.

"We rarely are, no matter how much we plan," she shares sagely. "Granted, at twenty weeks you're going to have a slightly steeper learning curve, but you strike me as a capable individual. I'm sure you'll manage and I'm happy to answer any questions you might have."

My eyes drift back to the screen, where I see what looks like a little fist by the face.

"Already sucking its thumb," Dr. Tippen explains. "A lot of babies start self-soothing in utero."

"Is that bad?" I manage, mesmerized by the sight.

"Not necessarily. There are different schools of thought on self-soothing and there's something to say for both sides of that coin. For what it's worth, babies generally know what they need instinctively, especially in the newborn stage. I'd say when in doubt, follow their lead."

Seems like sound advice.

I stare at the screen as her fingers click on the keyboard.

"Is that the heart?" I point out the dark pulsing shape.

"It is. Wanna hear?"

She reaches for a button on the monitor, repositions the wand through the gel on my belly, and the next moment the room is filled with the fast, steady beat.

Oh my God.

I'm still dazed when I walk out of the office half an hour later, armed with three black-and-white snapshots, a stack of pamphlets, and an appointment for a maternal screening test early next week. I remember Nella had one and that's how she found out her baby is a boy.

I mentioned to Dr. Tippen I wasn't sure I'm ready to know this baby's gender yet, but she assured me she'd keep the information to herself until I am.

Twenty weeks until this baby gets here. October seventh, or thereabouts.

This coming week we're already in May, which leaves me five months to get my life in order. The first thing I need to do is get my business up and running. With or without me. I already thought of a name last night—Pit Stop Engine Repairs—but I'm going to need to bite the bullet and hire someone. Maybe even two someones. I'll need a person who can manage the office side of things, and a licensed mechanic for the shop, because in five months' time, I'll be out of commission at least for a while.

Yowza.

Four

"Oh, come on. It's only lunch."

Marcie is persistent.

She caught me coming out of the Job Service Resource Center in downtown Libby, one block over from her real estate office.

I've had a few lunches with Marcie and all of them started in the middle of the afternoon and ended up sliding into dinner. On top of that, they were mostly liquid. Not a chance I'd get away not drinking without some kind of explanation, and I'm not ready for that.

"Come on. Cade wants to celebrate. Five baiting stations taken down in two weeks, that's some kind of record. Besides, you *know* he'll want to see you."

The Cade she's referring to is Cade Jackson, a conservationist with the DNRC—the Department of Natural Resources and Conservation—and founder of the Fair Game Alliance.

He would be the second reason for me to avoid going to lunch, seeing as I've been ignoring his messages.

He's around my age, decent-looking, passionate about his cause, and hasn't exactly made it a secret I caught his attention. We've flirted a bit back and forth—harmless enough—although last time it felt like he was working up to asking me out on an actual date and I bailed before he could. The flirting was nice exercise, but Cade doesn't strike me as a casual guy and I wasn't really interested in a committed relationship of any kind. At least not that soon after I got burned by Sully, only a year after my ex did his damage.

I'm like Pigpen, except instead of dirt I attract disaster. It seems to follow me around.

"I really can't. I'm supposed to be meeting my sister and go over some business stuff. As you well know, I need to get my auto shop off the ground. Which—now that I think about it—you actually might be able to help me with."

We're blocking the sidewalk so I pull her out of the way of some passersby.

"I just posted a couple of job openings. One for a part-time office manager with experience in an automotive setting and another for a licensed mechanic, but I recall you mentioning something about a guy who used to work for the previous owner?"

"Yeah, Ira Nelson. He's a licensed mechanic but I'm not sure he'd want to work for you. He was the only other person interested in the auto shop, but he wasn't able to wing it financially. At least not yet. He wouldn't have been happy finding out it sold from under his nose."

She makes a good point, he likely wouldn't be happy with me, unless I could make it worth his while. I'll have to think on that.

It takes me another five minutes to extract myself from

Marcie's clutches before I can hop in my truck. I want to catch my sister who—according to her husband—is at Bean There, a local coffee shop. Supposedly she's covering lunch for Kaylie, the young barista she's taken under her wing. Why? Fletch wasn't able to tell me, but I'm sure I'm about to find out.

I'm a little nervous when I find Nella's eyes on me as I walk in. I haven't seen her since I discovered I am pregnant. I've never been a successful liar and Nella is like a human lie detector. I'm worried she'll take one look at me and know before I get a chance to tell her.

While she deals with a customer, I take a seat at a small table for two near the cash register. From here I can observe her. I'm still getting used to the fact my sister is wearing jeans all the time now, let alone maternity jeans. In the last six months she's shown a whole new side to her I'd never really seen before, and I somehow feel closer to her.

I never questioned her love for me but before it expressed itself in motherly concern, despite only three years between us. However, since both landing here in Libby, she is more direct, more open, and definitely more relatable. Not that she's a different person exactly, but she's definitely come out of her shell. Fletch probably has something to do with it. Her pregnancy certainly has.

Or perhaps the change is in me.

"Vanilla latte."

Nella slides a takeout cup in front of me. My favorite. I haven't had coffee in over a week and my mouth waters at the sweet scent.

"Thanks." I take a small sip, mostly foam, trying to avoid my sister's observant gaze. "So what's wrong with Kaylie? How come you have to cover for her?"

"She had to drive her mom to the hospital for a procedure."

"Oh dear, I hope she's okay."

Nella leans forward over the table, clearly not wanting the folks at the only other occupied table to overhear.

"Routine colonoscopy."

"Ah, gotcha."

I take another careful sip of the brew, wondering if indulging in one coffee would harm the baby. I should've asked Dr. Tippen this morning but I had other priorities.

"How'd you know where to find me?" Nella suddenly asks.

"Fletch. You weren't answering your phone and I wanted to make sure everything was okay so I called him."

"As you can see, I'm fine." She tilts her head slightly. "But I get the feeling that's not why you're here."

See?

"You know that sixth sense of yours is not normal, right? It's downright creepy and I pity that kid of yours. He'll never know the secret pleasure of a snuck Halloween candy or the joys of a good hide-and-seek."

She grins wide. "Quit beating around the bush and spill, what are you up to?"

"Actually, I'm in the process of hiring a mechanic and someone to help run the office. I want to open up the shop."

Yes, I know I'm being evasive, but I figure it won't hurt to soften her up with this information first before easing into the big announcement.

"You got your work visa?"

"No, not yet, but I figure I own the place, I'm paying utilities, I may as well start building some clientele."

"Wow. But didn't you say you wanted to run it by yourself for a while before hiring anyone?"

"True, but who knows how long it'll be before I can actually start working."

I'm not lying, but it's a half-truth at best, because that isn't the reason I'm suddenly in a hurry. The dubious look on Nella's face tells me she knows I'm holding something back.

Time to put my big-girl panties on.

"That," I continue, "and also the fact there's been a slight change in my situation."

"Oh?"

A look of concern steals over her face and I'm afraid her imagination may be worse than my reality, so I forge ahead.

"I'm pregnant."

≈

Sully

"If you want, I can drop it off for you. I was heading out anyway."

Alex, who was already shrugging on her coat, stops and looks at me.

"Are you sure?"

"Yeah, it's not a problem."

I don't mention it was my intended destination to begin with. I found out from Fletch that Nella had seen her sister this afternoon and Pippa should be back at the farmhouse. After an interesting exchange I had last night at Pulpit Mountain, I definitely want a word with her.

Alex hands me the bag of powdered milk supplement

for a young foal at the rescue, providing me with an excellent excuse to stop by.

"Want us to save you some dinner?" Thomas asks from his perch at the kitchen island.

The smirk on his face makes it clear he couldn't care less whether or not I eat. Nosy old fart. I don't bother with a response—he's not really expecting one anyway—and make my way to the door, his teasing chuckle following me.

Her motorhome is parked beside the small horse trailer and her pickup is in front of the house. The two dogs run up to my truck, barking, and Lucy is heading this way from the corral as well. I greet Chief and Scout before I pull the bag of supplement from the back of the truck.

"That's perfect," she says, taking it from my hands. "Floyd isn't gaining as much as he should."

"You named Hope's colt Floyd?" I ask disbelievingly.

"So? It's a perfectly fine name for him."

Poor little guy, but I know better than to argue with Lucy so I let it slide.

"Pippa around?"

Lucy jerks her head toward the back of the property. "She took a ride to the creek."

The creek would be Swamp Creek, which borders the north side of the property.

I became very familiar with the lay of the land here when we were hunting down a bunch of domestic terrorists last year.

"She left half an hour ago. I don't think she'll be too long," Lucy continues, shooting me a funny look. "She took Ladybug, who doesn't spook. She's as docile as they come."

Not sure why she's sharing that information. I know Pippa can hold her own in the saddle.

"Mind if I head back there?"

"Be my guest."

I don't get very far. As soon as I clear the copse of trees behind the back meadow, I can see her coming toward me and I stop to wait. When she comes within thirty feet of me, I can tell she's been crying and I'm instantly alarmed.

"What the hell's wrong?" It comes out harsher than I intended and I immediately try to soften the impact. "Is everything all right? Are you hurt?"

"I'm fine."

The response is curt and I have to grab on to the horse's reins when she threatens to ride clear past me.

"Hey...hold up."

"What do you want, Sully?"

I don't like the dejected tone of her voice.

"We need to talk."

She surprises me by barking out a laugh.

"Afraid it's a little late for talking," she mumbles before urging the horse forward.

Forced to let go of the reins, I let her go but follow behind as she returns to the barn. She's already disappeared inside by the time I get there.

I'm about to step in the barn door when I pick up Lucy's voice.

"It's him, isn't it?"

Him? Is she talking about me? Am I the reason she was crying?

I can hear Pippa responding but I can't make out what she says. Whatever it is seems to stall the conversation and I continue through the door.

Scout—the more inquisitive of the two dogs—makes a beeline for me as soon as I step inside. The moment Pippa sees me, she grabs the saddle off Ladybug's back and carries it into the small tack room. I glance over at Lucy, who is sitting on a hay bale, a pretty black foal tucked between her knees as she tries to feed it from a bottle. She doesn't look up.

I'm pretty sure I walked in on something but it doesn't look like either one of them is eager to fill me in. Pippa appears and, without looking at me, walks over to Ladybug, unties her, and leads her right past me and out of the barn.

Her evasiveness is starting to piss me off.

"Pippa!" I call after her and I'm about to follow her—again—when Lucy speaks up.

"Go easy on her. She's got a lot on her plate."

Lucy is a bit of a hard-ass, so her sudden display of sensitivity is a bit of a surprise. There is definitely something going on with Pippa.

I catch up with her just as she takes the lead rope off Ladybug's halter and slaps her rump, sending her cantering into the field to join the small herd.

"We need to talk," I repeat my earlier words as I block her way back to the barn.

She shuts her eyes and exhales on a harsh sigh.

"What do you want to talk about, Sully?"

"For starters, how about your association with the Fair Game Alliance."

That seems to startle her. She looks genuinely surprised.

"Fair Game? What about it?"

"You're involved with that group?"

"Uhh...yeah. Why? There's nothing illegal about Fair Game. In fact, we work together with the game warden and the sheriff."

"I know, I met a friend of yours last night; Cade Jackson."

I tell her about going up on Pulpit Mountain at the request of the game warden's office and encountering

40

Jackson there. He's the one who reported suspected bear baiting going on up there and had a pretty good idea where the feed barrels may have been placed.

It took me less than half an hour to get the Matrice up and pinpoint the location, despite Jackson's ongoing commentary. I brought the bird back in and called the game warden with the coordinates for the barrels. While we were waiting for one of the wardens, he filled me in on his Fair Game group and their most recent calls.

That's when Pippa's name came up.

"You're taking risks getting involved with shit like this, Pippa," I tell her. "Some of these guys you have it in for wouldn't hesitate to hurt you. Camping by yourself off the beaten path is one thing, but doing surveillance on poachers and rogue operators like these guys? And you were just out there for almost a week again, making a fucking target of yourself."

"Actually, I wasn't," she snaps back, her temper flaring. "And who the hell do you think you are anyway?"

"Someone's clearly gotta look out for you," I fire back.

Her eyes bulge and her mouth falls open, but only for a moment, then her expression tightens up as she steps into my space, her index finger waving under my nose.

"You? Don't make me laugh. The same guy who came on to me, took me home, got his jollies off, and proceeded to claim it was all a big mistake. You could barely manage to look in my direction for four fucking months, Sully. Now you wanna look out for me? Give me a break."

She shoves right past me and stalks toward the house.

Oh yeah, she's pissed, but if I'm not mistaken, I'm picking up on something else as well. Hurt? The woman is confusing and infuriating at the same time.

I catch up to her in a couple of long strides, hook her

behind the neck, and pull her close. Before my mind has a chance to catch up, I kiss her.

Hard.

The next moment the air is sucked from my lungs, and my vision goes blurry with the hot blast of pain doubling me over.

She fucking kneed me in the nuts.

Five

PIPPA

"Thanks a bunch, Marcie."

I tear the piece of paper with the phone number for Ira Nelson from the pad on the kitchen counter.

"Not a problem. He's expecting your call. And, by the way? You missed a good time the other day. We ended up at the Mint. Woody showed up as well. Oh, and Cade was asking about you."

Sounds more like I dodged a bullet if they ended up at that local watering hole. The one place in Libby where you can drink until two in the morning. Not my cup of tea, even if I were able to drink.

Maybe I'm simply getting too old for that kind of scene, or it's too reminiscent of my former life. Drinking, partying, schmoozing with the in-crowd was part of the life my ex introduced me to.

Cash Curran—still can't believe his name didn't raise all kinds of red flags—was charismatic and always drew people in. An attribute I can't deny helped build our business.

That small automotive repair shop was mine. I'd worked hard and scraped together barely enough to hang up my own shingle when I met my ex. Like I said, he was charismatic, and I fell head over teakettle for his mysterious charm and rock star appearance. He'd wandered into town calling himself an automotive artist and claiming he was looking for a change of pace in the mountains.

He definitely was an artist. I had a rusty old 1972 Oldsmobile Cutlass at the shop I'd planned to fix up one day, but he offered to do some work on it and turned it into a thing of beauty. I was starstruck and didn't blink before I said yes to the marriage proposal that followed.

Nella never liked him. She definitely didn't like that I changed the name of the shop to Curran Car Concepts—that was Cash's idea—or the fact I signed over half ownership to him. Not that it was worth much at that time, but it certainly was worth a whack five years later when I discovered my sister had been right.

It took me two years to get out of a mess it had taken me less than two months to get into.

"Pippa?" Marcie's voice pulls me from my thoughts. "I said, Cade wanted to know if there was a problem with your phone since you haven't returned his calls."

"I've had my hands full."

Not a word of a lie there, both literally and figuratively. Although, it's mostly my mind that is full.

"You should just let him know you're not interested," my friend suggests.

I should, but the last thing I want is another person pissed at me. I've had my share of confrontations in recent days and it's starting to leave bruises.

I haven't spoken with Nella since I told her I was pregnant a couple of days ago. After her initial shock, she got a bit teary-eyed. Then, when I didn't want to share the name of the father, she got upset. Not that she said anything, but it was obvious I'd hurt her feelings.

Late that same afternoon I had a run-in with Sully that left him doubled-over and pissed, and me confused and vulnerable. I'd barricaded myself in the house after that incident and watched from my bedroom window as I saw him briefly talk to Lucy before getting in his truck and driving off. Lucy never said a word to me but I caught an occasional look of concern.

I thought I might've chased Sully off for good until I found out from Jonas's father today the team had been out near Troy on a search. Ama had called me in to check on a small skid steer the ranch hands couldn't get started. My stomach had been tied in knots and I was mentally geared up to apologize to him, when Thomas mentioned the guys weren't there.

I'm already carrying more guilt than I care to and I'm not about to add Cade to my list.

"Or maybe he should take a hint," I retort a little sharply, immediately regretting it. "I didn't mean to snap at you. I'm just..." I blow out a tense breath. "I've got a lot going on."

"I can tell. You know I'm here if you need an ear or a shoulder, right?"

"I know and I appreciate it, Marcie. You've already been helpful getting me that number."

"No biggie. Look, my eleven o'clock appointment is here. We'll touch base later, okay?"

After ending the call, I pour myself another tea and walk out onto the front porch. It's a nice day—actually quite warm in the sun—and I want to take a moment to collect my thoughts before I give the mechanic a call.

Lucy is in the corral working with one of her clients and Ladybug. In addition to running the day-to-day operation of the horse rescue, she also started offering equine therapy recently. In fact, I was the crash test dummy for those new services. Not that there was a lot of crashing, Ladybug is a sweetheart with nerves of steel. An explosion wouldn't shake her.

She's good with the horses. Not in the same way Alex is, but Lucy has a patience and quiet confidence they seem to respond to. What is really surprising is that the otherwise abrupt and somewhat gruff woman seems to have that same gentle way about her when dealing with her clients.

With the sun almost at its highest point, it's getting really warm out here. I take off my sweatshirt revealing the T-shirt underneath, and stretch my bare arms to the sun. As someone with olive-toned skin, who is outdoors a lot, I tend to tan easily. Unfortunately, the majority of the past seven months I've spent recovering was indoors leaving me with a pasty complexion.

For a few minutes I soak up the rays with my eyes closed and let my body relax. A moment of reprieve I indulge in before I get back to business.

"Yeah."

With only that single word I can tell Ira Nelson is not in a good mood.

"Hi, Ira? My name is Pippa Freling and I was given your—"

"Marcie. I know."

Alrighty then. Off to a swimming start. I'm guessing the man may be harboring some bitterness toward me for buying the garage.

"Then let me cut right to the chase. I'm sure Marcie told you I purchased what used to be Standish Automotive. I understand you worked for Standish for many years and have a special connection to the place. I happen to be in need of a good reliable mechanic, who is able to carry a lot of responsibility, and you come well-recommended. I was hoping perhaps we can come up with a mutually beneficial arrangement."

There's an extended pause on the other end, and for a moment I wonder if he's ended the call.

"I'm listening," he finally says.

Not exactly resounding enthusiasm, but I'll take it.

It takes only five minutes to organize a time to meet with Ira at the shop tomorrow. No time like the present.

Which reminds me, I need to get up to Cranbrook at some point and empty my storage unit. It holds a few of Nella's things, but most of it is stuff I stored when I took off with my rig. It seems silly to pay for that unit when both of us are here. Nella's got plenty of room for her things and I can probably store my stuff in the shop for now.

At least until I find a more permanent place to live.

"Wow."

I look up to find Lucy coming up the steps of the porch, eyeballing me. To be more specific, she's staring at my midsection.

"What?"

"Can't believe I didn't notice before. Look at you."

I glance down at the suddenly prominent swell of my baby bump under my shirt. The hand I quickly put there doesn't cover it.

"Won't be a secret for long," Lucy says, lifting her eyebrow as she looks at me in passing.

Her point is clear, but at least she spares me another lecture like the one she gave me the night Sully was here. I'm going to have to fess up soon, but first I want to have a solid plan in place.

~

Sully

"That's a good girl."

I run a hand over her distended belly.

Thomas had been waiting for us when we pulled up this afternoon. Alex was tending to Sunny, who'd gone into labor earlier in the day.

I'd been exhausted from the almost forty-two hours we spent scouring the woods northwest of Troy, looking for a local teen gone missing, but adrenaline kicked in as I followed Thomas into the barn. Jonas checked in briefly as the other guys were bringing in horses at the other end of the building. I waved him off when he suggested I come back to the house for a meal and some sleep.

We'll probably be out there searching again at first light tomorrow because we hadn't found the sixteen-year-old kid yet. We'd finally found some tracks, trailed him south for the better part of a day, but then we lost him when we got to Callahan Creek.

This time of year, the water had still been swollen with winter runoff and moving faster than normal. We split off into two groups to see if we could pick up his trail again, but had no luck. Nobody said anything out loud but we were all thinking the kid might well have been washed downstream, but we still need to find him. Dead or alive. But we first needed a chance to eat and recharge and so did the horses.

"Here comes another one," I warn Alex, who is monitoring Sunny's progress.

The poor mare is getting tired, I can tell when she barely reacts to the strong contraction going through her body.

"We need to call Doc. She's gonna need some help," Alex confirms my suspicions.

It's close to three in the morning when Sunny finally delivers her foal with a substantial amount of help from Doc Evans. It's a pretty little filly with similar coloring to her mother.

"You did good."

I rub Sunny down with some clean straw as Alex walks Doc Evans back to his truck.

"Pretty little thing," Jonas comments as he walks in.

"You're up already?"

"I had almost eight hours of sleep and am well rested. Besides, I want to have the horses loaded and be on the road by six." He claps me on the shoulder. "You, however, look like shit. You need to get some rest."

I shake my head.

"Nah, I'll have a shower, grab something to eat, and I'll be good to roll."

"I don't think so, my friend. You know how it works; the chain is only as strong as its weakest link. We're all rested and you're likely going to slow us down. Let me get Dan up, he can keep an eye on these two, but you're gonna rest up."

Ouch. But it's nothing I haven't said to one of the other guys at some point myself. Ego has no place in a good team, so I concede and head over to my cabin.

My phone ringing on the nightstand wakes me up. A quick glance at the screen tells me it's Fletch calling and it's a little after ten. I slept for almost six hours. Must've needed it.

"What's up?"

"Need a favor. Nella's stuck at home. She has an appointment at the clinic, and her van won't start. She can't get ahold of Pippa and Ama is apparently in Kalispell with Thomas."

I'm already out of bed, shoving my legs in a pair of jeans.

"On my way. Any luck out there?"

"Found a boot."

I freeze up at that with a heavy feeling in the pit of my stomach.

"One boot?"

"Yeah. Stuck on a fallen log in the water."

"Fuck."

That's not good. At all.

"Yeah," Fletch says. "Gonna give Nella a heads-up you'll be there soon."

"Five minutes."

"Appreciate it."

Nella is sitting on their porch when I pull up. I'm not liking the way she's hunched over.

"You okay, darlin'?" I call out as I leave my truck running and walk up the steps.

"I'm good. Just give me a minute."

I'll be damned. She's early. A little over four weeks early by my calculation.

I rush to her side, right in time to help her stand.

"I'm guessing you didn't tell Fletch you were having contractions?"

She waves me off.

"It's probably Braxton-Hicks, but my doctor wants to check me quickly. No need to get Fletch riled up when he should be focusing on finding that boy."

I bite my tongue, this is not my woman and not my

business, but if I was in Fletch's shoes I wouldn't be too happy when I found out. Instead, I hold her arm and lead her to the passenger side, helping her up in the seat. Then I drive like a bat out of hell to the clinic she gives me directions for.

The clinic is in a larger medical building and the parking lot is pretty full. My eyes lock on a spot being vacated right by the entrance and manage to snag it, right as Nella starts breathing heavy. It's been about ten minutes since I caught her mid-contraction on her porch.

"Stay put," I order Nella, who throws me a deathly glare.

If she doesn't call Fletch, I fucking will. Even if it turns out to be a false alarm, I'm pretty damn sure he'd want to know. It would only take me half an hour to get out to Troy, and maybe another fifteen to take the forestry road to where the team left the trailer. Only problem is, I don't know how far the team is from there or if they still have a phone signal. Luckily, I have a radio in my truck.

I open Nella's door and she holds up a finger, indicating for me to wait. A few seconds later she blows out a big breath and takes the hand I offer.

Inside the clinic, I follow Nella to the reception desk.

"Nella Boone to see Dr. DeMario. He told me to pop in when I talked to him earlier. I don't really have an appointment."

"Not to worry," the perky young blonde behind the desk assures her. "He told me to expect you. You can come straight back with me."

Nella turns to me with a worried look on her face.

"Do you mind waiting?"

"Not going anywhere."

Like I'd leave her here, Fletch would deck me.

I take a seat right next to the hallway Nella just disappeared down. The perky blonde returns, giving me a wide smile, and I quickly glance at the magazines on the small table beside me. My choices are *American Baby*, *New Parent Magazine*, or *Baby & Toddler*. Not a single copy of *Outside Magazine* in sight. I grab one blindly— not really caring— simply to have something in my hands.

I pick up a woman's voice heading this way.

"...a week, maybe a week and a half if the lab is busy. I'll let you know if there's anything to be concerned about. And you don't want to know your baby's gender, right?"

"I'm not sure yet."

The magazine slides from my hands and hits the floor with a slap when I recognize the second voice.

What the fuck?

Six

PIPPA

"Melissa, can you set Pippa up an appointment for two weeks from now?"

Dr. Tippen aims a smile my way.

"If there's anything to report I'll call, and remember to keep an eye on your salt intake."

As she turns to head back to her office, her eyes catch on something behind me. Or someone, judging from her polite nod.

It takes me a moment to recognize the short-buzzed hair. I'm used to the black Stetson. But there's no mistaking the clear blue eyes narrowed on me.

Oh shit.

What the hell is he doing here?

I want to run, but my feet are rooted as I look down at him.

My day was going so well up to this point. I met with Ira earlier and although the man has a serious personality issue and a giant chip on his shoulder, he genuinely seems to want to work at the shop. I got the impression the prospect of basically working by himself for the foreseeable future was appealing. I was able to call a few references and they all gave him glowing recommendations. We agreed on a salary and he even offered to come in and paint this week so we can open after the weekend.

A great morning so far, but I should've known it wouldn't last. Not with my luck.

Sully slowly rises to his feet and is now towering over me. It makes me feel even smaller.

"Wow. Talk about a shock to the system, you're not really showing," he observes before I can think of something to say. "That knee in the nuts makes a lot more sense now."

"What are you doing here?" my mouth finally forms, completely disregarding his comment. Or maybe I'm ignoring it on purpose.

"Fletch is out on a search and your sister's van wouldn't start. She needed to get checked out by her doctor and wasn't able to get ahold of you."

I realized my first visit here that Nella's OB-GYN, Dr. DeMario, is part of the same practice as Dr. Tippen.

"Wait, you said she needed to get checked out? Is she okay?"

"I think some cramping." He seems uncomfortable with the topic, but his next words imply his discomfort is with me. "I'll wait for her in the car."

"That's okay, you don't have to hang around. I'll wait for her."

Anything to get out of this awkward situation, since I'm not going anywhere without knowing my sister is okay.

Sully nods, fits on his hat, and starts walking to the door. There he stops and turns around.

"I'm sorry for the other day. I didn't know you were involved. Best of luck to you."

Then he pushes through the door and disappears from sight.

It takes me a moment to realize he hasn't clued in to the fact he's the father. At least not yet. I'm sure he will soon enough.

Yeah, I wasn't prepared for this today.

Five minutes later, Dr. DeMario walks out with Nella, who is surprised to see me. But before she can ask me how I got here, she winces and bends forward. While she's handling what looks to be a contraction, Dr. DeMario instructs the receptionist to alert the hospital and then turns to me.

"Are you her ride?"

"Yes, I'm her sister."

"Good. If you could take her, I'll meet you at the Labor and Delivery unit at the hospital. She's having premature contractions and looks to be dilating. I'd like to see what we can do to delay delivery."

"You need to...call...Fletch," my sister gasps.

"As soon as I get you in my truck," I announce, taking her arm. "Let me know when this one goes down and we'll hustle."

I manage to get her in the passenger seat and notice she's looking rather pale.

"Are you okay?" I ask, concerned.

She turns those pretty hazel eyes on me. I was always jealous of that color growing up. I ended up with the much less interesting drab brown eyes.

"I'm scared," she admits.

I totally get that. Heck, I'm scared now, and I'm not having any contractions. I cover her hand with mine.

"You'll be fine. You're the strongest woman I know, bar none, and, like everything you do in life, I have not a second's doubt you will rock this too.

"What if he's not ready? If his lungs aren't developed yet?"

"Stop. In one week no one would've blinked an eye if you'd gone into labor. Even if the doc can't slow this down, you'll be fine, and so will the little peanut."

I let go of her hand and start the truck, before adding, "I'm not worried about you two, but I'm not so sure about Fletch though. I think he might lose his shit."

Nella snickers beside me and I'm grateful she at least still has her sense of humor.

Instead of trying to reach Fletch, who is out in the field, I decide to get ahold of Sully. He's probably still behind the wheel since he answers after only one ring.

"Pippa?"

His voice is loud over the hands-free.

"I have to take Nella to the hospital. Can you get hold of Fletch?"

"Leave it to me," he says and abruptly hangs up.

"Charmer," Nella mumbles. "Where did he go off to anyway? Did he call you?"

"I had my maternal screening today," I explain. "I bumped into him in the waiting room and told him he didn't need to hang around."

"You sent the man packing?"

"Well, I'm sure he has better things to do than hang around a waiting room in an OB-GYN office."

It takes me a moment to realize she's studying me and I dart her a quick glance.

"What?"

"It's him, isn't it?"

How the hell does she do that?

I try to keep my face impassive but my nonresponse is probably confirmation enough for my sister. I hate to admit I'm relieved when another contraction hits her, keeping her occupied while I look for a parking spot at the hospital.

When we find the labor and delivery department, we're immediately hustled into a room. At Nella's request, I stay with her and am directed to a chair while the nurse helps her change into a hospital gown and starts an IV to administer fluids. Then she straps sensors onto Nella's belly to monitor contractions and the baby's heartbeat.

"Can you roll on your left side? I'll put a pillow under your hip for support. If you can keep this position, it can help slow down contractions. Dr. DeMario should be here shortly."

We don't have to wait long for the doctor. After introductions and another contraction, DeMario explains the plan.

"This is magnesium sulfite," he clarifies as he hangs a smaller bag onto the IV pole and inserts a line to the port. "I'm hoping it'll slow contractions. You're almost thirty-six weeks, at which point your baby's lungs should be mature enough to take that first breath, so if we can delay birth by those couple of days it would be preferable."

"Yeah, of course."

Nella nods her head at DeMario as he leaves the room and then her eyes come to me. She's worried, I can tell from the tight line of her mouth and the hand she reaches out to me.

I take her hand in both of mine and lean forward as her eyes slowly well up.

"You'll be fine. Fletch is gonna be here soon, Sully will make sure of it, and it is all going to be fine."

I hope I sounded convincing enough, because I'm really worried too.

~

Sully

I've been waiting at the trailhead where the HMT trailer is parked for about half an hour when Fletch emerges from the woods.

On my way here, I got in touch with Dan back at the ranch. He was going to hook up the small trailer and head here to pick up Fletch's horse, King. My initial plan had been to let Fletch take my truck and I'd take King to join the others. But when talking to my teammate it became clear it wouldn't be a good idea for him to be behind the wheel.

One glimpse at the expression on his face as he leaps off his horse tells me getting Dan over here had been the right call. My friend is teetering on the edge.

"Let's go."

He bangs his fist on my dashboard a few times.

"Easy, man, I'll get you there."

"Nella's not answering her goddamn phone."

She may not be able to. I can't recall seeing a cell phone on her, but now may not be a good time to point that out. Instead, I pull up Pippa's number on my phone and dial. It rings five times and I'm about to hang up when she answers.

"Hi."

Her voice is no more than a whisper and it sounds like she's moving around.

"Just checking in," I tell her. "How are things?"

"Sorry, I had to step out of the room. She's dozing a little."

"She's in a room? What's going on?" Fletch jumps in barking out questions.

"They have her on IV medication to try and slow down contractions. She'll be fine, but Fletch..." She pauses to make sure she has his attention. "...You're gonna have to rein it in. My sister's scared and the last thing she needs is you going off the rails."

I can tell she's trying to keep her tone level, but there is no mistaking the sharp edge to her voice. She's making it clear she will do what it takes to protect her sister, even from her husband.

Fletch hears it too and balls his fists and clenches his jaw, but still manages to promise he'll hold it together.

"Pippa? What room are you guys in?" I ask, breaking the tension.

"Room three in labor and delivery."

There's a small wobble in her voice which doesn't escape me. The better part of the past hour and a half I've been pissed at her, but the sound of that tremble has an effect on me.

"Okay, hang tight, sweetheart. We'll be there in less than half an hour."

I can't believe she's fucking pregnant. That was like another knee in the nuts, but this one really knocked me on my ass. I'm angry, but what really floors me is how much the idea of her with someone else hurts.

Not that I have any rights to her—I did a good job fucking that up—but I care about the woman. I just don't trust myself with her.

When you spend near eighteen years bouncing around from one high-octane assignment to another, always looking over your shoulder for the enemy, disconnected from every-thing that is familiar, bearing witness to atrocities that defy any form of humanity, it does something to you.

Your mind may be able to process—to categorize and file away—but the soul can't leave it behind. It becomes a shadow you carry with you, and no matter how much light you force into your life, all it takes is one moment of weakness for that darkness to creep in.

I know, I've seen it happen to many good men. And I've also seen the devastation it can leave behind.

Five years ago, my good friend, brother-in-arms, as well as brother-in-law, Nick, couldn't ward off that darkness any longer. In a moment of rage, he beat my sister so badly we weren't sure if she was going to survive. When he realized what he'd done, he took his gun, shoved it in his mouth, and pulled the trigger.

My then sixteen-year-old niece, Sloane, was the one to find both of them. Isobel made it, but both she and her daughter now have their own dark shadows to carry around.

I will not risk that. I can't chance causing that much damage. Not to anyone, but especially not to someone like Pippa.

"Did you know she was pregnant?"

The words are out there before I stop to think about it.

Fletch's head jerks around.

"Pippa?"

"Hmm," I hum, watching him from the corner of my eye.

"Yeah, Nella told me. Apparently, Pippa only found out herself last week."

"She seeing someone?"

Fletch's eyes narrow on me. I'm being too transparent, but I can't seem to help myself.

"Not that I know of. It upset Nella that she wasn't sharing who the father is. Turns out she's already halfway through her pregnancy and didn't know it. May have been some guy on the road. How fucked up is that?"

Halfway through her pregnancy? That's four-and-a-half months and puts the time right around...

Sonofabitch.

Seven

PIPPA

"Go."

I glare at my sister, who is all but shoving me out the door.

Fletch almost knocked me out of the way to get to Nella when he came barging in. Since I was busy trying to make room for him, I missed Sully stepping inside and ended up standing shoulder to shoulder with him in the process.

A weird energy seemed to zap around the man and the look he threw me when I glanced over was one I didn't recognize, but it had the hair on my skin stand up. But I didn't have the heart to move so I've been standing here with my back against the wall and Sully by my side for a while.

And now my sister wants me to leave with him.

"I can't simply leave. What if—"

"Nothing is going to happen. My contractions have slowed down, the baby is doing fine, and you need some rest. You can barely stand straight."

As soon as she says that, I feel Sully's hand firmly grab my elbow. I resist the temptation to shrug loose because the truth is, I am feeling a little woozy. It has to be close to dinnertime already and since the two slices of toast and decaf coffee I had for breakfast, I haven't had anything to eat or drink.

"Sully can drive you home," Fletch adds with a funny look for his teammate I'm too tired to try and decipher.

"I have my own truck here," I try in a last-ditch effort.

"Which you'll likely wreck if you try driving in this state," Nella snaps. Then she piles on the guilt. "Last thing I need is having to worry about you."

I make a face at her but she just raises an eyebrow, clearly unimpressed.

"I'll hold on to your keys, in case I need wheels tonight," Fletch contributes.

"Fine," I grumble, all but rolling my eyes when he holds up his hand for my truck keys.

Through all of this, Sully has remained stoic and silent. Something is up with him and it's making me uneasy.

Still, I don't object when he maintains a hold on my arm when we walk out of the hospital; I'm not that sure my legs would support me. This day has zapped the energy right out of me. I let him help me into his truck and don't even protest when he pulls into the Burger Express drive-thru a couple of minutes later.

My mouth waters when I see the menu on the board. It's been a while since I've had a juicy burger. Living with Lucy has dramatically cut down on my takeout habit. She is a phenomenal cook and I can't complain, but I've missed that first taste when you sink your teeth into a good burger.

"Cheeseburger, cheese fries, and a vanilla milkshake," I respond to Sully's questioning look in my direction.

I probably won't be able to eat it all—or I'll make myself sick trying—but right now my stomach feels like it could handle half a cow.

The smells from the two brown bags Sully dropped on my lap are killing me fifteen minutes later when he drives right past Hart's Horse Rescue.

"Hey. You missed my turnoff."

I turn my head to look at him when he doesn't respond. His eyes are focused on the road ahead and his jaw is set.

"Where are you taking me?"

An answer does not seem to be forthcoming, but I no longer need it when he turns into the High Meadow driveway. He pulls up to the cabin I know is his and turns off the truck. Then he grabs the bags from my lap and gets out, rounding the truck to my side, and opening my door.

I defiantly cross my arms over my chest and glare at him.

"We need to talk," he finally says. "We'll have privacy here."

"You seem to want to talk a lot," I snap. "But you don't tend to say a whole lot. If I recall correctly, talking hasn't provided much clarity between us."

"That's rich, having you talk about clarity."

Sarcasm drips from his voice as he turns his back and heads for the door. Unfortunately, he's taking my food so I have no choice but to follow him.

Curiosity momentarily trumps annoyance and hunger when I step inside and I stop to take in his space. The cabin is basically one large open living space with a pair of doors on either side. Bedrooms and bathrooms, I'm guessing.

The living room consists of a rustic stone fireplace, a large flat-screen TV hanging over the mantle, and a buckskin leather sectional sitting on a large Persian rug in deep reds and burgundies. No coffee table, no side tables, and the only light fixture in that area is a modern, brushed-nickel standing lamp by one side of the sectional, but the rug is a surprise.

Very minimalistic, very *Marie Kondo,* although I suspect she'd pooh-pooh both the sectional—which I see has cupholders—and the massive TV. She'd approve of the rest though. The kitchen has an L-shape and runs along part of the back wall, with the sink centered under a large window with a pretty view. It's a man's kitchen, sleek and uncluttered with upgraded appliances. I get the sense it isn't used much.

Sully has dropped the food on the island, which is basically open metal shelving underneath a stainless-steel counter, and is pulling a couple of slate gray plates from one of the cupboards.

The only clutter is a stack of mail, a few newspapers, and a thick hardcover book covering part of the simple rectangular dining table which separates the kitchen from the living space. The modern upholstered bucket chairs match the two stools that flank the island.

Despite the cool steel and sparse furnishings, this space is surprisingly warm and inviting. Not at all what I would've associated with Sully. The TV and couch are maybe the only two things that fit my impression of the man. I don't know about who that reveals more; Sully, with more layers and depth than I've given him credit for, or me, definitely short-sighted and judgmental, and shallower than I care to admit.

"You gonna stand there all night or are you gonna come eat?"

Eat, I guess. I slowly make my way over to where he's waiting by the island, his expression still strangely impassive. I'm hungry but also a little nervous about that talk he wants to have. The outcome seems inevitable.

I just hope I don't puke all over his immaculate kitchen.

~

Sully

I have gone through a whole range of emotions in the past few hours.

Heck, this entire day has been a fucking roller coaster from the moment I woke up. I'm wired, on edge, barely able to keep it all inside, and I'm afraid if I don't let up on this pressure soon, I'll explode.

I'm starting to second-guess if bringing Pippa back to my place was a good idea.

Hanging on to my temper, I keep my hands busy setting out the food. When I finally turn around and see her standing in my space, instead of anger, I feel something else settle over me.

A shift, almost like a realignment of balance.

I'm still pissed, still confused, but I don't feel like I'm coming apart at the seams anymore.

"How far along are you?" I bring myself to ask first.

Better make sure I have my facts straight before I start flinging accusations.

Her eyes flit my way and she reaches up to tuck a loose strand of hair behind her ear. Then she turns her focus on the wrapped food on her plate and methodically starts unwrapping it.

"I'm due October seventh," she says right before she takes a big bite of her burger.

It's evasive, both her response and the mouthful of food preventing her from saying any more.

"That means you're halfway there."

"Hmmm," she hums around the bite, not exactly helping.

I take a bite of my own, chew a few times, and then swallow the large, barely masticated lump, no longer able to hold back the accusation.

"You should've told me," I whisper.

She has a visible physical response with a slight jerk of her shoulders, so I know she heard me. Then she turns to look at me, her eyes weary.

"I only just found out."

"Bullshit," I counter. "You've known long enough for Lucy to have it figured out. That's what she was talking about the other night in the barn, wasn't it? Telling me about the baby?"

That thought had come to me sometime this afternoon when I was mentally backtracking the past months.

"Lucy knows, I'm sure your sister knows, although I'm surprised Fletch doesn't. He'd have floored me already otherwise. Why the fuck am I the last to find out?"

Suddenly not hungry anymore, I shove my plate away. A little too forcefully, as it slides across the smooth counter and shatters on the floor on the other side. The loud crash is startling, causing Pippa to jump off her stool and take a few steps back. The shocked look on her face is like a punch in the stomach.

"*Shit.* That wasn't intentional," I rush to say. "Sorry."

I move to the other side and duck down to pick up the pieces of the shattered glass and the remnants of my takeout.

Christ. I scared her. I didn't mean to, but I know I

fucking did. That look on her face... Add guilt to the cock-tail of feelings I can't really get a grip on.

Tossing the shards of china in the garbage, I turn around to see Pippa has taken a seat on the couch, while keeping an eye on me. I wash my hands and grab her plate.

"You should eat some more."

I hand her the plate and she gives me a shaky smile.

"I'm sorry," I repeat, leaving a bit of distance when I take a seat.

"It's okay." She shakes her head. "I should be the one apologizing. It's just...I'm still trying to wrap my head around this."

Like it's the most natural thing in the world, her hands automatically land on the swell of her stomach. I can't believe I didn't notice it before, and now it's all I can see. A fucking baby.

"For the record," she continues. "My sister knows I'm pregnant, but I haven't told her you're the father."

I abruptly lean forward, my head between my knees, waiting for the wave of sudden light-headedness to pass.

You're the father.

Words I never thought I'd hear in this lifetime. Holy shit.

"And Lucy made a lucky guess."

"How?" I finally manage, croaking like I recently woke up. I raise my head and look at her. "I mean, we'd both been drinking but I remember using a condom. Are you sure it's mine?"

Dammit, I know how fucking awful that sounds the moment it leaves my mouth, but I wanted to look her in the eye and know for sure.

"Without a single second of doubt," she says, the hurt evident in her voice and the way she looks back.

I know she's telling the truth.

It's like hearing the door slam and the key turning in the lock. Any hope of escape doused.

Time to man up.

Looks like I'm going to be a father.

I run a hand over my face. "Okay. All right." My mind is going a mile a minute, thoughts bouncing around like pinballs. "We'll go pick up your things tomorrow. I'll have to call my insurance company to figure out how to get you onto my policy. I can take the spare bedroom, and I'll clean out my office for the baby. Then maybe—"

I know I'm running at the mouth when I catch the incredulous expression on Pippa's face.

"Hang on there for a minute now, cowboy," she says, holding up a hand to silence me. "I'm not sure what you think is happening here, but I'm pretty sure I haven't agreed to any of what you just spouted."

Too much, too fast. Jesus, I'm out of my depth.

I get up and go grab a beer from the fridge. I'm about to ask what she wants when I spot her milkshake still sitting on the island. I pick that up too and return to the couch, handing it to her before I sit again. Taking a swig of my beer, I force myself to calm down. Otherwise, I stand to lose more ground than I was hoping to gain.

"Fair enough. I'm still trying to wrap my head around the fact you...*we*...are having a baby. I want to do the right thing."

Her expression softens slightly. "I'm not asking anything of you. You can walk away from this but you have to understand that's not an option for me. So I'm sorry if this doesn't work for you, but I will not let you make decisions about my life or my body."

I take another drink. This one for fortification. Then I

Eight

PIPPA

Co-parents.

That's the format we decided to move forward with last night.

Technically I decided, since Sully really had no choice but to follow along, but I think the concept worked for both of us. Knowing the boundaries and keeping the baby central certainly made our talk a lot less intimidating. Overwhelming, yes, but it felt like we were on the same side of the fence instead of at odds.

I was able to listen to him explain his thoughts behind the suggestion I move in. Most of that idea circled around health insurance and that part actually made sense. The only coverage I currently have here is my temporary travel insurance, which is geared toward emergencies and not ongoing care.

I already know I'll be getting a bill from the clinic and although I do still have some money in the bank to cover that, it won't last me long. Not when I also have to pay Ira, who is starting today. God only knows how long it's going to take for the business to start generating enough income to fully sustain him. In the meantime, I'll have to supplement out of pocket. It's a move I think will pay off in the end, but until then, it will likely leave me cash strapped.

Sully's proposal could actually relieve some of the pressure on me. From what he tells me the insurance coverage he has is pretty comprehensive. He's going to call them today to see if it's possible, what is needed, and what it would cost to have me added on to his policy. The whole issue of health insurance this side of the border is so different than what I'm used to, I'm happy to have him take the lead looking into that.

I also managed to quietly listen to him explain why moving in with him would be a good idea. He did add it could simply be temporary until after the baby is born, but I'm not yet sold on the idea. Oh, I can see the benefits—no living expenses, other than personal needs and groceries, always having someone around for emergencies—but I'm not sure it would be healthy for me.

Being in such close proximity to that man may prove to be too difficult. Not because I've been angry with him since the beginning of the year, but because he really fucking hurt me and has the power to do it again. I didn't even realize I had feelings for Sully until that night. Then within hours of that revelation, he managed to crush me. Sure, anger has been at the forefront of my emotions, but that doesn't mean the other feelings are dead.

So last night, I promised him I'd give the housing situation some serious consideration before I insisted on heading home. I ended up taking Fletch's truck, which he'd left parked at the barn.

It's early morning when I pull into the hospital parking

lot. I manage to slide Fletch's truck into a vacant spot beside my pickup, which I intend to leave with after I check in with my sister. Fletch can have his shiny truck back, I much prefer my classic.

There's no sign of Fletch when I walk into the room. Nella looks to be napping but when I tiptoe closer to the bed, her eyes snap open.

"Morning."

"Hey, how are you feeling?"

She shimmies up in the bed to sit up straighter.

"I feel fine. I still have the occasional contraction but the baby is great and dilation has halted, so it's all good. I'm kept on bed rest though." She makes an unhappy face. "I can only get up to go to the bathroom and every time I do it causes a contraction."

"That sucks. How long do you figure?"

Pulling up her shoulders, she answers, "I'm not sure. I think the idea is to get us to thirty-seven weeks at least, but that all depends on this little guy."

She places a hand on her prominent belly, a gesture that's becoming second nature to me as well.

"Guess he's eager to meet his parents. Speaking of which, where is Fletch? I brought his truck to swap for mine."

"He's just gone to grab a coffee and something to eat. I'm hoping I can convince him to go home and get some proper sleep. He's been watching over me all night in that chair, reacting to every little sound I make, and not getting any rest. I'm gonna go nuts if he stays and hovers all the time."

"Did you get the nursery done yet?"

Last time I was over at her place, they were still putting

it together at leisure. Things have become a little more urgent now.

"All the pieces are there. The crib and the changing table arrived the other day, but we haven't had a chance to put it together."

"Perfect," I announce. "Remind him the nursery is not ready for the baby and it's causing you stress. I bet he'll tear out of here to remedy that in a hurry. That man would move mountains for you if you asked."

I feel a twinge of envy, only a tiny one, but I shove it down. In truth, I'm thrilled my sister has found a man who adores her. Fletch is not exactly the most affable guy, but I love the way he is with my sister. She deserves to be adored.

She doesn't bother denying and instead turns the attention on me.

"What about you? How was your night?"

That question is way more loaded than it might appear, and I keep my answer simple.

"Good."

It's obvious my response annoys her when she rolls her eyes.

"You're being purposely obtuse," she accuses before asking me straight out. "Did you tell him?"

"I didn't get a chance," I admit. "He already figured it out."

"And?"

"After a bit of a bumpy start, we ended up talking. We're gonna take it step by step, keeping the baby central, sharing decisions. That kind of stuff. Co-parenting," I clarify.

Nella doesn't bother hiding her disappointment. I know she wants me to have what she found with Fletch.

"And what about you two?"

"It was a one-time thing, Nella, and we've barely spoken

since. That hardly makes for any kind of basis to build a relationship on."

"I was sure you liked him," she observes.

"I did, I do, but that has to be a two-way street."

That seems to surprise her.

"I was sure he liked you too," she states.

"Maybe, but even if that were the case, I don't think he was or is interested in anything serious."

"Well, then Sully is in for a surprise; becoming a father is serious business."

Behind me I hear the squeak of a shoe sole on the tile floor, and I watch Nella's eyes widen as she glances over my shoulder.

"That rat bastard," I hear Fletch growl behind me and I swing my head around. "I had a fucking feeling," he continues, glaring at me. "Knew he was sniffing around, but I had no idea that son of a bitch already went there. I'm gonna—"

I can pretty much guess what is coming after that, and I'm going to put a stop to it right now. I love my brother-in-law, I've been lucky to have seen his caring side, even appreciate his ingrained need to protect, but I could do without the knuckle-dragging, chest-pounding displays of aggression it seems to invoke.

"You will do absolutely nothing," I tell him firmly, getting up in his face so he'll understand me clearly. "I'm a grown woman, I made the choice to sleep with Sully, and I'll be the one dealing with the consequences. You need to know I'm gonna be mighty pissed if you make what is already a precarious understanding between Sully and me more difficult by throwing your weight, and—God forbid—your fists around."

I take in a deep breath before I hammer it home.

"I can—and will—make your life miserable if you interfere."

I can see the figurative steam coming from his ears as he glares at me, but then Nella clears her throat behind me before giving me her vote of support.

"And so will I."

~

Sully

"That's ridiculous."

I'm beyond annoyed, but it's not the fault of the insurance broker.

"Sorry I can't be of more help."

"That's okay. I'll figure it out."

Getting Pippa onto my insurance is not quite as straightforward as I'd hoped. It's not a problem changing to a family policy from the individual one I own. Her pregnancy is also not an issue, it used to be considered a pre-existing condition, but that no longer applies.

The problem we're facing is for her to meet the requirements of spouse. Her moving in with me is not going to be sufficient, and the fact she doesn't have her green card doesn't help. There's only one way to fix that, but I foresee that'll bring a whole new set of issues.

Luckily, once the baby is born, he or she would fall under my policy, but for Pippa the only alternative is to pay for her care out of pocket.

I do a Google search for the average cost of pregnancy and delivery. It's not as bad as I thought it would be. I'd need to do a little shuffling but I can afford it. I just don't know if Pippa will let me pay it all. I'll probably be lucky if she'll allow me to pay half. The woman is fiercely independent. But the problem is, I don't think *she* can afford it. She recently bought the garage, she hired a mechanic, and if she doesn't want to move in here, she'll also have to pay for a roof over her head.

I wanted to give her options, not force her into a corner.

Fuck. This is not going to be easy, is it?

"Who's ridiculous?"

Jonas is leaning against the doorpost to the office and I wonder how long he's been standing there. I haven't talked to anyone yet, but I want to be the one to tell my teammates. Out of respect for Fletch, I intended to tackle him first, but he's at the hospital with his wife and probably has other things on his mind right now.

Maybe it's not such a bad idea to start with Jonas.

"Health insurance."

"What's wrong with your health insurance?"

"I wanted to switch to a family plan."

He pushes away from the doorpost and walks in, taking a seat on the other side of my desk.

"Explain."

Jonas is direct, I know he'll appreciate the same from me so I'm not going to beat around the bush.

"Pippa is twenty-one weeks pregnant. I'm the father."

The words turn out to be surprisingly effortless for me, but hearing them has an obvious impact on Jonas. It's not often I see my friend lost for words, but he is now.

"What the fuck were you thinking, Eckhart?" he finally bursts out, leaning forward. "Four months ago? The woman would've barely recovered from her injuries. And she's Nella's sister. Practically family."

83

"I know that, J."

He gets to his feet, snatches his hat off his head, and slaps the brim against his leg.

"Fletch is gonna lose his goddamn shit."

"Probably. I plan to talk to him next."

Jonas shakes his head at me. "You'd better, my friend, because I won't stand for it if shit like that bleeds into the team."

"It won't," I promise, mentally crossing my fingers.

He leaves the room and comes back a few moments later with the bottle of bourbon he hides in his desk drawer and two tumblers. He pours a couple of shots, hands me a glass, and sits back down across from me. Then he looks up, the corner of his mouth twitching, and raises the glass.

"I trust you to do the right thing. Congrats, brother."

I raise my own glass and follow his example, tossing back the shot. The burn of the alcohol going down stings my eyes, and I suck in a sharp breath through my teeth.

Jonas simply winces and slams the empty glass on my desk before sitting back with a full-on smirk on his face.

"Butter my butt and call me a biscuit. Sullivan Eckhart... a fucking daddy."

My chuckle is inadvertent. It shouldn't be funny but Jonas is making me laugh. It's probably only nerves, or maybe the alcohol, but it takes me a moment to regain my composure.

"It's gonna be tough getting her added on my insurance unless she marries me."

"What are the odds of that happening?" Jonas asks.

I let out a snort. "I'd say pretty damn slim," I admit grudgingly.

"You not willing to take that step? You're not feeling it?"

"I'm feeling it and I wanna do the right thing, but I'm not so sure about her."

"Word of advice; don't mention 'doing the right thing' when you bring up marriage with her. I don't pretend to know much about women, but even I can tell you that'll be sure to annihilate any chance you might have."

I'm about to acknowledge what he says when my phone buzzes in my pocket. One look at the screen puts a smile on my face.

"Hey, sweetheart."

It's not often my niece calls me anymore. Not since she went off to college a few years ago. Too busy with student life to bother with her uncle.

"Uncle Sully? We have a problem."

Nine

"Wow. You're fast."

I walk through the waiting room and office attached to the garage. The paint fumes are minimal, courtesy of the non-toxic paint I paid a mint for, and the fact Ira has thrown every door and window open.

Rather than a pure white, I picked a warm pale gray, and Ira has done a good job painting all the walls in here. It looks really good.

He sticks his head out of the small customer bathroom.

"Doing the final coat in here with the dregs of the paint. Have you made a decision on those store shelves?"

The previous owner had a shelving unit and a small cooler against the far wall, according to Ira. He said they mostly sold drinks and snacks, but also things like air fresheners, motor oils, tire patch kits, antifreeze, that kind of stuff. The shelving unit was left behind, but the cooler had disappeared.

Ira offered to spray paint the shelving unit, to freshen it

87

up, but I'm not sure I want the hassle of selling merchandise. It would require at least one other person here, in addition to Ira, at all times and so far, I haven't had much luck finding part-time office help.

"If you have time to paint them, then go for it," I suggest. "But until I can find someone for the office, I don't want to make a decision on getting in merchandise. We can always use the shelving for storage in the garage though."

Ira grunts and ducks back into the bathroom.

A man of few words, but he works hard. It only took him a couple of days to give this place a fresh look. I peek into the garage to see if the new sign has been delivered. It's supposed to be dropped off today but it doesn't look like it has yet.

Ira had a tip and directed me to a signage place in town. Luckily, the old lighted marquee box was still working and all we needed was a panel with the new name. Still not cheap, but I decided to bite the bullet since these guys were able to promise a three-day turnaround. It's my own fault after doing nothing with this place for over a month after buying it to suddenly being in a rush to get it up and running.

You pay for speed and I want this place open after the weekend. I plan to be here but I have to fly under the radar since I'm not supposed to be working. Last thing I need is for someone to get wind of the fact I don't have a work visa and get it in their head to report me. That's why it's so important I find someone to do things like answer the phone and deal with the paperwork, at least part of the time.

I head back out to my truck to grab the bags of supplies and the old coffee maker Lucy gave me for the waiting room. Reaching into the rear of the cab, I hear the crunch of tires on gravel and look up to see an SUV pull in on the other side of the truck. I back out with my arms full and bump the door shut with my hip.

"Marcie told me I could probably find you here."

I silently curse my friend as I turn around to face Cade Jackson. The man whose phone calls I've been dodging for a while now.

"Oh wow," he says when he sees the load in my arms. "Here, let me give you a hand."

"That's okay, I'm—"

The coffee maker is plucked from my hands and so is one of the bags.

"Where to?" he asks with a smile, a little too hopeful.

I'm mad at myself. This is going to be an uncomfortable situation, and I could have prevented it if I'd only answered one of his calls. I can't really be pissed at Marcie, I figure he probably hounded her as much as he did me, and she did tell me a while ago I should let him know I'm not interested. I didn't want to bother, and now I have to deal with the consequences. I've kind of been avoiding Marcie recently as well.

All right, let's get this over with, but I'll feel more comfortable blowing him off inside within earshot of Ira.

"Inside. Follow me."

I walk up to the reception desk and lift the bags on the counter. He steps up beside me and does the same with the stuff he was carrying. He looks around the space with curiosity.

"Marcie told me you bought this place?"

"I did, last month."

He turns toward me and I wince at the pleased expression on his face.

"Good to know you've decided to stick around."

"Well, I have, but—"

"You know, I've been trying to get a hold of you," he starts. "Did you get a local phone plan?"

I take a deep, fortifying breath in.

"No, I haven't yet. I did notice you called a few times, but to be honest I've had my hands full. Trying to get this place open, among other things."

I put a hand on my belly. It's a cheap shot, but I have a feeling it'll take more than just words to dissuade him from his pursuit. Maybe this bump will get the message across without the need to actually tell him I'm not interested.

His eyes drop down to where I lightly rub the swell visible under my T-shirt. With the weather warming up, I've stopped wearing bulky sweaters and jackets, but I'm going to have to invest in some maternity wear because I'm fast outgrowing my wardrobe. People are going to know and I don't actively want to hide this bump, but I also don't want to flaunt it.

"Oh. Wow. I...uhh...had no idea. Yeah, I can see your hands are full. Wow," he repeats, clearly stunned. "I wonder why Marcie didn't mention this."

Shit. Marcie.

The moment he leaves, I'm gonna have to get on the horn before she finds out from him. She'll be upset enough I didn't share sooner, as it is.

"Actually, I haven't exactly had a chance to mention it to her. I only found out recently myself."

His eyes slowly make their way up to my face, and I feel a little violated to be honest. Then he suddenly darts a glance over my shoulder.

Without looking behind me, I know Sully just walked in the door.

I haven't seen him these past days, which sort of

puzzled me. I would've expected him to try and convince me to move in like he suggested, but he didn't even call me about the insurance, which he said he would do. Of course he would show up now, as I'm trying to let Cade down easy.

The entire atmosphere in here goes electric. I don't get a chance to turn around before he closes in behind me, sliding a hand around to cover mine on my belly.

Any other time I might've been moved, but this isn't a tender moment, this is a blatantly obvious public display of ownership. He could've yelled *'mine'* or peed on me and the message wouldn't have been any clearer.

"Hey, Honey," he mumbles, his lips brushing the shell of my ear.

I bristle with annoyance, but my body betrays me with a delicious buzz at his touch.

$\approx$

Sully

"That was unnecessary."

Her eyes flash with anger when she turns them on me.

I turn back to the window and watch that asshole, Jackson, pull out on the road. I want to make sure he's gone. In hindsight, I should've recognized the way he was talking about Pippa as interest the first time met I him out near Troy.

I did not like walking into Pippa's shop, catching him with his eyes on her body. Not only that, I could tell from her body language she wasn't enjoying this encounter. That really didn't sit well. So, my move to lay claim on her in a way he couldn't miss was very necessary.

"I could tell you didn't like him in your space, so I took care of it," I explain.

"Good move. I was about to step in there myself."

I turn around and see Ira Nelson walking toward us. That's right, Pippa mentioned hiring him. Libby isn't that big so I know the man, we bump into each other from time to time.

Right now, I'm grateful for the show of support because it looks like Pippa wasn't convinced by my explanation. On the positive side, she now appears equally annoyed with Ira.

"I was handling it," she says defensively.

"No, you weren't," Ira answers for me. "I heard your conversation and he doesn't sound like the kind of guy who gives up easily. Not tryin' to be an ass, but I'm not so sure that baby would'a scared him off." He cocks his thumb at me. "Man like Sully might."

I'm thinking I'm really going to like having Ira around.

"Ugh," Pippa grunts disgustedly before turning her back on both of us and walking into the garage.

"That baby yours?" Ira asks right as I hear a door slam in the back. "Bathroom," he adds by way of explanation.

"It is," I confirm, and I catch myself doing it almost proudly.

Ira nods and disappears through a door.

Now that the shock has worn off, I am starting to feel a bit excited. It helps I was finally able to pin down Fletch this morning and clear the air, so to speak. He spent most of his time in the hospital with Nella, so I ended up looking for him there. It worked out to my advantage, since that conversation went down beside Nella's hospital bed. No way he was going to bust my face with his pregnant wife looking on.

He had a few choice words for me, accused me of crossing the line, and I didn't bother arguing with him. Mainly because I agree. Not so much in sleeping with her, but in how I treated her after. I definitely crossed a line there.

He demanded to know how I was planning to look after Pippa and the baby. I told him in no uncertain words that was none of his business, that Pippa and I would work that out, but I did swear to him and Nella there's no way I'd fuck Pippa over.

That's what I came here for, to tell her I cleared the air with Fletch and to let her know about Sloane.

A whole other kettle of fish.

My twenty-one-year-old niece is having a meltdown because apparently my sister, Isobel—Sloane's mother—has a boyfriend.

I have to say it knocked me for a loop when she told me, I don't think Izzy has seen anyone since Nick. Not really a surprise, my sister may have survived her ordeal, but her trust in men received a death blow. In the past, I would've done a thorough background check on anyone my sister was seeing, maybe delivered a personal visit to ensure they knew to treat her right. But after what she's been through, I believe Isobel's own instincts would be a better measure.

The truth is, I'm actually glad she's seeing someone. She's got a lot of life to live yet to have given up on love.

Needless to say, my niece disagrees with me and wants me to pick the guy apart. She was able to tell me Isobel met him at the dog park, he's forty-nine, the vice principal at a high school, and his name is Steve Spence. Even his name sounds harmless.

I thought I'd calmed her down, assured her my sister knew what she was doing, and to give the guy a chance. That night Sloane sent me a snapshot of the guy getting into a mid-range sedan in my sister's driveway and added his license plate number. She's nothing if not thorough.

I have a feeling I haven't heard the last of her.

"I'm sorry, I had to make a quick call," Pippa says as she comes toward me. She avoids looking at me, when she adds, "And Marcie said I should be glad you're looking out for me."

"You were talking to your friend?"

"Well, I hadn't exactly told her about my condition yet and I didn't want her to find out from Cade, so I called her."

"And you told her about me?"

Her lips twitch as she glances at me from under her eyebrows.

"Sort of. Your name may have come up."

Something tells me whatever she shared about me wasn't very complimentary, but she doesn't elaborate and steers the conversation in another direction.

"But what are you doing here anyway?"

The smile on her face is friendly but reserved, and it hits me how much I fucking hate it. It's the way she might smile at someone she doesn't really know or trust. As much as I know I've caused that myself, it stings.

"I finally caught up with Fletch this morning."

I almost laugh when her eyes instantly scan my body, presumably to look for any damage.

"Oh?"

She's clearly curious what was said but doesn't want to ask, which is good because I wasn't planning on sharing.

Besides, I'm pretty sure Nella will fill her in at some point. I don't think there's much they don't share.

"We understand each other," is all I'm giving her before moving onto the next topic. "I also wanted to give you a bit of a warning. I have some family stuff which has popped up, courtesy of my niece who is not happy with her mother's life choices. I'm planning to give my sister, Isobel, a call and—seeing as she and Sloane are my only family—I'd like to tell her about the baby."

"Of course," she immediately responds. "I didn't realize you have a sister too. Younger or older?"

"Izzy is a few years older. Her daughter, Sloane, turned twenty-one earlier this year."

"Oh, I hope everything is all right?"

I'm about to brush her question off when I realize if I want Pippa in my life in any other capacity than co-parent for our child—if I want her to trust me enough to let me in—I should lead by example. After all, this woman is carrying my baby.

This still isn't easy to talk about so I focus on explaining it as fast and concise as I can. Like ripping off a Band-Aid.

"Five years ago, Sloane walked into the house to find her mother severely beaten and barely breathing, and her father with part of his head blown off as the result of a self-inflicted gunshot. Isobel finally started dating someone and Sloane is freaking-out."

Pippa gasps, slaps one hand over her mouth while spreading the other protectively over her belly, and widens her eyes, which are already brimming. Then she swings around and braces herself against the reception desk.

Fuck.

I was so preoccupied with getting the story out, I never

stopped to think how it might impact her. Clearly not that well.

I bridge the distance between us and press myself to her back, my hand seeking out the swell of her stomach as I whisper an apology in her ear.

A noise has me raise my eyes and I catch Ira poking his head around the doorpost.

Shaking his head.

Ten

Hormones.

That's what I blame my emotional reaction on.

As horrific as the entirety of Sully's story is—as awful the attack on his sister was—what is hitting me hardest is the thought of that poor girl walking into what must have been the scene of a nightmare. I can't imagine the trauma it would've left in someone at such a young age.

I try to regain my composure when I feel Sully behind me. The heat of his large hand sliding onto my stomach acts like a beacon for the coconut-sized little human growing there. She—I can't bring myself to say 'it'—reacts instantly, focusing a little kicking action into his palm.

I feel him stiffen.

"Is that...?"

I've only recently become aware the weird sensations I've been feeling aren't gas bubbles as I'd first thought, but the baby moving and kicking. I'm sure it would be an even stranger discovery for Sully.

"It is. She's been making her presence known," I inform him, wiping at the wet under my eyes before stepping out of his hold and turning around.

It's so tough not to lean on him—it would be so easy to let myself be tempted by the strength and stability he radiates—but I have to stand firmly on my own two feet. Be my own strength, create my own stability, not just for me but for this baby, because in the end, I'm the only thing standing between her and the world.

Sully still looks a little bewildered, staring at my belly like he's expecting something to leap out.

"Does it hurt?"

"It doesn't, it's just a little strange at first. It took me a while to clue in to what I was feeling. She moves a lot."

As if on cue, she starts moving again, so I reach for his hand and press it to where I feel her kicking. His mouth curves into a soft smile as he stares down at my belly. The look on his face steals my breath and I mentally file the moment away, along with the sudden wish to one day have a smile like that directed at me.

"She? You know the sex of the baby?"

His face betrays he wouldn't be averse to the idea of a little girl. I have to step away from his touch, which seems to draw me in as much as it does this baby. If I want my heart safe, I'm going to have to keep my distance.

"I don't actually know, but I'm supposed to see my doctor tomorrow and she should have the results of that test I told you about. Initially, I didn't think I'd want to know, but now I don't know...what do you think?"

It's funny, I find myself getting curious now. I guess the shock is wearing off. Maybe finding out the sex of the baby will provide a better connection. Something we can experience together. "You mean do I want to know?" He seems to think for a moment before answering. "Yeah, I'd like that."

"Okay, in that case what are you doing tomorrow at nine?" I ask him, decision made.

It took me all of two seconds to sabotage my own resolve to keep my distance. Then he throws me that smile, those dimples, the same ones that got me into trouble in the first place.

Dammit, they still get my heart pumping.

"I'll pick you up at twenty 'til."

I'm about to respond when the door behind us opens.

"I've got a delivery for ya."

The young guy with a Seahawks ball cap walks right up to Sully, handing him a clipboard. Instead of taking it, Sully cocks his thumb at me.

"Talking to the wrong person, this here's the boss."

The kid shrugs and hands it to me instead. "I've got your sign in the back of my truck. Gonna need a hand unloading."

I look over the order form, which is indeed for my signature. I'm about to head outside to make sure he's got the right one before we unload when Ira walks up and takes the clipboard from me.

"I've got it," he grumbles, following the guy outside.

When the door closes behind us, I turn back to Sully, whose eyes are on me.

"You've got your hands full, I'll let you get back to it," he says. "I'll see you tomorrow morning."

"Yeah. I'll walk you out," I offer, wanting to watch them put up the sign. Maybe take a few pictures.

I quickly grab my phone from behind the reception desk and follow him out the door.

Ira and the Seahawks kid are pulling the large sign from

the back of the truck, but to my disappointment it appears to be covered in white plastic. The design is quite simple, a black background to match the color of the rectangular light box, with bold, turquoise lettering. It has a bit of a retro feel, is masculine enough not to turn male clientele away, but with enough of me to feel genuine.

I'm not an idiot, I know there are plenty of guys out there—maybe more here in Montana—who would never step foot in this place if they knew it was owned by a woman. Hell, I dealt with my share of misogynistic rednecks like that back in Canada, which is why my shop back in Cranbrook didn't start getting traction until my ex signed on.

This time I'm building the business on my terms.

The kid announces he has more deliveries to make, so Sully ends up lending Ira a hand to hang the sign. I feel a ridiculous amount of pride when he and I stand back and watch Ira peel back the plastic.

"Pit Stop Engine Repairs," Sully mutters beside me. "I like it. It looks sharp."

Yes, it does.

I'm still grinning wide, pleased as punch, when I hear a vehicle pull in behind me.

"Looking good," Sheriff Ewing comments when he gets out of his cruiser.

Not sure what he is doing here, but I feel Sully closing in protectively.

"Sheriff," I greet him as he walks up.

"Social visit?" Sully asks, immediately taking control.

I'm not sure whether to be annoyed or grateful he's here. The sheriff doesn't exactly look like he dropped in to say hello. Ewing darts Sully a glance before fixing his attention on me.

"I have a few questions for you, Ms. Freling. It's about a report you made about barrel feeding wildlife."

Funny, we've bumped into each other enough, he usually calls me by my first name.

The truth is, I've made a few reports. I think three since February and Ewing should know about those. The last one I called in was a couple of days before Sully walked onto my campsite in early April.

"Which one? These past months I've made a few. I'm sure Fair Game has a record of them if the game warden's office doesn't."

"Yes, we spoke with someone of your group," he states. "This particular call would've been sometime in the second half of March."

I remember it. There was still some snow up in the mountains, but the weather forecast had predicted an unseasonably warm few days so I wanted to take my rig out. I picked a trailhead on Big Creek Baldy Mountain, about an hour's drive north of Libby.

"I remember that one. It was on a trailhead off Baldy Mountain Road, although I didn't stay long after discovering the place was overrun with black bear."

"Overrun, how?"

"Well, I rarely see four different ones within a twenty-four-hour period in the same place. They weren't shy either. Walked right up to the campsite. Well-fed. Unusually so. That, together with the recent tire tracks I noticed in the snow driving up there, I figured it was another baiting site. I called Marcie, gave her the coordinates, and then I left."

"Did you see anyone else up there?"

I feel Sully's hand slide up my back and under my hair where his fingers curl around my neck, giving me a light squeeze.

"What exactly is this about, Ewing?" Sully wants to know.

The sheriff appears annoyed at the interruption and shoots him an irritated glare.

An ominous chill runs down my spine.

~

Sully

"I'm following up on some information I received."

He's being evasive and it's pissing me off.

"Information about what?" I push.

"An investigation."

Yeah, he's not going to make this easy.

"Into what, exactly?"

I had a feeling by the way he addressed her that he was here on official business, and I'm not liking it. The questions he asked lead me to believe this has something to do with the dead hunters. I don't want Pippa answering any more questions until he clarifies what this is about, and why the fuck he's questioning her like she is somehow involved.

If he doesn't start talking, I won't hesitate to call Pippa a lawyer.

"A body was found not far from Big Creek Baldy Mountain a few days ago. Shot in the back, very similar to the other two victims. Predators had gotten ahold of this one though, so we didn't have a whole lot to go by, but we know that much. We also know it had been out there for a while."

He flips back his hat and runs a hand through his sparse hair.

few days before I bumped into her. That's when she reported Harper's license plate.

Finally, he asks her about the volunteer group. Who else does she know? Does she ever socialize with any of them?

"The body we found on Big Creek Baldy Mountain was Jeff Schumer. A local hunting guide, who'd been slapped with a few fines over the years, so he was known to the game warden. We have reason to believe he was the one responsible for that baiting site you found," the sheriff explains. "No one was actively looking for him because he rarely came into town. Harper's hunting buddies admitted John usually went early to start baiting. And the first body found near where Harper was found a few days later was another hunting guide, Rory Brent, from Moyie Springs, Idaho. All were shot from the back."

Wow.

"Hunters being hunted," I comment.

"Right," Wayne agrees. "And I hope to God there aren't more out there, but you and I both know folks go missing in these mountains and are never seen or heard from again."

Not a word of a lie there.

Ewing leaves not long after and I walk him to his cruiser.

"Next time you have questions, I expect a heads-up," I announce when he gets behind the wheel. I brace my hands on the roof and the top of the door and lean down so I'm eye level with him. "I don't care about the pressure I'm sure you're under, I don't give a flying fuck you're trying to solve this case before the feds come blundering all over your county again, but if you ever approach Pippa like you did today, we are going to have a serious problem."

Then I close his door for him and watch him drive away, legs spread and arms crossed over my chest.

Eleven

SULLY

"You must be Dad?"

I take the offered hand.

"Sullivan Eckhart."

"Nice to meet you. I'm Dr. Tippen, but you guys should probably call me Lindsey since we'll be seeing a lot of each other."

She gestures for us to follow her down the hall. I feel a little out of my element. Heck, that same blonde who was here when I brought Nella in was looking a little confused. The doctor shows us into an examination room, and my eyes catch on the table outfitted with the kind of stirrups I'm not that familiar with.

Holy shit. Talk about uncomfortable, especially when Pippa automatically sits on the edge of the bed.

"So, Sullivan, since I assume this pregnancy was a surprise for you as well, have you had a chance to get used to the idea?"

I keep an eye on the doctor as she wraps a blood pressure cuff around Pippa's arm.

"Working on it," I admit.

"Well, coming here is a good start. I may break out the ultrasound to give you a quick peek. That made things real in a hurry for Mom, didn't it?"

The latter is directed at Pippa, who is keeping an observant eye on me.

"It sure did," she responds.

"Blood pressure is slightly elevated. We'll try again at the end of the appointment."

She helps Pippa lie back and I dart a quick glance at the door, tempted to go wait outside, but when I turn back and catch Dr. Tippen's knowing grin, I dismiss that idea. I'm being tested and am determined not to fail.

To my relief—although I'd never admit it—only Pippa's belly is exposed. I'm suddenly mesmerized by the silky olive-tone skin stretched tightly over her abdomen. Her clothes hide a lot, this is a much larger baby bump than was visible from the outside.

The doctor gently palpates her stomach, commenting on the baby's activity level, and asking Pippa a few questions about her health. I listen with only half an ear, trying fucking hard not to get turned on by the mother of my child lying on a bed, which invokes a fantasy or two. It seems almost sacrilegious to have these thoughts, yet they persist.

"Why don't you pull your chair over here?" Dr. Tippen suggests, indicating a spot by Pippa's head. "I'm just going to grab the ultrasound.

"Wait," Pippa stops her. "The test, is everything okay?"

"Absolutely. I would've called you if there was anything of concern. Hang tight, I'll be right back."

When she's gone, I drag my chair closer and sit down by

her shoulder. Her stomach is still exposed. I reach out my hand, letting it hover over her smooth skin.

"May I?"

I glance over and find her nodding at me, the rich brown of her gorgeous eyes shining like jewels. She looks vulnerable, almost fragile, and every protective fiber in my body roars to the surface.

Then I touch her, feeling the heat of her body penetrate my calloused palm. Such a stark contrast between my rough, hard hand and her soft, delicate skin. Both protectively shielding the baby growing inside.

The door opens and the doctor rolls in an ultrasound machine, setting it up on the other side of the bed. I pull back my hand, but Pippa grabs on, curling her fingers around mine. My eyes lock on hers and for a moment everything else disappears, except for the silent communication between us.

The feelings masked by fear in her eyes, I know are reflected in mine.

When the clearing of a throat draws our attention to the grainy image on the screen, it feels like we've come to some unspoken understanding.

"There's the little one," the doctor says, her voice gentle.

At first, I don't know what I'm looking at until I see movement. Then I recognize a profile and what looks like a hand. The image shifts and I see a rib cage, part of a spine, and a darker spot pulsating quickly. The heart. Next thing I know, the sound of a heartbeat is audible, beating in tandem with the image on the screen.

I know it's there; I've felt it move, but being able to see it and hear it throws a switch in my brain. This baby is instantly transformed from a concept to a reality as tangible as the Stetson I have clasped in my other hand.

It takes me a moment to realize Pippa is asking a question.

"Dr. Tippen, is it possible to see the baby's gender?"

"You've changed your mind? Oh, and please call me Lindsey."

Her hand squeezes mine and she darts a quick glance my way before answering the doctor.

"We've decided we'd like to know."

"It's in the report, but let's see if this little one is willing to share the secret."

The image shifts again as she manipulates the wand sliding over Pippa's stomach.

"There, that's a good view."

I'm still trying to sort out what I'm looking at when I hear Pippa's sharp intake of breath.

"It's a girl?" she whispers.

"Sure is. Congratulations."

With quick, efficient movements, Lindsey wipes the gel off Pippa's stomach, tugging her shirt back down, before she unplugs the machine and starts rolling it out of the room.

"You can get off the bed. I'll be right back," she announces before walking out.

My heart was already beating fast but is now making its way up my throat.

I'm scared. Forty-four years old, have faced down brutal enemies, looked down too many gun barrels, felt the hot sear of a bullet penetrating my body more than once, but I don't think I've ever been this afraid.

A girl. A daughter to cherish and protect.

The thought terrifies me.

"Are you okay?"

Pippa lets go of my hand and swings her legs off the bed, sitting herself up.

"Sully?"

I pinch the bridge of my nose before rubbing a hand over my short-shorn scalp down to the back of my neck. My eyes pop open when I feel Pippa's cool touch on my cheek. She's leaning down, her nose almost touching mine, as her gaze searches my face.

"A girl..."

My voice is raw. Fuck, I don't even know what I'm feeling right now.

Pippa does. The vibrant smile on her face holds no secrets.

"Yeah. We'll have to start thinking of names."

Fucking hell.

It's like throwing a switch. Yesterday her face had been etched with worry after the sheriff's visit as she sent me home. Today—not twenty-four hours later—she's beaming and wanting to talk baby names.

I'm not that flexible, my mind is still set to worry.

Ten minutes later, I help Pippa into the truck before I get in behind the wheel. She has an appointment to see the doctor again in two weeks. The subject of insurance came up and I explained we're working on that. I guess there's no time like the present to tackle that issue.

"It's not a problem to switch my insurance to a family plan. I looked into the blood test for a license, but there's a consent form we can both sign to get around that. All it takes is a visit to the county clerk's office."

"A license?"

I turn my head and catch sight of the look of disbelief on her face.

"As in a marriage license?"

The pitch of her voice is even higher this time. She's pissed, which is a bit of a hit to the ego. I don't like the fact marriage to me seems to strike her as such an outrageous idea.

Then abruptly she dissolves into peals of laughter.

I'm pretty sure I like that less.

~

Pippa

His knuckles are white against the steering wheel as he turns the truck onto the road.

Maybe I shouldn't have laughed at his suggestion, although it wasn't so much at the marriage part as it was at the way he presented it. Like some kind of business proposal; exactly what every girl dreams of.

Still, I probably could've responded better, so I reach out and put a hand on his forearm.

"Could you pull over?"

Instantly his eyes dart my way.

"Are you okay?"

"I'm fine, but I really want you to pull over."

He aims the truck at the parking lot in front of the Smoking Gun restaurant. It's early and the place isn't open yet, so the parking lot is empty.

"What's wrong?" he asks as he shuts off the engine and turns in his seat.

"Let's talk about this," I propose. I don't bother clarifying, we both know exactly what I'm referring to. "You're suggesting marriage?"

"And you find the idea laughable," he replies, clearly butthurt.

It almost makes me laugh again but I manage to keep it under control. He's simply surprised me with these sudden displays of frailty in this past hour. My impulse to laugh is more from nerves than hilarity. I don't find his vulnerability funny; I find it dangerously attractive. Another layer to add to this strong, almost formidable man. Complex layers hidden by what I thought was an impenetrable shell honed by years in the military. The only parts of him suggesting a more approachable personality are the plentiful tattoos decorating his skin and the easy, irresistible dimples framing his mouth.

"No. The idea makes me nervous," I admit, watching the surprise on his face. "Last week we agreed to focus on parenting together, taking things a step at a time. This week you're talking about marriage, which is leaping ahead." I close my eyes and shake my head, not sure if I'm explaining myself right. "It almost feels like a business decision."

Then I feel him pick up one of my hands, covering it in both of his.

"My biggest concern is having you looked after. Both of you. Insurance is one consideration and a big one. We may be able to carry the cost of a healthy pregnancy, delivery, and baby, but what if not everything goes as planned? I need to make sure you are both covered in that event."

I open my eyes and find his closer than expected. He makes sense and clearly thought this through, but it still seems like a giant leap in a direction I'm not sure we should take.

"It's also the fastest way to get you permanent residence," he adds before he brings his point all the way home. "And finally, as your husband, I feel I'd be in a better position to stand up for you. Protect you."

Previously, I might've found that synonymous with

controlling me, but after yesterday's visit from the sheriff, I read it in an entirely different light. To be honest, I was scared out of my wits—still am—and well out of my depth. Having Sully there to stand up for me made it better.

By a lot.

"And I guess I'd be moving in with you?"

"You're making it sound like a sentence," he observes with a grimace. "But yes, it would make sense."

I get it and I'd have to agree, but that still leaves the bitter taste of a business proposal in my mouth, so I decide to address that too.

"What about feelings?" I bring up. "As convenient as a marriage would be, this feels like a business arrangement. I'm just trying to identify what this is."

His blue eyes deepen in color, warming.

"It's not an arrangement to me, Fillippa, it's a commitment."

I don't think he's ever used my full name before. I like it. I like the message it emphasizes too. But it's his next words that have my heart skipping a beat.

"And to answer your question, there are feelings. Right now, more than I know what to do with."

I barely have time to digest their meaning when my phone rings in my pocket.

"It's Fletch," I announce when I see his name on the screen before I answer with, "Hey."

"Need you to get your ass over here or you're gonna miss it."

A surge of excitement has my heart pounding and my skin tingles with excitement.

"Nella?"

"She's fine, making it look like a fucking tea party. Six

Twelve

"You've got a visitor."

My eyes drift past Bo in the direction of the main house. "Who is it?"

Instead of answering me, Bo's eyes widen slightly as he catches sight of something over my shoulder. Then he grins wide.

Here we go.

"Morning, gorgeous."

"Morning, Bo," Pippa answers from right behind me.

I reach back for her hand and pull her to my side, sliding an arm around her waist.

She stayed here last night, in my bed, while I crashed in the spare bedroom.

Yesterday afternoon after she took me to have a peek at Fletch and Nella's baby and congratulate the parents, I invited her back to the ranch. I knew Ama and Alex would likely have a celebratory meal ready, since Fletch had already called with the news.

The last kid born to a team member was James and Ama's youngest, Una, who is now a teenager and causing her parents' gray hair. All of us were still in the field then and didn't have a chance to celebrate.

This time was a little different, not in the least because of what it meant to Jonas's father. The old man was teary-eyed all through dinner, unable to hide his appreciation having the baby named after him. Jonas is his only child and doesn't have children of his own, aside from his stepson, Alex's adult kid.

In the same vein Thomas is a father figure to us all, I guess he considers every one of us his surrogate sons, so Fletch and Nella giving their son his name is a big deal.

It hadn't been too difficult convincing an emotional and exhausted Pippa to come back to the cabin after dinner. To my surprise, she snuggled into me on the couch and we rehashed the events of the day. That in itself was an alien concept for me, sharing your day with someone, but to my surprise I actually enjoyed it. Mind you, having Pippa plastered to my side might have had something to do with that.

I'd hoped we could maybe address the logistics of her moving in here, but it didn't take long for her to fall asleep on my lap though, and I ended up carrying her into my bedroom. There I got rid of her jeans, but didn't bother with the rest before tucking her in, and then I sent Lucy a text to let her know Pippa was here. As much as I would've liked to have crawled into bed with her, I ended up watching a bit of TV before I crashed in the spare bed. Next time I share a bed with her, I want us both to be very aware.

Any hopes I had for a one-on-one with Pippa over coffee and toast went out the window with Bo's knock on my door.

"Who is it, Bo?" I repeat, but an excited cry draws my

attention to the porch where I catch sight of a bright splash of color flying down the steps.

Fuck me.

"Uncle Sully!"

Barely seven o'clock on a Sunday morning and my niece is running this way, limbs, hair, and scarves flapping. *Christ.* The horses are going to have a heyday with Sloane, who likes dressing like a goddamn fortune-teller. She calls it Boho, but her style is basically a throwback to the flower-power era.

Love, peace, and harmony, my foot. She's far too passionate for that. It's the Italian genes she inherited from her sperm donor, because all she would've inherited from her mother and my side of the family would've been a Scandinavian cool head. We tend to be more reserved, cautious, and focused; all things Sloane is not. She lives for drama.

Pippa has the presence of mind to step out of harm's way, seconds before a human tornado in the shape of my niece launches herself at me.

"Jesus, kid," I grumble, when I find my footing and anchor her in my hold. "I'm getting too old and you're getting too big for that shit."

She immediately releases her hold on my neck and scowls up at me as she backs away.

"Are you calling me fat?"

A groan escapes me, which Bo seems to find amusing. I shoot him an angry glare as he slowly backs away from the impending train wreck I know is looming.

Sloane is primed for a fight. Any fight. She's frustrated with her mother, who has given up getting sucked into her daughter's moods, she can't get me to do her bidding, and so she shows up out of the blue, itching for some kind of confrontation.

I know it for sure when she catches sight of Pippa and

her eyes narrow. Apparently, Sloane's inability to share isn't limited to her mother.

"I'm not calling you fat," I try to draw her attention back to me. "I'm calling you no longer five years old."

My distraction doesn't work, since she's ignoring me and scanning Pippa head to toe. Her entire body jerks when she notices the baby bump.

"I don't know who you are," she addresses Pippa rudely.

I don't get a chance to put her in her place, Pippa beats me to it but she does it in a way that is more effective.

"Easily resolved," she says cheerily. "I'm Fillippa Freling, but call me Pippa, everyone does. And you are Sully's niece, Sloane. He's told me about you."

She's smart enough not to bother holding out her hand, probably realizing she would've been left hanging.

"Funny, he hasn't told me a thing about you."

Oh yeah, my niece is primed for a fight and it doesn't matter with whom.

"Enough," I bark, shocking Sloane.

I'm not in the habit of raising my voice, but it's clear she's on a tear and I don't much care to have more loaded to Pippa's plate than she already carries. Best my niece know right off the bat I will not put up with that shit.

"There's coffee in the kitchen, why don't we go inside and sort this over a cup," Pippa suggests, leading by example as she turns and heads in.

Sloane has a mutinous look on her face, but underneath I can still see the traumatized teenager whose trust in the world has been shattered.

"Come on, kid," I mumble, hooking her around the neck as I rub my knuckles over her short blond locks.

Pippa

Yikes.

That's a lot of anger radiating from one so young.

If Sully hadn't filled me in on her backstory, I would've given his niece a piece of my mind. But knowing what I know, I feel empathy for the girl.

When my parents died, it messed me up but I had my sister to provide the anchor I needed at the time. What Sloane went through is even more traumatic and I can see how—without an older sibling to guide her through—her experience would've resulted in this scared, insecure, and angry person sitting across from me. She's like a wounded animal, lashing out as she frantically tries to protect what is hers.

"What are you doing here, Sloane?" Sully asks her as he takes a seat next to me.

His voice holds a barely contained edge. He's pissed but he's holding it in. Good, because I have a feeling all hell might break loose otherwise.

"What? I can't come visit my family?"

I'm not the only one who hears the vulnerability under that sharp tone, and I'm glad when Sully's voice softens.

"Of course, sweetheart. Always."

Poor kid. She is a walking contradiction: from her short, functional haircut to the colorful, dramatic clothes, and from the sharp edge of her tongue to the sheen of insecurity in her blue eyes. She's a young woman unsure of where she stands, unable to shed her past or embrace her future. She's spinning in place.

I don't know her, but I recognize her.

"But shouldn't you be in school?" he asks.

"I'm done. Handed in my final papers a few days ago, packed up my room, got in my car, and drove here."

"From Utah?"

"Yeah. It's not that far," she says casually. "About twelve hours or so."

"Where's your stuff?"

"In the car."

"Your car? I didn't see it out there." Sully leans back to glance out the window.

"It's not. It's on the side of the road about fifteen miles south of here. Dead. I hitched a ride on a truck heading this way and got him to drop me off at the base of the driveway."

Sully's groan is loud as he buries his face in his hands.

"Tell me at least you told your mom you were heading here?" he mumbles.

Her eyes flit to me before drifting outside. When there is no response forthcoming, Sully sits up straight.

"Sloane?"

"Well, it's not like she lets me in on *her* plans," the girl returns defensively. "Besides, she's too busy packing up the townhouse to move in with *Steve* to care what I'm doing."

"She cares."

Sully's comment is met with stubborn silence and I don't feel it's my place to wade in. Not yet.

Instead, I get to my feet and head for the kitchen.

"I'm gonna make some breakfast," I announce. "I hope you have eggs."

I pull open his fridge to find the end bit of a piece of cheese, a few containers of yogurt, half a loaf of bread, a package of lunch meats, a few beers, bottled water, and a variety of condiments. No eggs, no vegetables or fruit, nothing I could use to slap together an omelet.

"Sorry," he mumbles right behind me. "I'm not much of a cook. I usually eat at the main house."

"You don't live here?"

I turn around to find Sloane standing by the kitchen island, observing us. It's the first time she addresses me since Sully told her off.

"No."

"Yes," Sully answers at the same time.

His niece looks confused.

"She's moving in today," he clarifies.

Admittedly, yesterday is a bit of a blur, but I'm pretty sure I would've remembered agreeing to that. However, I don't think this is the time to test Sully's patience, which appears to be stretched thin as it is. I was ready to give in on that point anyway. The past few days I've realized how much I've already come to rely on the support he seems surprisingly natural at providing.

Yesterday morning in the doctor's office, we shared a moment where neither of us had up any shields. I could see my swirling emotions reflected back at me through his eyes, and we seemed to come to an unspoken understanding. One where maybe we should start focusing forward instead of looking back.

Moving in would definitely be a step in the right direction. Perhaps a bit unconventional, and definitely fast, but nothing about Sully and myself, or this pregnancy, has been by the book. We're making it up as we go.

"I am," I confirm, more for Sully's sake than for Sloane's.

He looks at me. "Yeah?"

"Right after I go pick up a few groceries to cook us some

breakfast. Oh, and drop by the hospital to see my nephew," I add as an afterthought.

"Make me a list and I'll quickly drive into town," he offers.

Right, and leave me with his angry niece? No, I think maybe it's better if I make myself scarce for a bit. They could use some time without me being a distraction.

"You should visit with Sloane while I'm gone," I point out, realizing as I'm saying it I don't have my truck here. It's parked at the rescue. "I'll see if Bo can give me a ride to my truck."

"I can drive you," Sully offers.

"I'm going to need stuff from my car," Sloane interrupts, her eyes sharp on her uncle. "Besides, I'm not hungry."

This is a test, I'm sure, and I can almost guarantee Sully is going to fail unless I intervene.

"Okay. Change of plans," I suggest, clapping my hands together. "Forget about breakfast. You guys can simply drop me off at the rescue before you go pick up Sloane's things. I'll pack my stuff, run my errands, pick up some groceries, and meet you back here this afternoon."

I can tell Sully wants to object but he seems to read the look I send him.

Five minutes later, we're heading down the driveway toward the road. Sloane is quiet in the back of the crew cab as Sully checks his rearview mirror before glancing over at me.

"I can get groceries, you know."

I firmly press my lips together before my thoughts escape, because judging by his fridge his kind of groceries aren't the ones you can actually cook.

"That's okay. I'm heading into town anyway. I don't mind at all."

I want to tell him I intend to pay for all groceries as a contribution to the household since he won't accept any rent, but I don't want to get into a potential argument with his niece listening in. I'm sure we'll have a chance to work stuff like that out later.

"What is this place?" I hear Sloane's voice behind me when Sully turns up the driveway to the rescue.

"It's a horse rescue. It actually belongs to Alex, Jonas's wife," Sully explains. "And her friend, Lucy, runs it for her. This is where Pippa's been staying."

He pulls in beside my pickup in front of the house and gets out from behind the wheel. I'm already halfway out of the cab when he rounds the truck to help me down.

"Walk me to the door?"

"Was planning to," he shares, taking my hand in his.

"See you later, Sloane," I call out.

I don't get a response but I wasn't exactly expecting one.

On the porch I turn to face Sully, whose expression reads like thunder. I lift a hand to his face.

"Lose the scowl."

"She's out of line, Fillippa. Behaving like a petulant child," he grumbles.

My full name again, so I'll know he's serious.

"Maybe so, but consider she was still a child when she had to grow up in a hurry because her security was ripped right out from under her. You see a petulant child, and yet, I see a girl who is lost. Who is struggling with the fact she is no longer number one in her mother's life. So she comes running to you to assure herself she's at least still number one in yours, but finds me moving into your house. And to top it all off, I'm pregnant. Something I'm sure she's noticed but pointedly hasn't addressed. She's scared, Sully, to lose her place in the family she has left."

He stares at me for the longest time before he mirrors my touch with his hand against my cheek.

"You're smarter than I am," he says in a gruff voice.

"Nah...I recognize where she's at, that's all. Best thing to do is take the high ground and don't get sucked into the energy she's putting out. Stay calm and stay steady. That's what she needs most."

He nods once, bends his head to kiss me sweetly, and turns to head down the steps.

"See you later," he calls over his shoulder.

"Yes, you will."

Behind me I hear the door open and Chief and Scout rush out to greet me, followed by Lucy, who steps up beside me. The two of us watch Sully drive toward the highway.

"You're back earlier than expected," she says when his truck disappears from sight.

"I'm here to pack," I tell her.

"Hmm," she hums before hooking an arm in mine and turning me toward the house. "I'll make us some decaf and you can tell me all about it."

Thirteen

SULLY

"Yes, she's with me."

I get behind the wheel and glance over at Sloane, who is pretending to look out the side window. I'm sure she can guess who I have on the phone.

"Oh, thank God."

My sister blows out a relieved breath and I hear her relay the information to someone there. I assume her boyfriend.

"Yeah. Showed up this morning. She's fine."

"Jesus, Sully. I swear, that kid. Now that I know she's not lying dead in a ditch somewhere, I'm tempted to strangle her myself."

I bite off a grin and notice from the corner of my eye the subject of our conversation is paying closer attention than she'd like me to think.

"How about you talk to her instead? Here, let me put you on hands-free."

Ignoring Sloane's vehement head shake, I turn the key in the ignition and plop my phone in the holder.

"Isobel?"

"Still here."

Her voice sounds a little echoey over the truck's sound system.

"Sloane's right beside me."

I quickly put the truck in gear and pull away from the curb, afraid my niece might otherwise make a run for it. The tow truck hauling my niece's piece of junk to Pippa's shop took off right when my sister called.

"I was worried sick about you, young lady!" Isobel scolds her daughter. "We both were. You should've let us know."

I'm glad my sister can't hear Sloane's derisive snort. I throw her a look of warning at which she rolls her eyes. *Fuck*, if this is what having a daughter is like, I've got something to look forward to.

Christ help me.

"I'm twenty-one. I'm not a kid," is her response, her belligerent tone at odds with her claim.

"Then quit acting like one!" my sister is quick to point out. "I had to find out from your roommate you packed up all your shit in your car and took off. Not a word of warning to me. And then you clearly ignored the dozens of times I tried to call or text you. Did you know Steve spent the past twenty-four hours calling every hospital and police department from Provo to Ogden and in surrounding counties?"

By now my sister is so mad she's crying, which is unlike her. In the background I hear a deep voice in a soothing tone. Steve, I presume.

Beside me Sloane is staring out the windshield, her face a stoic mask except for the slight twitch of a muscle by the corner of her mouth.

"Come home." Isobel sounds a little more composed now.

"Pffft, what home?"

"Right here, Sloane. The apartment over the garage is all yours for as long as you want, we told you that."

"I don't want to move into Steve's house," she says, making it sound like something distasteful. "I want to live with Uncle Sully."

Whoa. A visit I can handle, but living here? Permanently?

It's becoming clear why she didn't call ahead, I would've done my damnedest to disavow her from this hairbrained idea.

"Have you asked your uncle about that?"

I sense her looking at me and glance over. Big mistake. She knows I have trouble resisting those big, innocently round blue eyes she turns on me.

Goddammit. I've successfully avoided sharing my space with women longer than a few hours at a time for many years. Yet here I am, facing a houseful of them. And only one by invitation. Well, technically one and a half.

"Sully?" Isobel addresses me. "Has she?"

My mind is scrambling. As we speak, Pippa is packing her shit to move in with me, but having my slightly hostile niece move in as well was not part of that plan. But maybe...

"Not in so many words." Or at all really, but it won't do any good to fan the flames. "But how about this? Is there any chance for you to come for a visit? We can sit down, like the adults we are," I add for the sake of my niece, "and talk through the options."

"What if I don't want to?" Sloane interjects stubbornly.

"If you want to spend any time here, you're going to have to."

"I'll just go somewhere else."

I remind myself of what Pippa mentioned earlier this morning when I dropped her off, that Sloane's afraid of losing her family.

"Can't stop you if that's what you want, kid. But make sure you understand that'll be your choice, not your mother's or mine. But if you're the adult you say you are, an honest discussion about your plans and options with family who love you shouldn't scare you."

Her face is turned away but her body language betrays a struggle and her almost whispered response confirms it.

"Fine."

By the time we pull up outside my cabin, we have a temporary plan in place until my sister can get here next weekend. I'll have to check with Jonas, but I'm sure he won't mind if I install Sloane in the guest cabin beside mine. There is still Fletch's old cabin, should anyone else need a place to crash. This way I hope my unexpected family invasion won't send Pippa running.

"Leave your stuff in my truck for now. You and I need to go have a word with Jonas first."

I'm not sure my niece realizes what being a grown-up means, and I think it's time she learned that as an adult you have to work for what you want. There are no free tickets.

She doesn't say anything but I can hear her footsteps behind me as I walk toward the corral, where I saw Jonas watch Dan working one of our young colts on a lunge line. The ranch hand has taken over a lot of the training. He's come a long way since Alex took him under her wing.

Jonas turns, leaning his shoulder against the fence as we approach.

"Heard you had a visitor," he comments, with a hat tip to my niece. "Good to see you, Sloane. How's school?"

"You too," she says, proving she hasn't forgotten her manners. "And I'm done. I handed in my final paper last Thursday."

"Congrats. So, what's next for you?"

Rather a loaded question, given the circumstances, but Jonas doesn't know that. Yet.

Sloane darts a glance my way, looking for a rescue.

"Actually," I step in. "That's exactly what we came here to talk to you about."

He turns his gaze on me, an eyebrow raised. "Oh?"

I shoot him a pointed look I'm trusting he'll pick up on.

"Yeah. Sloane was hoping to move here. I figure before she makes any decisions, she should have a trial run, but Pippa will be moved in tonight..." That earns me an approving grin from Jonas. "So I was thinking maybe Sloane could take the guest cabin next door, if you're okay with that, but you may want to fill her in on what would be expected from her, living at the ranch."

I'm trying hard not to look at my niece to catch her reaction, but the strangled sound beside me tells me enough.

"Sure," Jonas picks up, a dead-serious expression on his face. "It's pretty straightforward, everybody pulls their weight around here."

"What does that mean?"

I have trouble keeping a straight face at the hint of panic in her voice.

"I'm talking daily ranch chores; keeping the grounds, mucking the stables."

≈

Pippa

I'm still grinning when I hang up the phone.

That was Sully, calling to let me know he had Sloane's old clunker towed to the Pit Stop. He also filled me in on what was happening with his niece. Sounds like she'll be around at least for the foreseeable future, depending on how long she lasts. From what he shared, he and Jonas are going to make her work for it, which is what has me grinning.

It actually makes sense to have her take some responsibility. I can see where the adults in her life have sheltered her where they could, after what she went through as a teenager. However, ultimately, she has to find a way forward from that trauma on her own. Giving her the choice to stay—to have the safety of family next door, a roof over her head, and food in her belly—but making her work for it is a good taste of reality for her.

You can't bank on trauma of the past to sustain you in the future. I'm still learning that lesson myself.

The dogs come bounding toward me as I walk to the barn to check in with Lucy. She came out here after lunch to feed Hope's foal. I'm gonna miss these dogs. I know they have Max at the ranch, but he's Jonas's shadow. I wouldn't mind a dog of my own.

Another part of the dream I had long given up on.

A dog, a baby, a business I can call my own, and a man who is proving himself to be kind and supportive. A man I have feelings for and not only because he's the father of my baby.

The same man who is currently on his way over here to pick up the bulk of my stuff, so I don't have to haul it into town when I go to pick up groceries. Another check mark on a growing list of his qualities is his insightfulness. I didn't have to ask for his help, he offered, which makes a big difference.

"How is Floyd?"

Lucy looks up. She's sitting on a hay bale with the foal wedged between her legs. "Getting better at this, thank God. He's starting to fill out a little, isn't he?"

I run a hand over the animal's soft hide, noticing how his spine and ribs aren't quite as pronounced as they were.

"Handsome boy," I observe.

"He sure is."

"I know you've got a client coming, so I just wanted to let you know Sully is on his way. We're gonna load up his truck and as soon as he's gone, I'll be heading out too. I have to grab some groceries, is there anything you need? I could drop it off when I pass on my way back."

"I'm good. It's gonna be quiet here again."

"I'm sorry, I kinda feel like I'm abandoning you."

Lucy snorts and grins up at me. "I wasn't complaining."

I'm already on my way back to the house when I realize what she said and I burst out laughing. Lucy is honest to a fault. I love that about her.

When Sully gets here, he won't let me lift a finger, hauling my things to the back of his truck. It's packed solid when he drives off fifteen minutes later. There's nothing left for me to take in my pickup. The only thing I'm leaving here for now is my rig. We can get it another day.

I give the dogs a bit of love and wave at Lucy, who is working with her client on Ladybug. Lucy doesn't wave but she gives me a barely-there salute when she catches sight of me. She's not an easy person to get to know, but over the past months I've come to consider her a friend. Sure, I'll miss her, but it's not like I'm moving that far. I'll be right down the road and will drive by here every day going to the garage.

The Pit Stop is on my right side on the way into town. I'd already planned to stop and park Sloane's car inside overnight. I assume the tow truck driver dropped her keys through the slot in the shop door. It's easier to pull off and do that now than it would doing it heading home.

I immediately notice the damage and slam on the brakes.

My body is almost vibrating with anger as I pull out my phone and dial the Libby Police Department. But it's not the Libby PD that shows up only minutes later. It's Sheriff Ewing. Last week I would've been relieved to see a familiar face, but after what happened on Friday anyone else would've been preferable.

"What happened?" he asks when he walks up to my open driver's side window.

I pulled in farther but forced myself to stay in the truck, as much as I wanted to go out and check.

"Other than someone broke my brand-new, beautiful sign and smashed in my windows? I don't know. I haven't looked."

"Okay, sit tight here."

He walks toward the building, brushing the toe of his boot through the debris on the ground. Then he steps over and sticks his head through the hole in the large store window.

While I watch him try the bay doors and head around the side of the building, I call Fletch. When I talked to him earlier, I mentioned I'd be by after lunch, but now I don't know when I can get there.

"Where are ya?"

"At the shop. I've run into a snag and I'm not sure when I'll be able to get out of here."

I should've known my brother-in-law's antennae would pick up trouble.

"What kind of a snag? I thought you weren't opening 'til tomorrow?"

"Nothing I can't handle," I tell him before distracting him. "How's my nephew?"

"Good, eating like a champ. Nella is waiting for the doctor to stop in so she can convince him to spring her. She's itching to get out of here."

"I bet she is." I catch sight of the sheriff coming around the other side of the building. "I gotta go, but do me a favor, shoot me a text to let me know if you guys are heading home? And give my sister and my nephew a kiss."

I hang up before he has a chance to answer, right as Ewing steps up to the window.

"Doesn't look like anyone went inside." He cocks a thumb at the rusty Honda Accord parked out front. "Yours?"

"No, a customer's. Tow truck towed it here just this morning."

"This morning?"

He pushes away from my door and saunters over to Sloane's car, picking something off the hood. I slip out from behind the wheel and walk up to him.

"What is that?"

He holds out a shard of plexiglass, which I recognize as part of my sign.

"What time was the car dropped off?"

The words aren't out of his mouth when the crunch of tires has me turn around to see Sully's truck pulling in.

"You didn't call me," is the first thing from his mouth when he comes rushing up.

"No, I called the police like I'm supposed to, except the sheriff showed up. Who called you?"

Sully points at Ewing.

"He did."

"I heard the call come in over the radio, was in the neighborhood, so I volunteered to come have a look. I called Sully on my way over," the sheriff explains. "Now, can we get back to my question? What time was that car dropped off?" he repeats.

I don't know whether to be pissed with Ewing or grateful he called Sully. It was either infuriatingly sexist, or unexpectedly considerate...*and* sexist. Either way, I don't think I'm in the right frame of mind to point out I feel it was inappropriate either way. I'm already pretty steamed and I might say something I regret. I don't want to get on the sheriff's bad side.

"I'm not sure. Sully?"

"Probably around ten. I had Joe at Bighorn Towing drop it off here. He might be able to narrow down the time."

"I've got his number. I'll give him a quick call, check if he saw anything."

Then Ewing turns to me, his expression stern. Sully immediately takes a step closer and wraps his arm around my waist.

"In the meantime, I'd like you to think long and hard about who might have it in for you."

Fourteen

SULLY

She's killing me.

The scent of her shampoo, body wash, or whatever the fuck it is, lingers in the bathroom and seems to have stuck to my skin.

She's suddenly everywhere. Or maybe she already was and I was simply trying to ignore her existence.

I'm very much aware of her now; her scent, the sounds she makes, the way she moves, and the energy she radiates. My bland and modest cabin seems to come alive with her. Even after only a few days.

It's taking everything out of me to stick to brief kisses and modest touches, and then lying in bed alone knowing she's on the other side of the house. Maybe if life hadn't exploded on us these past few days, I would push things a little further, but not with stress already piled high.

I want us to work. As much as four months ago I couldn't imagine my way clear to any kind of relationship, it's now all I see when I look ahead.

145

I drop my cup in the sink and head for the door, just as Bo sticks his head inside.

"Are you coming?"

"On my way. And knock next time, asshole," I grumble. "So people can make sure they have clothes on before you barge in."

By people, I mean Pippa, not that she's been running around naked. Not yet anyway. Personally, I don't give a rat's ass if he catches me in the buff—wouldn't be the first time—but if he ever catches Pippa, I'm going to have to shoot him.

"Relax, brother. I saw the little woman leave earlier."

"I dare you to call her that to her face," I comment, grabbing my hat from the hook by the door.

I'd waited with my shower until she left for the garage. The walls are thin and I can be loud. It's not like when I was in my teens and twenties and was jerking off every damn chance I got, but with temptation living under the same roof, I need to relieve some pressure occasionally or I'll blow.

Pippa wanted to be at the shop early. She has one more contractor coming in to give her a quote on replacing the large window before the insurance adjustor shows this afternoon. Thank God she had insurance for the business in place. Still, it's a pain in the ass and will set her back some. It's also stressing her out, but there's not a lot I can do about that since she's determined to handle it on her own.

I pull the door shut right as he mutters, "I don't know anymore, man. I remember a time women would lap that shit up."

Barking out a laugh, I fall into step beside him.

"In what universe? Look, in a lot of things I'm as clueless as the next guy, but I can pretty much guarantee there

146

hasn't been a woman since the Nixon administration who appreciates being called 'the little woman.'"

"*Fuck.*"

I chuckle. It's not often I get to dole one out to Bo, who is the undefeated master of goading and taunts on the team.

Clapping a hand on his shoulder, I give him some free advice.

"Time you graduate from those John Wayne reruns, brother. Maybe give *G.I. Jane* or *A Long Kiss Goodnight* a try for a different perspective."

He swallows a retort when we're joined by Wayne Ewing coming up the steps to the main house.

The sheriff called this meeting.

I'm not sure what's going on, but Ama mentioned yesterday she noticed a couple of identical, black Chevy Tahoes parking in front of the sheriff's office, and thought she recognized Agent Wolff from the Kalispell office getting out of one. Looks like maybe the feds are back in town.

"What's going on, Wayne?" I ask as I hold the door open for him.

"A shitshow, that's what," he grumbles, walking past me.

A shitshow it turned out to be.

The feds showed up two minutes later, Agent Wolff in the lead.

Leroy Yokum—thirty-two-year-old son of Montana congresswoman, Janet Yokum—was last heard from on April twentieth when he left for his hunting cabin up near Snowshoe Peak. He was expected back in Helena for his mother's sixtieth birthday celebration, which was last Thursday, but he never showed.

Friends of the family came up to look for him, found his vehicle parked at the trailhead near Leigh Lake and his ATV with four slashed tires at the cabin, but no sign of Leroy.

The congresswoman alerted the feds, who had been monitoring the ongoing investigation into the three dead hunters here in Lincoln County. They didn't waste any time descending on Libby.

Needless to say, Ewing isn't thrilled, but at least he, along with the game warden's office, is still very much involved. It was the sheriff's idea to bring us on board in a more official capacity and Agent Wolff had no objections. The FBI agent has dealt with us before and he knows what we can do.

The plan is for an FBI dog team to go in this afternoon. Then tomorrow, I put up the drone and do a scan from the air. I'll be able to cover a much bigger area and will take the lead from the dog team. Anything they pick up; I can explore faster than they can on the ground. The team will stand by and as soon as we hit on something promising, we'll be going in on horseback.

I'm not happy about having to go out there. Not with Sloane showing up, Pippa moving in, and her business being targeted. It doesn't sit right with me to leave her to deal with all that by herself but with Fletch home looking after Nella and the new baby, we're shorthanded as it is. I'm counting on Ama, Thomas, and Alex to keep an eye on Pippa and my niece, but this job could not have come at a worse time.

I catch sight of Sloane coming from the side of the barn reserved for foaling. My guess is she's been checking out Sunny and her little filly.

"What'cha up to?"

She shrugs her shoulders. I'm still not back in her good graces, but I can live with that.

"How's the filly?"

That gets me a response and even a faint smile.

"She's cute. She needs a name though."

"I know. Got any ideas?" I ask her. "I was supposed to come up with one since I was there when she was born, but I'm drawing a blank."

"When was she born?" Sloane asks, looking back at Sunny's stall.

"Beginning of the month."

I saunter over to the half door and wait for Sunny to join me. I don't have to wait long before her silky nose nudges my arm.

"Hey, girl. How's motherhood?" I mumble.

"Blossom," Sloane says right behind me.

"Sorry, what?" I look over my shoulder.

"A name for the filly—Blossom—since she was born in the spring. I don't know. It's stupid—"

She starts turning away, but I put a restraining hand on her arm.

"No, it's not stupid, I like it. Blossom. It suits her."

This time the small smile is directed at me.

Progress.

"Listen, I have to go out with the team on a search tomorrow and we might be gone for a couple of days. Do you think you could keep an eye on Pippa for me?"

I'm not sure what prompted that idea, but I'm rolling with it. I'll feel better knowing Sloane is looking out for Pippa instead of making her life harder. Maybe it works.

"Why?"

Okay, maybe not.

Perhaps it's time to break through that attitude with a little dose of reality.

"Because she's been through a lot, more is piled on her

daily, her business was just vandalized to top it off, and she won't ask for help. All that when she's twenty-two weeks pregnant with my baby, and I care about her. But more than anything because you're my family, but so is she. I don't want to be out there worrying about what is going on at home when I should be focusing on finding a missing person."

"Okay."

She says it so softly I almost miss it.

~

Pippa

"Here's your copy."

The deputy hands over the incident report and I fold and tuck it away in my bag.

"Thank you. You managed to send it over?" I ask to make sure.

"Sure did."

I'd been in earlier, around lunchtime, hoping to catch Ewing but he wasn't expected back in the office today. This same deputy said he'd need to talk to the sheriff before handing me a copy, but I couldn't wait around for that because the adjuster was due at the shop any minute. Luckily, he wasn't too difficult, handed me his card, and told me the sheriff's department could send it straight to his office.

"I appreciate that. Thanks again."

I take the card he hands me back, shove it in a side pocket and, with a friendly smile and a nod, head for the front doors. Right then the game warden comes walking in.

"Hey, Woody."

He stops and holds the door open for me.

"Pippa. What brings you here?"

"Oh, you know. Same shit, different day."

He chuckles, then drops his eyes, and gestures at my baby bump.

"Marcie mentioned something about that. Said you'd be taking a break."

"Oh, no, nothing to do with the alliance," I quickly clarify when I realize he thinks I'm here about that. "I'm just picking up an incident report. Some yahoo did some damage at the garage."

"Right. Heard about that too. Sounds like you're still attracting all kinds of trouble."

"Yeah, you're not kidding," I say as I slip by him and out the door, waving a hand over my shoulder. "Catch ya later, Woody."

"You bet."

Woody reminds me a little of Bo, not so much the flirting—at least not with me—but he's got the easygoing teasing down. He does a lot of that with Marcie and I strongly suspect there is more going on with those two than they're willing to admit. I'm still grinning when I get behind the wheel.

It was a hectic day and I'm ready to get home. This baby is taking more out of me than I would've thought. The past few nights I crashed on the couch right after dinner. I have a feeling tonight won't be any different. For someone who technically can't work, I sure seem to be busy.

Fortunately, I can sleep in tomorrow. I've already given the go-ahead to the contractor this morning. He was the only one who was able to do the work tomorrow. Besides, Ira knew the guy and was able to vouch for him.

The place I bought the sign from luckily has the design on file. They think they'll have some time to replicate it this week, in which case they should be able to deliver it by Friday.

The only thing I have to do tomorrow is find someone who can put in a security system, some outdoor lights, and maybe a camera or two. Nothing too fancy, I don't want that big of a dent in my nest egg, but I need to do something.

To my surprise, I find Sully and Sloane sitting on the small front porch when I drive up. I'm half expecting the girl to jump up and disappear to the cabin next door when she sees me, but she doesn't look like she's going anywhere.

Sully does get to his feet, drops a kiss on my lips, and lifts my bag from my shoulder, indicating for me to take his chair. I note he's having a beer and Sloane is sipping on some kind of vodka mixer.

"Want some iced tea, Honey?"

"We have iced tea?"

"Sloane made some. She cooked dinner too."

The girl has her head down and is picking at her nails, clearly uncomfortable. I'm dying of curiosity to know what brought about the change.

"In that case, I'd love some iced tea," I tell Sully instead, and as soon as he disappears inside, I lean over a little and add softly, "That's really kind of you, Sloane. Thank you."

"No problem," she mumbles.

"I actually have some news for you. Ira, my mechanic, had a look at your Honda today. He says it shouldn't take that much to get it back on the road."

In truth he said the effort wouldn't be worth it, but I don't want to tell her that. I had an epiphany today, but that requires me to have a little leverage in the form of her vehicle.

"What was that?" Sully steps outside and hands me a glass before he leans a hip against the railing.

"I was just saying Ira thinks the Honda is fixable."

"What would that run me?" Sloane wants to know.

I shoot her a grin. "Well, that depends. How are you with computers? We could negotiate a barter, if you have a few hours to spare this week to help me set up a system at the shop? I'm hopeless."

My eyes flit to Sully, who seems amused.

"How about you guys talk about that over dinner, because I'm starving," he announces.

"That was inspired."

I tilt my head back to look up at him.

We're on the couch—the way we've been the last couple of nights—and again I find myself snuggled up against him, fighting sleep. His arm is draped around me, his fingertips brushing lightly over my stomach, and every so often the baby responds with a brief flurry of movement under his hand.

Sloane went next door after her hearty dinner of spaghetti and meatballs. I suggested she think on my offer before making a decision, but I get the impression she'll be taking me up on it. We'll see how it goes once Sully leaves for the search tomorrow.

"Nah, she simply needs to feel important. Useful. She'll come around."

He drops a kiss to my forehead and I'm a little blown away by how natural all this feels. All this...togetherness.

"She will," he confirms. "She's a good kid, smart too, she'll make waves in this world."

I'm sure she will, I've noticed her making a few right here with the way she seems to have caught the eye of young Dan. Not that she's noticed, or Sully for that matter, but I'm not about to enlighten either of them.

"I was thinking," he mutters, rubbing his nose in my hair. "As soon as I get back, we should get marriage taken care of."

I can't help the chuckle that escapes. "Stop, please. I don't think I can handle this much romance."

His mouth twists in a lopsided smirk as he wiggles one eyebrow.

"You sure? There's much more where that came from." Then he lowers his head so his lips touch the shell of my ear. "I have a whole night of romance planned."

Suddenly the air is heavy with promise and an electric charge ripples over my skin as his fingertips brush the waistband of my leggings and dip underneath.

I've thought about it, stood in the kitchen in the middle of the night after my bladder woke me up and stared at his door, wondering if he'd welcome me or whether it would only be another mistake. I wanted a sign, something to tell me this isn't just Sully doing right by the mother of his child. Bruised self-esteem and a lingering touch of insecurity had me craving to be wanted for me. I wanted him to look at me and see the same woman who took him to her bed four, almost five months ago.

As his fingers slip between my legs and he groans sliding a digit through my wet heat, I let my head fall back and look at him. His eyes, now almost midnight blue, burn into mine.

"Fuck, Fillippa. You—*this*—it's all I've thought about since that night. Heck, even befo—"

I cut off the rest of his words when I suddenly climb on his lap, take his face in my hands, and kiss him like my life depends on it.

In this position we both have our hands free to roam. Without thinking, I map his body with my touch, brushing my palms over the ridges of muscle, and dipping my fingers in grooves and folds. I moan when he lifts my shirt and discovers my sensitive breasts, plumping them with his hands as his mouth abandons my lips for a nipple.

I feel the bristle of his stubble against my skin and hiss as the strong pull of his mouth shoots straight down to my core. I read something about an increased libido during pregnancy and dismissed it as a myth. It's not. I don't think I've ever been this turned on.

First, I pull my T-shirt over my head before grabbing a fistful of his and start tugging on it.

"Off. Everything off," I mutter urgently as I push off his lap and shrug out of my leggings.

I need him inside me. Now.

He barely has a chance to get rid of his shirt and unbutton his fly before I push him back on the couch and climb back on.

"Easy," he mumbles when I firmly wrap my hand around his cock.

Then I sink down until he's buried inside me to the root.

So full—so fucking good. It's like every nerve in my body is vibrating every time I raise up and bounce back down.

He hisses as his fingers dig into my hips, trying to get me to slow down, but I can't. I'm like a coil, wound too tight, and I couldn't stop if I tried. My heart beats like a drum riff, so fast I'm afraid it might stop, but there is nothing I can do as instinct has my body hurdling toward climax.

"*Fuck*, Pippa," Sully cries out as he bucks wildly underneath me.

But I'm already flying off the edge, blood roaring in my ears, and black dots blurring my sight. A free fall that ends with me boneless, breathless, and speechless, draped across Sully's sweat-slicked body.

Where I promptly fall asleep.

Fifteen

SULLY

Almost forty hours since I left Pippa asleep in my bed.

So much for being able to focus better once I had some relief from the sexual tension between us. It's a joke. I still can't stop thinking about her and every time I do I get hard.

Christ, she's magnificent. All lush curves, dark, long hair, and untamed passion.

"Coffee's hot," James calls over.

Jonas had us set up camp for the night when the sun started going down. I'm making sure the horses and Hazel are looked after before we settle in. The others are already sitting around the small fire James built.

Yesterday, one of the FBI dogs had hit on a scent a bit north of Yokum's cabin. They followed it for about a mile and a half before losing it at the edge of a creek. I took the drone up and searched the area for most of the day yesterday before I spotted something from the air. Nothing more than a speck of light, but enough to catch my attention.

The low sun had caught on something reflecting off a

159

smooth shiny surface, out of place in the rugged surroundings. I flew the drone over for a second, lower pass, but couldn't identify the object. Still, since it's the only location of interest we've been able to pinpoint since the dogs lost the trail, it's worth checking out.

This morning the team set out early. It's nothing to fly quite a distance over rugged terrain, but it's not quite so easy to traverse the same path on horseback. Those few miles as the crow flies turned into many more on the ground.

I grab my mug from my saddlebag, walk over to where the others are gathered, and pour some coffee from the kettle next to the fire.

"We're not far," I announce, taking a seat on a boulder and pointing at the ridge behind us. "Right over that crest is a shallow canyon with what looked from the air to be a small water basin. The vegetation around it is denser than on this side."

Where we are is pretty exposed. The few firs provide a little shelter for the animals, but other than that it's mostly rock up here. We're used to sleeping under worse conditions than this, but at this age, I'd much prefer my bed than a night under the stars with nothing more than a sleeping bag between me and the rock-hard surface.

"We'll head out at first light. Fingers crossed we find something. A storm is supposed to come through late tomorrow and I don't want to be stuck another night on this mountain, especially in bad weather."

Weather up here can be unpredictable. A simple rainstorm in the valley can produce a foot of snow up in these mountains. Even in May.

After a dinner of barely passable MREs, I roll out my sleeping bag and crawl in. For a while I listen to James sharing his daughter's latest escapades before my thoughts drift back to my favorite subject, Pippa.

Knowing Jonas wants us back at base camp sometime tomorrow gives me hope I may actually make it home before my sister and her boyfriend get here on Saturday. Don't want to load that mess on Pippa's shoulders, she has enough on her plate.

I fold my arms behind my head and look up at the clear night sky. A familiar sight, no matter where in the world we were at any given time, providing a bit of comfort regardless of the dire circumstances we might find ourselves in. A moment of respite in a fucked-up world when it was safe to let my mind drift.

"Hey, Sully," Bo calls my attention. "Guess this means your woman is no longer on Ewing's radar?"

I push up on my elbows and look over to the fire.

"How do you figure that?"

"If the feds' suspicion the disappearance of Yokum is connected to the case of the dead hunters is correct, then there's nothing linking it to her or that animal rights group."

"Depends," Jonas pipes up. "Yokum's disappearance could have everything to do with baiting. Congresswoman Yokum may spend most of her time in Washington these days, but she's still one of the most vocal proponents of legalizing wildlife baiting. Just because we haven't found any evidence yet doesn't mean her son didn't do his own share of baiting. It wouldn't surprise me."

"Don't think Pippa was ever a serious suspect in Ewing's eyes anyway," James contributes. "But you've got to admit, it looks like more than a coincidence that group is somehow involved."

I'm not going to argue that. The first person to come to

mind would be its founder, Cade Jackson, although I may be negatively biased toward him. I have no doubt he's being vetted by law enforcement, like I'm sure the entire group is.

At least I hope so.

"Looks like those are his."

Bo holds up the pair of glasses he just found on the edge of the water. The distinct glasses look like the pair Yokum was wearing in the picture Agent Wolff showed us. One lens is cracked but the frame appears intact.

"Tom Ford?" Jonas asks.

Bo checks the writing on the inside of the temple. "Yup."

That was the brand listed on Yokum's description. For the life of me, I can't imagine wearing a five-hundred-dollar pair of glasses traipsing through the wilderness, but then I also didn't know designer hunting gear existed. It does, and it's the most ridiculous fucking thing I've ever heard of, but Leroy Yokum is decked out in it, tip to toe.

To be honest, I didn't think someone like him would get as far as he did—at least without leaving tracks all over the place—but apparently, he is more of an outdoorsman than his designer garb might suggest.

"I've got a shell."

I twist in the saddle to see James crouching on the opposite bank of the small, shallow basin of water I'd seen from the air yesterday.

"Two of them," he corrects.

I dismount Cisko, pull my camera from my saddlebag, and walk over to snap a few pictures. Whenever we're helping out law enforcement, we try to record whatever we encounter in terms of evidence.

"Two sets of tracks coming over the ledge over there, but only one set on this side of the water," Jonas indicates, keeping his eyes on the ground as he guides his horse, Sugar, to the opposite side of the canyon from where we came in.

"Someone was hunting, and it wasn't for game," Bo observes.

Sure looks that way. It would be a fair guess in this case Leroy Yokum was the prey, which would suggest this is indeed connected.

I make sure I record the shells before walking over to the sets of tracks. I start snapping pictures of those, putting my phone beside them for size comparison, when Jonas calls out.

"Bring that camera over, Sully. We've got blood."

Not only did we have blood, we found Yokum curled up behind a fallen tree, twenty-five feet farther. It's clear he was trying to find shelter and a miracle he was even able to make it that far with the two bullet wounds in his back.

We were able to raise base camp on the satellite radio and are now waiting for the FBI helicopter to get here. There's a level section of rock at the top of the ridge where it should be able to land. There was no way Agent Wolff was going let us haul Yokum's body out on a mule. If I were him, I'd want to see and collect every piece of evidence myself.

When Congresswoman Yokum finds out her son has been murdered, the shit is going to hit the proverbial fan. I just hope I can be home before Saturday morning.

～

Pippa

I keep my eye on my side mirror where I can see my pickup following me.

It actually hurt me to hand over my truck keys to Sloane, but it was the only way to get the rig to the ranch. The only thing scaring me more than her driving my pickup, is the thought of Sloane behind the wheel of my motorhome.

I wanted to get it over with before Sully's sister arrives tomorrow. I don't know when Sully will be back, I don't know how things are going to go between Sloane and her mother, but I do know I'll feel better with an escape route, should I end up stuck in a shitshow by myself. I won't hesitate to hop in my rig and find a quiet spot to hide out until things settle down, I have enough going on as it is.

A heavy breath of relief escapes me when we pull up to the cabins. I tuck the rig as far out of sight of the ranch as I can get it, between Sloane's cabin and the empty one at the end. Call me ridiculous, but I like having my home-on-wheels nearby. It has been my gateway to the world this past year and a half. My path to freedom, and despite the fact I seem to be setting roots down here, it gives me comfort to know it's within reach should I want it.

"When can we go camping?" Sloane asks when I join her by my pickup.

I grin. I'm not so sure camping without amenities is something she would enjoy—from what I've seen the girl is quite attached to her phone and social media—but if she wants, I'm happy to let her tag along if and when we get a chance.

She's actually been a pleasant surprise. Very savvy on the computer, which has been a blessing, since I'm not. The past two days she's gotten more done than I likely would've in a month. I'm pleased I was right and Sloane simply needed to feel like she had a place and a purpose. Her whole demeanor has changed almost overnight.

It wouldn't be a hardship to take her out with me for a few days, but it'll have to be on a weekend when the Pit Stop is closed and we don't have things on the schedule. Heck, she may not even be here after this weekend if she and her mom can resolve their issues.

"I wish I knew, but if you're still around next time I go out, you're welcome to tag along."

"Oh, I'll be here," she states firmly.

I decide to let it go and pluck my keys from her hand.

"Come on. We should get going."

Ira already has the big bay doors open when we pull into the Pit Stop. It's not quite nine in the morning and already it's getting warm. According to the forecast, we're supposed to have a bout of unseasonably warm weather over the weekend and well into next week. They expect temperatures could hit the nineties and with no AC in the shop, keeping the air flowing is about the extent of what we can do.

The new window is installed and when the sign goes up this afternoon, we'll be back on track. Despite the damage to the place, we've had a pretty decent first week of business. Mostly coming from folks either familiar to Ira or to me. Ira hasn't been bored yet, so I've taken over work on Sloane's Honda. Ira helped me drop the engine and I've decided to rebuild it. The after-market parts I ordered should be here by Monday and between Ira and myself, I think we can have it back up and running the second half of next week.

Technically I'm not supposed to be working, but I'm

only doing a favor for a friend. The cost of parts is less than I would've had to pay for someone other than Sloane to set up social media accounts and design a website.

Besides, I get the sense local law enforcement has their hands full with more important things at this time.

I leave Sloane in the office and walk into the shop to find Ira coming out from underneath the Subaru he has up on the hoist.

"Hey, I thought they were picking that up this morning?"

He scowls as he walks toward me.

"Not anymore. We had another visitor sometime overnight."

"What?"

I swivel around and look for anything broken or damaged I could've missed.

"A little more subtle than that this time," Ira clarifies. "If it wasn't for the fuel tank door left open on the Outback, I would'a missed it."

"Missed what?"

"Water. And it wasn't just the Outback, all three cars parked outside had a wet spot underneath the fuel tank door."

Shit, Sloane's car was inside in the farthest left bay, but we had two vehicles dropped off yesterday that were parked outside. Those were supposed to get oil changes this morning.

Water in the gas tank can kill an engine if you try to drive the vehicle. The fix can be as simple as draining the tank, but that takes time and is very inconvenient. The worrisome part is that if Ira hadn't noticed and those cars went back to their owners, it could've done serious damage not only to the vehicles but to the reputation we're trying to build.

"Did you call the police?" I ask him.

"Yup. They said it could be a while before someone can come out."

To be honest I'm not surprised.

"Yoohoo!"

I turn to the open bay door and see Marcie heading this way.

"What are you doing here?" I ask when she reaches me, dropping air kisses that never reach my cheeks.

"Can't I come by to check how a friend is doing? I haven't seen you in ages."

I haven't exactly lived in Libby 'ages' and Marcie is not a clingy person, so I'm calling bullshit.

"More like a month. Maybe," I counter, staring her down. "And I talked to you last week."

She doesn't hold out long before she caves, rolling her eyes at me.

"Okay, fine. I've got a headlight out. My regular mechanic doesn't have time to fix it before the weekend, and I was going to take the trailer out to this new spot on Lake Koocanoosa I found on the satellite map, a little south of Eureka. I don't wanna get pulled over by some overzealous deputy. I swear that sheriff has it in for me."

I chuckle because Marcie drives like a maniac and has collected at least four speeding tickets since I've known her.

"Don't start with me," she mutters. "He's been on my case with all that stuff about Fair Game having anything to do with those bodies they found. I've been so busy pulling all the reports, call logs, putting together timelines, I've barely seen the inside of my real estate office."

"It's not merely the sheriff anymore," I share. "The FBI

is involved in the case now, and Sully and his team were called in to help find another missing hunter they think may be connected."

"No shit?"

"That's what I heard."

"Wow. Can't believe the feds are involved now."

I shrug. "Kind of inevitable when it's the son of a well-known politician who's missing."

Behind me I hear Ira cough as I watch the blood drain from Marcie's face.

"Are you okay?" I ask her, putting a hand on her arm.

She doesn't respond but instead asks me a question.

"Do you know who the politician is?"

"Someone by the name of Yokum."

Marcie takes a step back and pulls her arm from my hold.

"The congresswoman?"

"I believe so."

I'm not up to date with the different political roles here in the United States but that sounds familiar.

Then Marcie backs out of the garage.

"I should be on my way. I forgot I have an appointment."

Before I can stop her, she darts toward her car, gets behind the wheel and, spraying gravel, peels out of the parking lot.

"Was it something I said?" I mutter, turning back to where I left Ira standing.

But he's no longer there.

Sixteen

PIPPA

"Thank you. I appreciate that."

Ending the call, I drop my phone on the counter and pour the freshly brewed tea over the pitcher of ice, I drop in a handful of fresh mint and drizzle some honey, giving it a good stir before pouring some in my water bottle. Then I head out on the back deck, where I can sit in the shade at this time of the morning.

I finally got the call back from the retired cop turned security specialist I left a message with on Thursday. I got his number through Ama's sister, who apparently works for the Libby Police Department. The guy is coming by the garage on Monday, and I hope to God nothing happens between now and then.

Yesterday was a crazy day with Marcie tearing out of here, Ira disappearing out back, and the Libby PD cruiser pulling into the driveway. All within a matter of minutes.

It turns out, Ira went outside because he noticed the hose intended to wash vehicles behind the shop was left uncoiled along the back and side of the building. He figured whoever messed with the gas tanks used our own water. The officer who showed up agreed with him.

I left Ira to deal with the cop while I tried to get a hold of Marcie to see what happened to her, but never got through. Then the rest of the day was spent flushing out the gas tanks of the three vehicles, doing the two oil changes, and picking up groceries since people will need to eat this weekend. Back at the ranch, both Sloane and I helped Ama get the empty cabin ready for Sully's sister and by the time we had that done I was too exhausted to eat dinner and went straight to bed.

Last night, Ama was able to tell me the guys wouldn't be back until sometime today and I know Isobel and her boyfriend likely won't arrive before noon. So, with Sloane still sleeping in the next cabin over and no one knocking down the door yet, I'm taking advantage of the peace and quiet. Something tells me it won't last.

I lean back in the patio chair, lift my feet up on the empty planter I'm using as a footstool, and close my eyes for a moment. Enjoying the light breeze on my skin and the scent of fresh mountain air, I let myself drift off.

I'm not sure how much later it is when the pain wakes me up. It's so sharp it takes my breath away and I'm instantly panicked, wrapping my arms around my middle.

Holy shit. That can't be good.

The moment it abates a little, I get to my feet and make my way inside, where I left my phone on the counter. But before I can dial another pain hits and I have to hang on to the island to keep my feet under me.

Oh no, please no. Fate wouldn't be so cruel, would she?

I know this baby wasn't planned, and I know it took me some time to get used to the fact my life would be forever changed, but I want her. I want the new life I'm only now starting to believe in.

"I was just about to call you," Nella says when she answers.

"I think I'm having contractions," I tell her, still recovering from the last one.

"When did it start?" she asks, her voice instantly calming.

"Like, five minutes ago? It woke me up."

It's quiet for a second and then she comes back with, "When you say contractions, how many did you actually have?"

"Two. I think."

"Hmmm," she hums, and I'm starting to think maybe I overreacted. "What are you? Twenty-two, twenty-three weeks?"

"Twenty-three today."

"That's when they started for me too," she says. "Braxton-Hicks. Remember, I'd have them on occasion? They're only practice contractions."

"That was practice?"

My voice sounds shrill, even to my own ears, but apparently Nella finds it funny. She's chuckling in my ear.

"You'll know when you're having a real contraction."

I'm not sure I want it to get any more 'real' than what I just felt.

"I'm gonna need drugs. Lots of them," I emphasize.

"If there's time," Nella cautions. "With Hunter, things went so fast I never had the chance."

Wonderful, just what I want to hear.

"I don't know why I called you," I grumble as I pinch the bridge of my nose.

"Would you rather I lie?"

My sister; always so damn reasonable.

"By the way," she continues, "any twitches since we've been talking?"

My hand automatically goes to my belly.

"No. Nothing."

"Braxton-Hicks," she confirms. "You'll get used to it."

I'm about to retort when I hear my nephew exercise his lungs in the background. He's got a decent set by the sound of it.

"Sounds like the boy is hungry. Duty calls," I point out.

Nella sighs loudly. "I know. That's all I've been reduced to—a walking buffet."

As soon as she ends the call, I try Marcie's number again. In identical fashion as the other times I've tried to get hold of her since yesterday morning, I am bounced to her voicemail.

"Okay, you are starting to worry me now, Marcie. Call me back as soon as you get this."

As relaxed as I was fifteen minutes ago, is as restless as I am now. To give my hands something to do, I strip both Sully's bed and the one in the spare bedroom, and grab all the towels from the bathroom. I get the laundry started in the stacked washer dryer combination in the small mudroom next to the back door.

Then I head for the smaller of the two bedrooms on the other side of the open living space, which Sully uses as his office. I stand barely inside the door, feeling a little guilty for invading his inner sanctum, although he invited me to. This is supposed to become the nursery. It's a light room, with a window at the front and one on the side of the house. A crib might look good in the corner between the two windows. Right now, they're covered with plain old blinds, but I could imagine floor length sheers, softening the light. Maybe a soft lilac on one or two walls, keeping the others white, and the space definitely needs a new light fixture. It's not usually my style, but one of those faux mini chandeliers would be pretty for a girl's room. Better than the functional ceiling light the room has now.

Maybe I should start making a list of things we're going to need for this baby. It feels like time is flying and with everything else going on, this kid is going to end up sleeping in the laundry basket unless I get my butt in gear.

I'm standing on a dining room chair, trying to unscrew the brackets holding up the second set of old blinds when Sloane walks in forty minutes later.

"Pippa?"

"I'm in here!"

She sticks her head around the door. "What are you doing?"

"Taking down these ugly things."

"Why?"

"Because this is supposed to become the nursery."

She regards me with her head slightly tilted. "You know if my uncle catches you standing on a chair, he's going to have a shit fit, right?"

To be honest, I'm not a hero with heights on the best of days, and right now I don't feel too stable. Sloane walks over to help me down.

"Someone has to do something. This baby is gonna come whether we're ready for her or not. I feel so unprepared."

"So, make a list. I'll help you. There's probably some templates available online. Let me have a look." Before I can object, she sits down at Sully's desk and wakes up the computer. "If you're worried, Uncle Sully offered me the use of his because my laptop is old and slow and he mostly uses the one in the HMT office. Come on, pull up a chair."

I fetch one of the kitchen chairs and set it beside her on the other side of the desk. Then I sit down and glance at the screen. I'm surprised to see the website for Fair Game Alliance.

"Whoa, did you pull that up?"

She gives me a sassy glance from under her eyebrows.

"I have good ears, I'm graduating with a degree in criminal justice soon, and I'm an ace with computers. What do you think I'm doing? I'm looking into them. I'm curious by nature."

She turns and points at Cade Jackson's publicity shot staring back at us.

∾

Sully

Fuck.

The dark gray Nissan Altima my niece had taken a snapshot of in her mother's driveway is now parked in front of my place.

I'd so hoped I could beat my sister home, but we didn't leave the canyon where we found Yokum until late yesterday afternoon and were forced to spend another night out in the field.

I'm tired, hot, I reek, and I was counting on having a shower before getting sucked into family drama, but it looks like that isn't going to happen. Hope Isobel didn't give Pippa a hard time. My sister can be protective and it would've been a shock to see a woman in my space, let alone a pregnant one.

The front door opens and I watch Pippa slip outside at the same time I get out of the truck. She's carrying a big plastic bag as she hurries over to me.

"They just got here ten minutes ago. So far, no bloodshed, so I've got it covered for now. You can grab a quick shower in Sloane's cabin."

She shoves the plastic bag in my hands. It has a towel, my soap, and clean clothes. There are a million things I want to ask, but she's shoving me with some force in the direction of the cabin next door.

"Hurry."

I shower in record time, get dressed, and head to my place, leaving the bag with my dirty shit on the porch. Then I walk in where an icy reception awaits me.

"Were you planning to tell me at *any* time?"

Isobel is not happy with me. I guess it means her anger is focused on me and not Sloane, but I'm sure it's only a matter of time before it's my niece's turn.

I close the door, keeping the air-conditioned cabin cool, and move toward Pippa, who is doing something in the kitchen.

"As a matter of fact, I was gonna give you a heads-up before you got here, but then we got called out on a search," I tell my sister as I walk up behind Pippa, slide a hand over her belly, and bend down to press a kiss to the side of her neck. "Hey, Honey. Whatcha doing?" I look over her shoulder at the wooden board she is loading cheese and deli meats onto.

"Charcuterie board."

Don't know what the hell that is, but it sure looks good. She tries to slap my hand when I reach over and snatch a slice of salami, stuffing it in my mouth. Only then do I turn around and look into the living room.

Sloane already has us all tuned out as she scrolls through something on her phone, Isobel's mouth is hanging open, and the tall guy from the picture standing behind her is wearing a grin. It's him I head for first.

"You must be Steve."

He shakes the hand I offer. A nice firm shake, nothing challenging, but strong and steady. I like him already.

"And you are Sullivan."

"It's Sully," my niece mumbles from her perch on the couch, without as much as looking up.

I see she's still cultivating her snit but rather than give it any credence by reacting to it, I ignore her and turn to Isobel instead, opening my arms.

"Sis."

She tries to hang on to her scowl—guess where Sloane gets it from—but finally caves and steps up for a hug.

"You're having a baby," she mumbles against my shirt.

"That's right."

"I'm still pissed at you," she says, pushing out of my hold.

"You can be pissed all you want but that's not gonna change anything. Hope you didn't give Pippa a hard time though."

"Why would I do that? Her I like, it's you and Sloane I'm upset with."

I look over at my niece. "Hey, sweetheart? Think you could put your phone down for a minute? We've got some air to clear."

It was a long fucking afternoon. Pippa's cheese and salami board helped, as did the six-pack of beer Steve brought. So many damn tears, angry ones, sad ones, preg-

178

nant ones. Every time my sister or my niece would get emotional, Pippa joined in. She finally gave up and went down for a nap.

The good news is, by the end of the afternoon mother and daughter were actually talking. Giving me a chance to get to know Steve a bit better. He's a good guy. I believe him when he says he wants the best not only for Isobel but Sloane as well.

The three of them went out for dinner in town. I passed, wanting some time to catch up with Pippa since we haven't exchanged more than a handful of words, and we have a shitload of things to discuss.

I brush the hair back from her face.

"Hey. Wake up, Honey."

She squints up at me through heavy eyelids. Then she rolls to her back and stretches her body like a cat, raising her arms and arching her back.

"What time is it?"

"Five thirty."

"Oh, shit."

She scrambles to sit up, the side of her face she was sleeping on flushed with a pillowcase imprint on her cheek, her hair a tangled mess, and those big brown eyes slightly unfocused. She takes my fucking breath away.

"Why did you let me sleep so long?" she complains with a shove to my shoulder.

"I figured you needed it."

She's furiously trying to smooth down her hair.

"What your sister must think of me," she mutters, disgruntled.

"Fillippa, relax. She's the one who told me to let you sleep. Says she remembers how tired she would get." I help her off the bed. "Besides, the three of them left for dinner."

179

That perks her up.

"All three?"

"Yup. And I popped a frozen lasagna in the oven."

That's about the extent of my cooking skills, but from the beaming smile on Pippa's face you'd think I'm cooking her a five-course gourmet dinner. I grabbed something from the freezer so we'd have time to cover some ground talking.

"Good. I'm starving."

I have her sit on the couch while I get us something to drink. Sitting down beside her, I pull her feet on my lap and massage her arches while she updates me on what's been happening here.

A lot, evidently, but I focus on the water in the gas tanks.

"You need some cameras," I interrupt her.

"Yes, I know. I've got someone coming on Monday. A former cop friend of Ama's sister."

Good. That's probably Barkley, same guy I would've suggested.

"Anyway, as I was saying, Marcie peeled out of there at the mention of the congresswoman's name and I haven't been able to get a hold of her since."

That is pretty strange. I'll give Ewing a heads-up on that, maybe he can keep his eyes open. I just hope her friend's absence isn't going to interfere with the plans I have for us on Monday.

Seventeen

PIPPA

"This is crazy."

I blink against the bright sun when we walk out of the courthouse.

It's just the two of us. We talked about the possibility of having family there, but that would've meant coordination and organization. Given that we don't have a lot of time, and could do without the added stress, we decided to simply pop into the courthouse in true shotgun-wedding fashion and without fanfare.

I'm not at all disappointed I had to forego a wedding dress. I already had my white gown once and vividly remember not particularly enjoying it back then either. Besides, it would've looked silly with my baby bump, although I wouldn't have minded seeing Sully decked out in a suit for a change.

As it is, we're both dressed casually, as if we're only in town to run some errands. We didn't get rings either, partially because there was simply no time, but mostly because neither of us have the kind of profession where wearing jewelry is advisable. I did, however, opt to take his name.

Mrs. Fillippa Eckhart. Holy hell. That sounds pretty good.

"Doesn't feel any different." Sully grins down at me.

"You say that now. Wait 'til it sinks in," I warn him as we walk up to his truck. "I just hope you won't regret it."

The grin evaporates from his face as he turns me with my back against the passenger door.

"I'm not going to regret anything," he says in a low voice. "All I could think about while we were out there these past days was getting home to you."

It would appear I pushed a button with my lame joke.

"Hey..." I lift a hand to his face. "Bad joke. Must've hit a bit of a sore spot."

He closes his eyes and drops his head, our foreheads touching.

"Could be I'm worried you'll be the one regretting it."

"No."

He lifts his head. "No?"

I grin up at him. "Not a chance."

If you'd asked me a year ago, I would've told you I'd never get married again and give up my hard-found freedom. Yet today—with my life in disarray, my future in flux, but with this man by my side—I welcome the promise of stability.

Of course, the other part of that equation is unsolicited protectiveness, which means my brand-new husband not only insists on being present for my meeting with Bill Barkley, but completely takes over.

When he walks back into the shop after taking Barkley around the outside, indicating where he thinks cameras should be mounted, I shoot him a pointed look but he doesn't appear to notice.

Barkley does and addresses me.

"So, I'll price this out, give you a quick call this afternoon, and with your okay, be here first thing tomorrow morning for installation."

I grab the opportunity and smile big at the burly man. "Actually, you should probably call Sully and get his okay," I suggest in my friendliest voice. "Since he ordered it, he'll be paying for it too."

Behind me I hear Ira bark out a laugh, but poor Bill looks a little uncomfortable.

"I really appreciate you coming on such short notice," I quickly add, offering him my hand as I sense Sully stepping in close behind me.

He reaches around me and shakes Bill's hand as well.

"Look forward to hearing from you," Sully rumbles before dropping his hand to my hip, giving it a little squeeze.

The moment Bill gets in his truck, Sully's voice sounds right by my ear.

"Message received, Honey."

I catch Ira's amused look and send him a wink.

Sully yells goodbye to his niece before grabbing my hand. "Walk me out?"

He leads me around his truck to the driver's side, which is out of view of the garage. Then he boxes me in against the door.

"Married for less than an hour and already I managed to piss you off. In my defense, I know Barkley and I know a little about security."

"Which is why I didn't object when you said you wanted to be here," I inform him. "I would've valued your input. What I didn't count on was you taking over,

185

completely sidelining me. Just because I've chosen to take your last name, doesn't mean I've handed over my independence."

May as well be honest. Some women may be fine letting a man take over—good for them—but I promised myself I wouldn't let another man erode my sense of identity. The Pit Stop is a big part of that. The garage is mine, I want its success to be mine, as its failure would be too.

"So noted," he grumbles, following it with a self-deprecating smirk and a quick, "Sorry."

I smile back and pat his chest. "It's all good. Give me a kiss, I need to get back to Sloane's car or I'll never get it done."

Isobel and Steve left first thing this morning for the long drive home to Salt Lake City, but they'd come to an understanding with Sloane. She wants to stick around Montana for the summer before she decides what her next move will be. With her degree she should be able to join any law enforcement department, but she hasn't figured out yet whether she wants big city or small town. Once she and her mother set aside hurt feelings and got down to actually communicating, they found common ground easily.

"It's all good? That easy?" Sully wants to know.

"Sure. Now are you gonna kiss me or not?"

This time he doesn't need any further prompting, and I'm glad we're hidden from view by his truck because the kiss goes from zero to full speed in seconds.

Both of his hands are on my ass, holding me, lifted off my feet, my back braced against the truck, and my legs wrapped around his. He rolls his hips, pressing the hard ridge of his cock right where I crave it most and my moan escapes down his throat.

That seems to bring him back to his senses, although I'm a little slower to clear the lust-filled fog I find myself in.

"Think I'm gonna like married life," he comments, a satisfied smirk on his face.

"Enjoy it while it lasts," I fire back, my own mouth twitching as I pat my belly. "I have a feeling this little pea may put a crimp in any sex life."

His smile deepens. "It simply means we'll have to put the time we have left to good use." He drops a light kiss to my lips. "I'll see you at home."

"Gross," Sloane comments when I walk into the office a few minutes later.

The goofy smile Sully put there is still plastered on my face.

~

Sully

"Hey, girl."

I rub Sunny's soft nose.

She showed up at the fence the moment I walked up. Behind her the little one is bouncing around like a goat, giddy on fresh air and freedom. After spending most of the afternoon in the hot and stuffy breeding barn I can sympathize, I came out here for a little fresh air myself.

It's hot, I'm sweaty, and I'm ready to be done with this day.

It started off on a high but has gone downhill since. I hadn't planned on making any kind of announcement about getting hitched. Would've probably let it slip at some point as a matter of record. I did, however, need to call the insurance company to change over to a family plan right away.

Bo walked in, right as I was feeding the court-stamped record of marriage through the scanner. His voice booming out congratulations carried down the hall and into the kitchen where Jonas, his father, and Ama were having lunch. Jonas didn't say much, I guess he was expecting it, but Thomas and Ama had plenty to say.

The old man told me off, accusing me of skirting my responsibilities if I wasn't willing to stand up for Pippa publicly. Ama added insult to injury, claiming I was treating my new wife like some business arrangement and she was worth more than that.

I walked right out of the fucking house; I was so pissed. It hurt, to be honest, they'd think so little of me. These people are as much family to me as my sister and my niece are. I didn't even bother arguing with them.

Spending an afternoon in the barn with Dan got my blood settled down some, but the bitter taste lingers.

"You did what?"

Great.

Either some big mouth called him or Pippa talked to her sister.

I turn to find Fletch stalking toward me and getting right up in my space.

"Easy, brother," I caution him, my hand up.

"I trusted you to treat her right, you asshole. Do you know how hurt Nella's gonna be when she finds out?"

Just like that I'm done. Over it.

"What is wrong with you fucking people?" I blow up, backing Fletch up a step without touching him. "Treat me like I fucking forced her, put a gun to her head or something. You honestly think she'd let me get away with that? Do you even realize how you're all insulting Pippa with your asinine assumptions?"

I notice Jonas behind Fletch, leaning against the barn door. He appears to be casually observing, but the tension in his body is obvious. He's ready to get involved at any untoward move from either me or Fletch. But I'm not going to use my fists on my brother, no matter how much I'd like to.

"This was something she and I both agreed on, doing it now, and doing it alone, no fuss. Not that it's any of your fucking business."

With that I brush past him, but I don't get past Jonas.

"You've got twenty minutes to get your shit together. Have a cold shower or whatever the fuck you need to do to cool down. Got a heads-up from Ewing a minute ago; Agent Wolff is on his way with a search warrant."

"What the fuck for?" Fletch asks, beating me to it.

But Jonas's eyes stay on me and an uneasy feeling crawls up my spine.

❧

"This is bullshit."

Yeah, this day is not getting any better.

I'm standing on my porch, facing off with Wolff and two other agents. To think I liked the fucking guy. Well, at least he has the decency to look moderately guilty.

"We understand this is Ms. Freling's main domicile?" The agent with the stereotypical reflective Ray-Ban sunglasses is the one asking the question.

I get the sense he and the other guy decked out in a

similar suit may outrank Wolff, who remains a step behind them.

"It's Mrs. Eckhart, and yes, it is. What's it to you?"

One of the guy's eyebrows shoots up. "Married? That's an interesting development. Must've been recent?"

"This morning, as a matter of fact," I fire back, wanting them to know if they fuck with Pippa, they'll have me to deal with.

"Convenient," the asshole mutters.

"How would that be convenient?"

If he's gonna make suggestive comments, he better have the balls to spell it out.

"Would allow you to claim spousal privilege in the case now, wouldn't it?"

I do my best to stare him down, but it's hard to stay focused without seeing his eyes. Besides, I'd like to get this over with before Pippa gets home. So, I check the copy of the warrant he shoved in my hand when he got here.

"As you can see the search warrant includes her motorhome as well."

Jesus Christ. What the hell is going on?

"You're aware my wife is five months pregnant? She's already been questioned and cleared by Sheriff Ewing. You're barking up the wrong fucking tree."

"We had an anonymous call come in," Wolff pipes up, drawing dirty glances from his fellow agents. "Probably a bull-shit call," he continues, ignoring the looks as he focuses on me. "But as you can imagine the pressure has been turned up since finding Yokum and we've gotta run down every lead."

"Seems pretty thin," Jonas speaks up for the first time. "A warrant based on an anonymous call?"

"Not that hard when her name was already on file as a

person of interest," Agent Ray-Ban explains. "Now, I believe we've wasted enough time chitchatting, I suggest you step aside so we can get on with our job."

I do as he asks and step away from the front door.

"The only reason I'm not fighting you on that is because I don't want my wife to walk into this."

As the asshole moves to the door, he turns his head and grins at me.

"Oh, she already knows. I've got another team searching her auto shop as we speak."

Before I realize what I'm doing, Jonas has me turned around, my arm pinned behind my back, and his voice is hissing in my ear.

"Don't do it. Don't give him the satisfaction."

Behind me I hear the agents walking into my house and then I realize I don't give a fuck what they do here, I need to get to the Pit Stop.

"Pippa..."

"Fletch can take you. I'll keep an eye on these guys."

My brother is standing at the base of the steps, his expression is granite as he nods at me. The moment Jonas loosens his hold on my arm, I swing around.

"Don't let them fucking wreck the cabin or the camper. Her keys are on top of the fridge."

We barely make it down the driveway when my phone starts ringing. It's Sloane and she's crying.

"Uncle Sully, you have to come right now. The FBI—"

"Already on my way, sweetheart. Is Pippa with you?"

"They have her in the back of an SUV and took her phone. Uncle Sully, they put her in cuffs."

Rage boils through my veins.

"Ira?" I grind out.

"He's trying to reason with them. I managed to sneak away to call you."

"You did good. I'm gonna hang up now, I'm only a few minutes away." I end the call and turn to Fletch. "Floor it."

There are two nondescript SUVs and a van parked in front of the building. Ira is standing beside one of the SUVs, and I catch sight of one of the agents coming out of the office carrying a desktop computer. As we pull up, Sloane appears on the far side of the building, running toward Fletch's truck.

I catch her in a hug right as Ira yells my name. When I run over and glance inside the back of the vehicle, I see Pippa is curled up on her side in the back seat, her hands cuffed behind her.

"She was fine a minute ago," Ira says, worry in his voice.

The fucking door handle won't budge when I yank at it.

"Hey! Get this fucking door open!" I yell at the agent, who just loaded the computer in the back of the van, and is on his way back to the office.

He looks back at me before darting a glance into the open garage door, then he continues on his way. A second agent walks out of the open bay.

"Step away from the vehicle!"

Fletch steps in front of me and calls back, "Open this fucking door or I'll do it for you. She's five months pregnant and something is wrong with her."

I can't see the agent but I hear the click of the doors unlocking. I have it open and dive inside, brushing her wet hair away from her face. It's a fucking oven inside the SUV.

"Fletch, help me get her out. Ira! We need water!"

She's out cold.

Eighteen

PIPPA

"I'm fine."

What I am is embarrassed.

It was my own fault. I got in the FBI agent's face, poked a finger in his chest when he tried to move past me, so they put me in handcuffs and threw me in the back of the SUV. Also, they hadn't realized I'm pregnant, and they couldn't have known I hadn't had a drink since breakfast this morning. That was all on me. I guess we can blame locking me in the back of a hot vehicle on the agent.

I passed out not only from the heat but also from dehydration, and I was loaded into an ambulance before I was even aware of what was happening. Dr. Tippen was waiting for us when I was wheeled into the ER—Sully called her from the ambulance—and made sure the baby was okay.

Still, Sully blames it all on them. He's out in the hallway, facing off with the FBI agents who apparently wish to speak with me. He's not exactly quiet about it either, which is how

I am now finding out the agents claim to have found a rifle in my rig. Me, with a rifle, it's too ridiculous to contemplate.

Before I have a chance to lose it over that, the doctor walks back in to see how I'm doing, which I hope means I'll be heading home soon, where I can hide from this madness.

"You're not fine," she disagrees. "You passed out. That's not fine. Your blood pressure is high, you're clearly not drinking enough, and unless you want to end up on bed rest, you have to cut back on some of this stress."

Suddenly that strikes me as hysterically funny—or maybe I'm simply hysterical by now—which is why I'm snort-giggling when Sully walks in, his face one giant scowl. That has me laughing even harder.

My life is pretty much a joke. I'm flying by the seat of my pants, trying to get some solid ground under my feet, but wherever I turn I seem to land in quicksand. I got married this morning with two county clerks as witnesses before my new husband dropped me back off at the auto shop someone has it in for, while I'm desperately trying to get it up and running. I'm well over the halfway mark of an unexpected pregnancy and haven't yet bought a crib, a car seat, or even a newborn onesie, which already is not winning me a mother-of-the-year award. And to top it off, my business, our home, and my rig have been deep-searched by the freaking FBI, who seem to think I'm capable of chasing down and shooting four accomplished hunters when I don't even know how to fucking hold a gun. Yet a rifle was apparently found, which must make it true.

So yes, I'm laughing hysterically, and crying at the same time. It feels like I landed in a particularly cruel version of *Candid Camera* and I keep waiting for someone to jump up and yell, "You've been punk'd!" Since that hasn't happened, it's becoming clear I'm not equipped for this life. Not even a little.

I pull the sheet up to cover my face in a feeble attempt to block it all out.

"Take her home," I hear Dr. Tippen say. "Make her rest. Tie her up if you need to."

"I can do that," Sully replies. "But I'll need your help getting rid of the two federal agents out in the hallway. They insist on speaking with her."

"Over my dead body," the doctor replies, which strikes me as hilarious as well.

By now my shoulders are shaking and tears are streaming down my face, so I roll on my side toward the wall as I try to get myself under control. Sully's familiar hand rubs soothing circles on my back and suddenly nothing is funny anymore. Only deep, out of control sobs remain.

"Easy, Honey. You're going to make yourself sick."

It's no use, I've officially lost it.

It's already dark out when we pull up to the cabin.

I was a little embarrassed when Jonas was waiting outside the hospital to give us a ride home. I'm sure I looked a fright when Sully insisted on lifting me into the passenger seat, but he nodded and told me he was glad to see me okay.

Before I have a chance to get from the truck to the front door, Sloane comes flying outside and has me wrapped in a bear hug. A far cry from the angry girl I met just over a week ago. I can't believe it's barely been eight days; it feels like a few months' worth of stuff has happened in that short time.

"I was so scared," she hiccups, her face buried in my hair.

"I'm fine, the baby's fine. We're all fine," I mumble, feeling oddly empowered I can give her that reassurance. Twenty minutes ago I was a basket case.

"Let's her get inside, sweetheart," Sully tells Sloane, peeling her gently off me.

Behind me I hear Jonas's truck pulling away and I realize I forgot to thank him.

Another fail that almost has me lose it again, until I give myself a mental slap in the face. Enough of that. Things are what they are and I have no choice but to deal. To underline that, the baby does a few somersaults and I press my hand to my belly.

I hear you, little one, I promise I'll get my life sorted before you get here.

Sloane busies herself with something in the kitchen, while Sully insists I install myself on the couch with my feet up. I don't argue too hard because I'm tired. Exhausted, actually; emotional breakdowns wear you out.

"I'll be right back," Sully announces.

Then he bends down for a peck on my lips before he heads for the kitchen, where he exchanges a few words with his niece before disappearing out the back door.

Sloan walks over with a plate and a glass of what looks like iced tea.

"What's this?" I ask when she hands me the plate holding a substantial slice of cheesecake.

"I called your sister to find out your favorite," she admits with a shrug of her shoulders. "Got some of the ingredients from the big house. You've gotta eat something, it might as well be something you love. Especially after a day like today. Consider it your wedding cake."

That's sweet. So sweet it gets the waterworks going again.

198

When Sully walks back in a few minutes later, tears are still leaking but two-thirds of my cheesecake is already gone.

Not exactly the memorable wedding day you'd hope for, but definitely one we're not likely to forget.

And Sloane's cheesecake is the bomb.

~

Sully

Thank God this fucking day is over.

I glance beside me at Pippa, who was asleep the moment her head hit the pillow. Her face is puffy from the crying that didn't seem to stop. Then again, neither did the hits, they keep coming and there's nothing I seem to be able to do about them.

At least she's sleeping, even if I can't. Too much going through my head, not the least of it the FBI's arrival on our doorstep, which I know will be inevitable. Pippa's doc did a good job getting rid of them, but as soon as they return to the hospital tomorrow and discover she's not there but resting at home, I'm sure they'll come straight here.

I gave Fletch a call last night to let him know we were home. In the background I could hear Nella announce she was on her way which, as I mentioned to her husband, was not a good idea. I suggested coming by tomorrow instead. Or rather, today, as a quick glance at my phone on the night-stand indicates.

In hindsight that may not have been a good idea either, now that I've had time to think on it.

Fuck.

Rubbing a hand over my face, I swing my legs out of bed. Not going to get much sleep like this. I grab my shirt off the floor, and a pair of sweats from the dresser. A last look at the bed shows Pippa hasn't moved an inch and I pull the door closed behind me.

I watch some *Justified* on Netflix with the sound practically off before I get too restless to sit. It's already close to four when I grab a beer from the fridge and head out on the front porch.

The night is bright, a nearly full moon already starting to slide down in the sky. I'm surprised at the cool temperature, a relief after today's heat. A slight breeze carries the familiar smells of horse, hay, and mountain. Leaning back in the old wooden rocker, I take in the view of the ranch. The single light outside the barn spreading to the corral and the field behind. I can make out the silhouette of a horse, its swishing tail the only thing moving.

I consciously push the tension from my body as I attempt to blank my mind, inhaling deeply. It's an exercise the therapist I saw briefly after arriving back Stateside recommended. Back then, it was to deal with some of the nightmares and temper flares I came back with, but it works for stress just as well.

I breathe in deeply again, but this time the slightly acrid scent of cigar smoke catches my attention. Glancing over at the main house, I see the faint light of an ember. Someone is smoking on the porch. Guess Jonas can't sleep either. Wonder what's got him up at this hour.

Grabbing my bottle by the neck, I get to my feet and make my way down the steps. Maybe talking things through with him wouldn't be such a bad idea.

Except when I get closer, I realize it's not Jonas on the

porch. He would've spotted me already. Instead, I recognize the shorter, slighter stature of Thomas.

I shake my head and grin at myself. Thomas, who isn't supposed to be smoking. If either Ama or his daughter-in-law, Alex, get wind of this he's in for a world of trouble.

The old man almost leaps to his feet when I climb up the steps.

"Dadgummit, boy...ya got me jumpin' like fleas on a farm dog," he mutters as he tries to hide his cigar behind his back. "What the heck are you doin' up?"

"I would ask you the same, except it doesn't take a genius to figure out that cigar you're trying to hide is the reason you're out here this time of night," I tell him, hitching my hip on the porch railing.

Knowing he's been made, he sits back down and tugs on his cigar, smoke billowing from his lips as he aims a challenging look in my direction.

"You gonna tell on me?"

"Nah. Guess we all have our way of coping with life."

I take a swig of my beer and look out at the mountain range barely visible by the light of the moon. Behind me I hear Thomas take another drag.

"So you never said why you're out here."

I swing around to face him, intending to feed him a line. Then I reconsider. Why not unload on him? Wouldn't be the first time Jonas's father had some sage advice to impart.

"I got married today," I start.

"Yeah, I heard. Congrats." He tilts his head to one side. "Regrets already?" he teases.

I grin. "No. But I'd hoped it'd settle life down a bit for her, but that hasn't happened."

"Heard about that too. Don't think whether she's

married or not would've made a lick of difference with this FBI business. A bunch of bull, if you ask me, but I'm sure it'll resolve itself with time." He pulls another drag and his face disappears behind a cloud of smoke. "You already know the outcome, simply let it run its course, not a lot you can do to speed it along, but you don't want to slow it down either."

"Easier said than done. Her doctor tells me I need to get her to rest, but how the fuck am I supposed to do that? She doesn't only have the FBI breathing down her neck, Thomas. Someone clearly has it in for her. They knew where to find her motorhome, managed to hide a rifle in there, and called in an anonymous tip. Law enforcement is busy following bogus leads, and in the meantime, I'm supposed to be looking out for her. Instead I feel useless, and those fucking agents will be knocking on our door demanding to speak to her in a matter of hours."

"Take a breath, son. You're not gonna fix it this morning. That filly's already shown she's made of sterner stuff. Besides, you made sure she doesn't stand alone, but you're forgetting that you don't either. You've got a band of brothers...hell, you've got an entire family here standing with you. Every one of us happy to carry some of that load weighing ya down."

The screen door opens and the old man curses under his breath when Jonas walks out.

"Hand me the lighter, Dad," he mutters, holding out his hand.

Grumbling, Thomas fishes the item from the pocket of his pajama top and hands it over. Then Jonas lifts his own cigar to his lips with his other hand and lights it before taking the vacant seat beside his father.

"For the record," he rumbles. "You haven't been fooling anyone. Shoulda picked a different spot, my damn bedroom is right up here and Alex likes the window open summer and winter. Good thing a cannon wouldn't wake that woman because I could hear every damn word."

"You don't tell on me, I won't tell on you," Thomas negotiates, narrowing his eyes on Jonas's cigar.

"Could'a done that the first time I heard you out here, old man." Jonas grins. "I'm saving the information for when I need leverage, and for the record, there's nothing you can tell Alex about me she doesn't already know."

Then he turns to me.

"First light I'm going to have a word with Wolff. If that doesn't get me anywhere, I'll be getting on the horn with Ewing. Make sure, even if the feds become myopic in their hurry to pin this on someone, the sheriff's department won't stop looking. Don't forget we've got some friends in high places."

Fuck, I hate depending on others—at least when we're not in the field—but I'm willing to swallow my damn pride for Pippa...and our daughter.

"Appreciate it. Means a lot."

Jonas waves me off with a hand. "Shoe's been on the other foot too, my friend. And Dad's right, you and Pippa both have people at your back. In the meantime, go back to bed. Try and get some rest while you can. Lord knows you're no fucking good to anyone without your beauty sleep."

"Fuck you, J," I fire back, but I do it smiling as I straighten up. "And thanks for the ear, Thomas."

"You bet, son."

Nothing's been resolved but when I walk back to the cabin, my step is a lot lighter.

Nineteen

Pippa

Could the timing be any worse?

It's a good thing this cabin is open concept or we wouldn't be able to fit all these bodies in.

First, my sister showed up right as we were sitting down to breakfast, which Sloane and Sully had prepared while I was in the shower. Fletch trailed in behind her carrying the baby and looking a little sheepish. Nella was on a tear, not hesitating to give me the big sister talking to about looking after myself. She got up into Sully's face about not looking after me, which I didn't appreciate, but by then she was on a roll, insisting I'd have to move in with her so she could make sure herself I was properly looked after.

Then she burst into tears and almost got me going, just as Jonas and Bo arrived on the scene. Jonas alerting us to the fact the feds were coming up the driveway.

Which brings us to now, nine adults and a baby packed in a relatively small space. Six guys glaring at each other, the air heavy with testosterone—despite the fair amount of pregnancy and postpartum hormones in the room—and baby Hunter so overwhelmed by the thick atmosphere he starts crying.

Agents Wolff and Powell, two different agents from the ones who showed up at the garage yesterday, but some of the guys seem to know them. It didn't take me long to figure out these two were the ones searching the cabin and my rig.

"We'd like to speak to you alone," Powell announces to me.

"Not gonna happen," Sully growls before I can respond. "Anything you want to ask her you'll have to do in front of us."

Powell throws him a look. "We could always bring her in for questioning."

"Not without her lawyer," Sully retorts.

"Interesting that you feel your wife needs a lawyer. I wonder why that is?"

"Because I don't trust you fuckers. You handcuffed my wife, stuck her in the back of a hot car, and left her there. She ended up in the fucking hospital."

Yeah, this isn't going anyplace good. I put a hand on Sully's arm to remind him I'm fine but I'm not sure he notices.

"Need I remind you we found a weapon in your wife's possession?" Powell brings up.

"That's not hers and you know it," my sister throws in for good measure, beating Sully to the punch.

I can feel my anxiety building and my blood pressure creeping up. Time to take charge and put a stop to this.

"All right! That's enough," I intervene. "This is not productive."

The last is for Sully's ears in particular. He needs to tone down on the big, bad, protector schtick because all he's doing right now is antagonizing Powell.

"I will answer any questions you have, but I'll do it here," I address the agents before looking around the room. "I'd suggest anyone who thinks they can't keep their thoughts to themselves leave now. I appreciate the show of support, but I won't hesitate to kick you out later if needed." Then I pin Sully with a glare. "And that includes you."

Someone starts chuckling but I don't bother looking who it is, my eyes are locked on Sully. His look tells me he wasn't expecting that and he opens his mouth to protest, but I beat him to it.

"Look. Me, you, and everyone else here know the FBI is barking up the wrong tree," I tell him. "Eventually they will come to that conclusion as well. Let me just get this over with."

The only one who leaves is Bo, with a nod and a wink for me. But the others all remain.

Most of the agents' questions are pretty straightforward. Where did I get the gun? Nowhere, since it's not mine. Who had access to your motorhome? Anyone with a key or a decent lock-pick set. Could I account for my whereabouts from May fourteenth to May twenty fourth? Had I lent out my rig to anyone? What would I say if my fingerprints were found on the weapon?

I can feel the angry vibes coming of Sully, but it's Nella who speaks up.

"You didn't find her fingerprints, did you?" I'm tempted to cut her off like I promised I would, but I'm actually interested to hear what they have to say, except Nella is not done. "There wouldn't be any, because my sister didn't touch any gun, and whoever planted it in her motorhome wouldn't want theirs found. I bet you the gun, as well as the storage locker, showed no prints at all," she concludes.

From the sour look on Powell's face, she struck a nerve with him, but the other agent seems amused. He ends up the one to respond.

"Both were clean," he admits.

"We don't know that. Not until forensics has a chance to go over the camper and the gun," Agent Powell provides.

"When do you figure I'll get my rig back?" I direct my question at Wolff, since he's the one more likely to give me a straight answer.

"Provided they don't find anything of concern, you should have it back in a day or two."

I hadn't noticed it missing until this morning when I spotted a receipt for everything the FBI collected yesterday. I'd been shocked to see they'd taken Sully's computer, but according to Sloane they'd taken the one from the office at the Pit Stop as well. Not sure what they're expecting to find, but it's an annoyance.

By the time the agents leave—Powell with a warning for me not to leave town—I'm already exhausted, though it's not quite ten in the morning. Jonas walks the agents out the front as Sloane ducks out the back door, with the announcement she's got 'stuff to do.'

Nella, who had disappeared into the spare bedroom at some point to feed a fussy Hunter, walks in with the baby over her shoulder. My chest blooms with love for my sister, who not only pushed that chunk of delicious baby into the world only ten days ago, but doesn't let that slow her down or stop her from trying to slay my dragons for me.

"You rock," I tell her when I pluck the mini-hunk from her shoulder and transfer him to mine.

"You're pretty fierce yourself," Sully observes, sliding a hand on the small of my back while he brushes a finger softly over Hunter's downy cheek.

Not to be left behind, Fletch adds, "No one messes with the Freling sisters."

Damn.

They're going to have me bawling again.

~

Sully

The dogs run up to my truck barking, as I pull up to the farmhouse. They easily recognize me when I get out and their fierce barks turn into eager whines as they battle for my attention. I sink down on my haunches to give them just that.

Where the dogs are, Lucy isn't far behind, and vice versa. The animals are protective of her, which is good. May not be a bad idea for us to get a dog at some point. It would make me feel a bit better about leaving Pippa if we're called away on a job. Something else to ask Lucy about.

"To what do I owe this pleasure?"

I grin up at the blond firecracker. I like Lucy, she's a force to be reckoned with, like every other woman choosing these rugged mountains to settle down in. A tough exterior hiding a vulnerability for another man to discover. I may have an idea who'd like a shot at that, but I fear he'll have an uphill battle on his hands.

Lucy isn't one to beat around the bush so I don't either.

"The FBI is looking at Pippa for the murder of four hunters, including Congresswoman Yokum's son."

"What the fuck?"

"They found a rifle they think may be the weapon in an outside storage compartment of her motorhome."

"And you want to know if anyone could've gotten access to it while parked here," she finishes for me, proving she's not only smart, she's a good friend to my wife as well. Not even a moment's hesitation to come to the conclusion someone is messing with Pippa.

"Got it in one."

"I'm gonna have to think, because it's been here for quite a few months in total."

If it is in fact the rifle that shot those hunters, whoever planted it must've done so after Yokum was shot. He'd been dead at least a couple of days, if not longer, when we found him.

"Only the past month, I'm guessing."

"Why don't you come in, I've gotta check the schedule."

I follow her into the house where she heads straight for the kitchen, pulling a calendar off the fridge door. She drops it on the counter and starts flipping through pages.

"Had a total of six different clients, a feed delivery, a horse drop-off, and two visits from the vet, according to this. I don't see how any of them would have anything to do with this. They don't know Pippa, other than maybe seeing her here," Lucy volunteers.

"What about people who do know her? Did she have visitors while she was living with you?"

I would've asked Pippa herself, but after the feds left this morning, she crashed and I left her with Sloane to keep an eye out. I was actually on my way to the garage to catch up with Barkley, who is supposed to be installing cameras today, and happened to look over when I passed the rescue, noticing Lucy's truck out by the barn.

"A few. Her sister, of course, and her friend, Marcie, she came by a few times. I can't remember—wait, there was this guy from that anti-baiting group she's part of." She shakes her head. "I can't remember if she told me his name. I think it was after some kind of group meeting. She'd had a couple of drinks so he dropped her off here."

My mind immediately goes to that idiot who showed up at the garage with a hard-on for Pippa.

"Cade Jackson ring a bell?"

"Only Jackson I know is Jackson's Automotive in town. That Jackson worked on my previous truck a few times, but I haven't been there since I got the new wheels last year."

I never thought to connect Cade Jackson to the only other garage in town, but now I do. That guy already popped up in my mind as someone who might be messing with Pippa at the Pit Stop. That might make even more sense if it turns out he's related to the Jackson of Jackson's Automotive.

"Not the same guy?"

"The mechanic is probably in his late sixties or seventies. The guy who dropped Pippa off was younger and I haven't seen him since."

Lucy may not have seen him but that doesn't mean he wasn't here at some point.

I think maybe I should look into Cade Jackson. I could see him doing petty shit like breaking windows or dropping water in gas tanks, but this might mean he could be a killer hunting down and cold-bloodedly shooting his victims in the back.

I thank Lucy, get back in my truck, and head over to the

Pit Stop, where I find Ira working on Sloane's Honda. It's the only car in the garage.

"No customers?" I ask him when I walk up.

"Two cancellations and a no-show this morning," he grumbles. He looks as pissed as I feel. "Small town. Word gets around."

"Or someone is helping it go around," I suggest.

Fuck. This'll set Pippa back even further.

"I see we're of one mind," Ira says. "But in this case, it legit could've been anyone driving by here yesterday. It was a bit of a circus."

He's not lying. The number of vehicles parked out here, a forensics van, and at some point the ambulance as well, I'm surprised someone wasn't selling tickets on the side of the road. Nothing much happens in Libby without the whole fucking town knowing.

"Did Barkley not come around?"

I notice his truck isn't parked outside. If he bailed on Pippa as well, I will not be too pleased.

"He was here. Hung the cameras but couldn't do much more without the computer the feds hauled off with."

Christ, every damn day it's a new snag. Whoever has it out for Pippa is doing a damn fucking good job. I'm going to have to give him a call.

"You familiar with Jackson's Automotive?"

His response is to clear his throat, turn his head, and spit a loogie out the rolled-up bay door. Nothing ambivalent about that answer.

"Is Cade Jackson connected to Jackson's Automotive?"

"It's his uncle's."

"You don't say..."

I think it's high time I paid Wayne Ewing a visit, make

sure he's still looking farther than his nose is long, and that he's not missing possible leads.

And just in case the sheriff is preoccupied with something else, I will be doing a little checking myself.

Sloane does not get her computer skills from a stranger, and my fingers itch to dig a little deeper into what makes Cade Jackson tick.

"You know all this is bullshit, right?"

Ewing looks up from his desk and the moment he sees me, he drops back in his chair, his eyes rolling to the ceiling.

"What do you want, Eckhart? You know this is out of my hands," he shares, exasperated.

"You're telling me you don't have any input? I thought you were part of the task force."

"That was before we found Leroy Yokum dead. The moment the congresswoman was informed, it became an FBI case. I only know what they want me to know, which isn't a hell of a lot. The only person who doesn't treat me like I'm suddenly an enemy of the state is Wolff."

I drop down in one of the visitor chairs on the other side of his desk.

"What about the vandalism at the auto shop? Is that still your case? Because I think the same person planted that rifle in Pippa's RV."

"You're looking at me to undermine the FBI's case against your girlfriend," he accuses, leaning forward, his elbows on his desk.

I'm not in the least offended because I'd make a deal with the fucking devil at this point to protect Pippa.

"She's my wife, and no, what I am asking you to do is the job you were elected to do. What does that plaque on your wall say, Wayne? *Committed to our community*? Fillippa is part of that community as well. An innocent woman—a member of the community you're supposed to be committed to—is being railroaded."

Ewing hunches over and bangs his forehead on the desk a few times.

"You're killing me, Sully," he groans. "Retirement is eighteen fucking months away and you want me to start rocking the boat."

"You bet I do. Starting with Cade Jackson."

Twenty

Pippa

"Go. I'll be fine."

Already the hovering is driving me insane, as does the feeling of being restricted.

I didn't mind yesterday, was able to catch up on a few episodes of a Netflix show I've been watching, read a couple of chapters of a book I'd been anticipating, and had at least three naps.

Sloane stuck around again yesterday, keeping me company in everything but my naps, but today she's back at the garage. There was an older computer at the High Mountain Trackers office Jonas offered, so we could at least get Sloane back working on the website and have Barkley come back to finish up security. I suspect it was Sully's idea. He just helped load the desktop into my pickup, which Sloane is driving for now.

Another reason why I'm starting to feel a bit claustrophobic. I have no means of transportation anywhere with my rig still in the hands of the FBI and now my pickup missing as well. Sure, Sully offered to drive me wherever I want to go, but that's not freedom, and now he's wanting me to come to the main house with him so I don't have to be alone while he works.

Guess he forgets I actually *like* being alone and I haven't had a lot of opportunity lately.

"You sure?" he asks for the third time.

My pained eye roll is accompanied by a tortured groan.

"Really? How can I put this in clearer terms? I. Am. Fine. And if you don't leave in the next two minutes, I may actually consider inflicting bodily harm, and then Agent Powell will really have something to pin on me."

Sully is already treading on dangerous ground with that smirk tugging at the corner of his mouth.

Then he opens said mouth.

"Don't think the FBI wastes time with assault, Pippa."

Good God, what do I have to do to get the man out of my hair? I squeeze my eyes shut when I feel the burn of frustrated tears. If I let him see those he'll never leave.

I hear him take a step closer and then his lips are on my forehead.

"Okay, Honey. I'll go, but promise me you'll call if you need anything."

"I will." If I absolutely have no other choice, but I don't say that out loud.

He hooks a finger under my chin and I lift my face, opening my eyes. He looks into them for a moment and then focuses on my lips, right before he kisses me sweetly. Next, he walks out of the door and I sigh a breath of relief.

All I want is some alone time to see if I'm still limber enough to shave my legs, which I haven't done in a while. Maybe give myself a pedicure if I can reach my toes. It's warm outside—flip-flop weather—and right now my feet would scare away small children. I'd also love to not have to worry about bodily sounds. I read online my innards are rearranging themself to make room for the baby, which could be why I've felt gassy the past few days. It's getting painful to try and hold it in, and I feel like we haven't quite reached that phase where you can fart in front of each other without concern.

It's one of the drawbacks of being in an expedited relationship, things don't have a chance to develop organically.

I'm also acutely aware, before too long, I'll have zero privacy when this baby announces herself, but until then I'd like to limit the emission of bodily gases, fluids, or solids to times I can do so while maintaining a little modesty.

Forty-five minutes later, I walk out the back door, aiming for a trail running along the back meadow I spotted from the kitchen window yesterday. I believe it leads toward Fisher River on the east side of the ranch.

I filled my water bottle, packed a sandwich, some fruit, and my phone in my small backpack, and left a note for Sully on the kitchen table. I wish I had my camera, but it's stored in the motorhome, along with most of my gear. My phone has a decent camera built-in should I encounter something picture-worthy.

The stifling heat from earlier this week has been replaced with infinitely more tolerable spring temperatures. Much more suited for hiking, not that I intend to go far.

I suck in the mountain air as I make my way along the fence line, feeling much better right away. Out here I feel like I can breathe, recharge my batteries, which have been running very low. As I exercise my muscles and fill my lungs, I do my best to clear my mind.

A small herd of horses grazes along the fence up ahead and a few raise their heads when they notice my approach.

One of them breaks away from the group and comes to check me out, sticking his head over the fence. I hold out my hand, palm exposed, and smile as soft lips explore my skin, maybe hoping for a treat. Not finding anything, he pulls back, snorts as he shakes his head, and turns back to the herd as I continue on my way, following the trail into the woods.

The river is wider than I thought, divided into separate streams meandering around a number of rock plateaus forming elongated islands in the water. Every time the sun appears from behind a cloud, the light hits the surface, turning the streams into silver ribbons.

It's beautiful here. Peaceful. I kick off my runners and roll up my pant legs. The water isn't too deep and I stick a toe in to test the temperature. It's a little chilly, not cold, and I carefully make my way across to the first island. A massive log, which I'm sure washed downstream at some point, got hung up between two rocks. A perfect place to sit and have my lunch. The view from the middle of the river is stunning, no matter in what direction I'm looking.

Fresh air makes my simple cheese sandwich and grapes taste so much better. I can see myself coming back here often, maybe with Sully, and once this little nugget is born with her too.

I'm about to get up when I hear my phone buzz in my pack.

"Hey—"

"Where the hell are you?"

~

Sully

"Want to try that again?" she snaps.

I groan, lifting a hand to squeeze the back of my neck. I need to get a grip on my temper and catch my breath.

When I was walking back to the house from the barn, I saw the black SUV coming up the drive and turning toward the cabins. I broke out in a run to try and beat them to the door, but they were already banging on it by the time I got there.

"Honey, where did you go?"

"I left a note."

"Which says you went for a hike, but not where."

My eyes slide to the two agents standing in my living room. Powell didn't say anything other than they need to speak to Pippa and it can't wait. I have a bad feeling about this. I need to know where she is so I can go get her.

"Fillippa?" I prompt.

"I took the trail behind the cabins down to the river. I was about to head back," she finally responds.

That's at least a thirty-or-forty-minute walk. I can feel Powell's eyes burning in my back as I turn to look out the kitchen window.

"Stay put," I tell her. "I'm coming to get you."

"That's ridicu—"

"Please...stay put. I'll be right there."

Maybe it's something in my voice but instead of more objections, Pippa's response is suddenly a subdued *okay*.

Tucking my phone in my pocket, I turn on my heel and head for the door. It'll take me less than ten minutes to get to the river if I grab one of the ranch's ATVs.

"Where is she?" Powell asks, blocking my way.

"If you step aside, I can go get her."

"Why don't you tell us where she is and we'll go get her," he counters, stepping into my space.

I notice Wolff closing in behind him.

"Over my dead body," I grind out.

I really don't fucking like this guy, and I'm not about to let him blindside Pippa with whatever it is he so urgently needs to speak to her about.

"Don't tempt me," Powell growls, leaning forward.

Apparently, the feeling is mutual.

Luckily Wolff intervenes, pulling Powell back before it can get out of hand, which it will if the guy shoves his face any closer to mine.

"Let him go get her," Wolff tells his fellow agent calmly.

I'll be damned if I wait for Powell's response, and reach past him for the front door.

Minutes later, I'm heading toward the trail on one of the quads I got from the shed on the far side of the ranch house. The trail Pippa took is one I use often in the summer if I want to do some fly fishing for trout, which the Fisher River is good for. I go later in the afternoon, after work, when the sun is low in the sky. It's beautiful back there. Sometimes the old man joins me, but if Pippa likes it out there, maybe she wants to come along. Good fishing from the middle of June through September, so we could get a season in before the little one gets here.

I find her standing on one of the rocks in the middle of the river, her eyes on me as I clear the trees. With her running shoes in her hand, she starts wading toward me.

"What's going on?" she asks when she's within earshot.

"Agents Powell and Wolff showed up at the cabin looking for you," I inform her.

"Did they say what they want?"

I shake my head before bending down to brush her lips.

"Powell is pretty intense though. He was ready to come look for you himself."

Her shoulders pull up and her mouth tenses.

"Do you think they found anything? Are they gonna arrest me?"

I take her face in my hands.

"They may have, and I don't think so."

I hope I'm right about not taking Pippa in, but I get the feeling from Wolff he's not as keen on Pippa as a suspect, as his colleague is. I'm pretty sure he would've indicated if an arrest was the purpose of their visit. Had that been the case, I don't think he would've suggested letting me pick her up.

Still, my instincts tell me to get her on the back of the ATV and get her the hell away from here. Plenty of places I could hide her, but in the end that would make her look guilty when she isn't.

She searches my eyes with hers before finally nodding sharply.

"Okay, then let's go find out."

Not sure what Wolff said to Powell while I was gone, but he's not as aggressive with Pippa as he was with me. I'd say that's a good thing, but there's an underlying intensity I feel coming off the man that has me wonder if he's simply lying in wait, ready to pounce.

"Yes, I've used the computer at the garage. Mostly to place orders, check my emails, stuff like that. I did try to set up a website but failed miserably, but Sully's niece is working on that for me."

Powell scribbles something in his notebook before returning his attention to Pippa.

"What about the computer here? Do you use that?"

"Not really. I have my laptop but that's locked in my rig. Wait...I did use the one in the office once, with Sloane. We looked up a template for a list to print out."

"What kind of list?"

"Uh, just...baby stuff." She darts a glance my way. "That room is supposed to be turned into the nursery and we were just trying to sort out what we'd need."

Fuck. I need to get my head in the game. I should've been working on clearing out that room already, maybe paint, but shit keeps happening. If we could have a week or two without any disruptions or surprises, we could get a ton done.

"What about you, Mr. Eckhart? Used the computer in your office recently? Or the one at the auto shop?"

"Neither. Never used the one at the garage and the last time I was on the one in here was probably a few months ago. I use either the desktop or my laptop in the office in the main house," I reply, although I'm getting the sense he's narrowing in on something. "Why are you asking?"

"We found some interesting evidence on both the computer we took from your house and the one from your wife's business," Powell explains.

"Interesting, how?" Pippa wants to know.

"Someone has been looking at the Fair Game Alliance, checking on some of the key people in the organization. Doing background checks. We discovered a ton of research on bear baiting, political opponents, but more interestingly, proponents. Like, for instance, Congresswoman Yokum, as well as her son Leroy," Powell says smugly.

"Impossible."

That's gotta be a bluff of some kind, because no one else has access, at least to my computer. Unless...

"*Oh no*," Pippa mutters, looking slightly concerned when she looks at me. "She said she was only looking into some stuff, I was gonna mention it. She wanted to help."

Fucking hell. Guess who's doing some investigating of her own.

"Are you suggesting Mr. Eckhart's niece?" The disbelief in his voice is unmistakable.

"Sloane recently finished her degree in criminal justice," Pippa explains as I contemplate strangling my niece. "Like I said, she was only trying to help. She has nothing to do with any of this."

"If that's the case, why would she hack into Ms. Watts's social media accounts?"

"Marcie? I don't understand."

Neither do I. I have no fucking idea what goes on in Sloane's head anymore. Hacking into social media is illegal. A criminal record could be a career killer for her before she even gets her feet on the ground.

Goddammit.

"How do you know Marcie Watts, Mrs. Eckhart?"

"She's a friend. She was my realtor first, then got me involved with Fair Game, and ended up being a friend."

"Would you happen to know where we could find Ms. Watts?"

"Marcie? I assume she's home, or at the office. I don't really know because she hasn't been answering my calls all week. I left her a couple of messages, but she hasn't gotten back to me."

"When was the last time you saw her?" Wolff takes over in a more sympathetic tone.

"Last week sometime. No, I remember, it was on Thursday."

I notice the two agents exchanging a look. Somehow, I

sense we've come to the real reason for their visit and I don't like where this is going.

"How did Ms. Watts seem at the time? Did she say anything about going away?"

Pippa turns to me with fear in her eyes. She can see it coming too.

"She mentioned something about this new spot on Lake Koocanoosa she found. She wanted to take her rig out there for the weekend."

"Was she going alone? Going with someone?"

"She didn't say. She left in a hurry."

"Why in a hurry?"

At this point, he's simply badgering her and I've had enough.

"What is this about?" I interrupt before he browbeats Pippa into saying or admitting something that might put her in a bad light.

Powell can't resist the smug smile as he shocks the hell out of me and pulls the rug from under Pippa's feet.

"Ms. Watts was reported missing on Tuesday and it sounds like your wife was one of the last persons to have seen her."

Twenty-One

PIPPA

I'm still reeling from yesterday when we walk into the medical clinic.

These past two weeks have literally flown by, but my world hasn't stopped spinning since before I discovered I was pregnant. Now I'm over halfway to having a daughter, am married to a man I didn't think was interested in me, and I find myself the prime suspect in not only four murders, but the disappearance of a good friend.

Agent Powell told us Marcie hasn't been seen since she tore out of my parking lot the week before. She didn't show up at her office on Monday and when she didn't show again on Tuesday—missing a few important appointments—her secretary went to check at her apartment. No one answered but her car was still parked in the parking lot, so the police were called in to do a welfare check. Apparently, her phone was charging in the kitchen, car keys left on the counter, but no sign of Marcie and her purse was gone. The thought something may have happened to her has me sick to my stomach.

Agent Wolff was kind enough to inform us they'd be checking in with other members of Fair Game as well. It made me feel a little better, knowing I wasn't their only focus.

"Pippa? Follow me, please? I'm just going to do your weight and blood pressure."

Wonderful.

I follow the doctor's assistant into the small room where she has me get onto the scale.

Funny, before my pregnancy the scale would be the part I'd be most concerned about, but what worries me is the next part.

The effects from the fresh mountain air, the sound of babbling water, the sun on my face, my entire relaxing lunch by the river didn't last long yesterday. Add to that the rather restless night I had, I'm pretty sure my blood pressure has reached new highs.

"One thirty over eighty-five. That's a little on the high side."

I was afraid of that, although it could be worse, I guess.

"Been a crazy week," I comment with a shrug.

She hands me a small urine jar and smiles sympathetically at my wince.

"Sorry, I know it's a drag, but especially with the elevated BP, we should make sure everything checks out."

I know from my sister that because of my age I'm at higher risk for preeclampsia, among other things, which is why I guess they're keeping a close eye on my blood pressure.

I do as asked and leave the jar in the designated basket on the shelf next to the sink. Then I wash my hands before returning to the waiting room and take a seat next to Sully, who insisted on coming.

"Everything okay?"

"BP little high, that's all."

I hate waiting as much as the next person, but it's even worse when someone came with you who, you know, is hating it more than you do. It's making me antsy and restless.

I shift in my seat for the twentieth time when Sully's hand lands heavy on my knee.

"Relax. It's only been ten minutes."

"Pippa?"

This time it's Dr. Tippen. We follow her into the examination room where she doesn't waste any time doing a quick exploration of my stomach. When she's satisfied, she pulls up a rolling stool and sits down, her face serious.

"You need to be cautious," she starts. "Your BP doesn't quite fall into the hypertension range yet, but it's damn close. You measure on par with twenty-four weeks. Your weight gain is appropriate, and your urine looks clear, so it looks like everything is fine. So far," she adds sharply. "Because that can change on a dime. I wasn't joking when I said to avoid any stress."

Sully makes a sound like a stifled snort and it triggers a bark of laughter from me.

"I'm sorry, Dr. Tippen, I know it's not funny."

"Please...Lindsey," she reiterates.

"Lindsey," I confirm. "Trust me, if I could avoid stress I would. It follows me."

She looks at me dubiously, but Sully backs me up.

"She's not kidding," he says. "It's been a little intense."

"There's a lot going on right now that I don't have any control over," I contribute.

Lindsey already knows of the FBI's involvement with my visit to the hospital earlier in the week, so I decide to fill her in on the latest. I'm a little surprised how easily she dismisses any claims law enforcement thinks to have and immediately she aligns herself with me.

"I could admit you, have you put on straight bed rest, they wouldn't be able to get near you without my say-so," she offers.

I was already struggling with my lack of freedom in the past few days of staying at the ranch, so the thought of having my movements restricted further—in a hospital setting, no less—is far from appealing. I'd almost rather deal with the FBI.

Something on my face must've betrayed my thoughts, because Lindsey grins and shakes her head.

"Guess that's a no. But all kidding aside, regardless of circumstances, you need to find a way to relax. Is it possible for you to get away? Even for a few days? Somewhere you're not poised for the next knock on the door?"

"Unfortunately, I still don't have my motorhome back, otherwise I'd know exactly what would relax me," I inform her.

Nothing like a couple of days camping in a remote place where the sounds of so-called civilization can't reach me. Nothing but the lens on my camera between me and the great outdoors. Fresh air, no noise pollution, and the peace and solitude I've come to crave.

"Wouldn't have been a bad idea," Lindsey says. "As long as you didn't go too far."

"We'll find a way," Sully states.

Sounds like maybe my days of camping alone have come to an end. Scratch the solitude I guess, as long as I can have the rest of the perks, I'm good.

We leave the office shortly after, with an appointment in another two weeks.

"I'm going to take some leave."

I turn to face Sully, who has both hands on the wheel and his eyes fixed on the road ahead.

"Leave?" I echo.

"Until this is sorted."

"Look, I don't know if that's necessary."

He darts a glance my way, takes one of his hands off the wheel, and reaches for mine. Palm to palm, he entwines his fingers with mine.

"I do," he asserts. "First and foremost, I don't want to let you out of my sight. Not," he adds quickly when I start pulling my hand from his hold, "because I don't trust you, but so I can look out for you. Run interference or offer support when Powell comes knocking again, which I'm sure he will. The bastard is relentless."

He lifts my hand and brushes my knuckles with his lips. An achingly tender gesture which—in its simplicity—makes me feel treasured in a way I've never experienced before.

Sully

"But also," I continue. "I need to track down my niece and have a word with her about her independent investigations."

Sloane called last night, announcing she'd gone to stay with a friend. Apparently, the agents had shown up at the Pit Stop when she was out on a test drive with her Honda to see how it ran. Ira—who's not a fan of the feds—told them he had no idea where they could find her. As soon as they left, he called Sloane and warned her.

Then my niece decided to buy herself a little time and drove straight to Kalispell where one of her college friends lives. The moment I started grilling her on what the hell she thought she was doing hacking people's social media, she hung up. I tried calling, but she wasn't answering.

I was furious, but Pippa pointed out I could've handled that better and convinced me to cool off before trying again in the morning.

Which is now.

"Try not to bark at her. The more you treat her like a child, the more she'll behave like one. Try treating her like an adult and you might be surprised to find out she is one."

I glance over again, noting the slight twitch of her lips.

"Very sage of you, Honey."

Her lips spread into a smile I haven't seen in a while.

"I have my moments."

"Yes, you do," I admit before getting us back on track with, "I also need some time to look into the vandalism at the garage. Sloane doesn't have her affinity with computers from a stranger, and I want to dig into Cade Jackson a little deeper. I'm worried Ewing has bigger priorities and won't give him a second look, but I'm convinced there is something off about the guy."

"Are you sure that's necessary?" Pippa questions. "Sure he had trouble hearing no, but he's also not the most socially attuned person I know. He could've simply misread the signals."

"I'm digging," I insist. "I'll do it in a way that if I turn out to be wrong, no one will be the wiser."

"But us," she adds.

"But us. Which brings me to my final reason for wanting to take some time."

"Which is?"

"You and me. I want to spend some time with you while I can before our daughter arrives." She opens her mouth to say something, but I hold up my hand. "Let me finish. I know we seem to be in the middle of a giant mess, but you and I both know there is always going to be some kind of crisis to deal with. That's life. However, I want to make sure you and I are as solid as we can be to take those hits together."

There is stuff I want to tell Pippa and things I want to know from her. It's important for her to know my buttons and I'd like to understand hers. This isn't about looking back to drag whatever baggage we bring with us; it's about being properly equipped to move forward and leaving the crap behind.

"As much as I like that idea, I'm worried we don't have anything for the little one yet. No clothes, nowhere to sleep. Heck, we haven't even talked about names yet."

Pippa's voice goes up as she talks, a clear indication this is part of what is causing her stress.

"Those things aren't mutually exclusive. In fact, how about for our first outing together we head to Kalispell this afternoon? There are a couple of baby stores we can check out."

I'm getting the feeling she's on board with that idea when she beams a smile at me.

"Sounds like a plan." Then the smile turns into a smirk. "And I guess it's a convenient happenstance Sloane is supposed to be in Kalispell?"

"Who says happenstance?" I ask, trying to distract from the fact she seems to know me so well already.

"I do."

When we get back to the cabin, I go in search of Jonas to talk to him about taking some time. I find him in his office in the main house.

"How is she?" is his first question.

He'd stopped by yesterday after he saw the agents leave, so he's already up-to-date on what was happening. I'd also told him about the doctor's visit this morning and that I'd be in later.

"Baby seems okay, Pippa's blood pressure is too high. She needs to take it easy, which is part of what I want to talk to you about."

"Take whatever time you need," he says without hesitation.

I haven't had the chance to ask, but that's what made him a good leader in the field and a great boss now. He has a good read on people.

"Only off the ranch schedule. If any searches come in, I'll do my part. Don't want to leave you shorthanded."

"We'll be fine. Fletch is back and I've been looking into hiring some extra hands anyway. We can use the help this summer."

He makes a good point. When the new barns were built, we expanded the breeding program, which is taking off.

"Wouldn't be a bad idea. I'm sure Dan and the guys would welcome a few more bodies."

"It's partly for the ranch, but I have plans for possible team expansions as well."

"HMT?"

"Yup." He studies me closely as I try to process what he's saying. "This is something I want to discuss with you guys in detail at some point when shit stops hitting the fan, but I've given the team a lot of thought the past few

236

months. We're getting older. I don't want to get to a point where we don't have fresh blood ready to step in when one of us has to step out."

Good point. It's not that it never occurred to me we aren't spring chickens, but the days one of us actually is no longer able to do the job still seemed light-years away. Still, if we wait too long there won't be anyone to fill the empty spot we leave behind.

Christ. Nothing like listening to your unborn baby's heartbeat and discussing your impending decline in the same day to have you contemplate your mortality.

"When I pick someone to hire for the ranch," Jonas continues, "I want to do it with the team in mind as well. Someone young, smart, and physically capable. Someone like Dan. I'd like him to be the first one we train."

I rub my face with my hands. "Yeah, I guess. Wow. I mean...great idea, it's just..."

It's been the five of us on the team for as long as I can remember. It's hard to wrap my head around Dan—who's always been more like a little brother—as one of us. Not that I doubt he'd be capable, but it doesn't quite compute yet.

"Let's revisit this later," Jonas jumps in. "This was the wrong time to bring it up. Go, take as long as you need. Oh, and for your information, I paid Wayne Ewing a visit last night. Caught him and Agent Wolff at his office and I can tell you, neither of them seemed particularly enamored with Powell. I discovered a few things that should put your mind at ease: they found a single fingerprint on a round the rifle was loaded with. It does not appear to match Pippa's prints. The round itself is the right caliber, but according to Wolff you couldn't shoot a bear in a porta potty with the rifle. The barrel is warped."

That is an interesting development, I wonder if they had this information before they showed up at the cabin yesterday and badgered Pippa.

"So it's not the murder weapon?" I confirm.

"Doesn't look like it, although they don't have the ballistics report back yet."

"Whose print was on the round?"

Jonas shrugs. "If they know, they weren't telling me. Wolff did mention they intend to release the motorhome tomorrow."

"It's a start. They're wasting their time on Pippa."

"They're figuring that out, my friend. Patience."

Right. Except I don't have any patience left.

Twenty-Two

PIPPA

I can't stop myself from smiling as I glance over my shoulder for the fifteenth time since we left Kalispell.

The back seat bench is full of bags and in the back of the truck, bungee cords hold a pile of boxes in place.

We bought an entire nursery.

Crib, changing table, dresser, car seat, sheets, diapers, and that's only some of it. The eyes of the sales woman in the store bulged out of her head when we told her to ring everything up. Granted, there was a little kerfuffle at the cash register when both Sully and I pulled out our credit cards. I think the poor woman had visions of the biggest sale of the month slipping through her fingers, so she quickly proposed having one pay for the furniture and the other for the rest.

"I still say a car seat is furniture."

My eyes slide to the grumpy man behind the wheel. He would not have been happy with anything other than letting him pay the whole bill.

"Give it up, Eckhart. It's ultimately all coming out of one pot, isn't that what you tried to tell me the other day?"

I bump his shoulder when he grunts in response, knowing it's not really me or the car seat he's grumpy about, it's Sloane. She's still dodging his phone calls and he's getting ticked. Although, I'm pretty sure the shopping hasn't helped his mood either. I'm not a huge shopper myself, but this was fun. Costly, but fun.

However, I was shopped out myself, so when the sales woman suggested I go check out the maternity store next door, I passed. Not because of Sully—I'm sure he would have muscled through that as well—but because I was done. Besides, most of my clothes are built for comfort. Yoga pants, stretchy leggings, roomy cargo pants, and loose-fitting tops. Anything that doesn't require any special care and can withstand a good washing. I got rid of all my party clothes when I got rid of my ex-husband. In addition, if it should become necessary, I'm sure Nella would be happy to lend me any maternity clothing she has.

I'm feeling good. Better than I have in days, which is a direct result of getting something done. Finally, an item I can cross off my massive to-do list. I figure if everything around this baby is taken care of and under control, I'll feel better equipped to deal with all the other stuff swirling around in my life.

Leaning back in my seat, I let out a deep sigh. When I glance over at Sully, I catch him looking, his handsome face no longer grumpy.

"Pleased?" he asks.

"Very. I'm actually feeling a little accomplished. With so much going on, it's been hard to focus on one thing and see it through, so yeah, I'm happy we got this done."

"Peace of my mind too," he admits. "Although, overall, I still feel woefully unprepared for any of this."

I pat his knee, grinning at him. "We'll figure it out together."

Another quick glance from him, this one accompanied by a little smile. "I like the sound of that."

"You know..." I start when we drive past the Marion Grille, the small roadside restaurant we stopped at for a quick lunch earlier. "Something else we should figure out together; a name. Or names if we want to give her more than one. Any preferences?"

"Haven't really thought about it."

"No family names we could use for inspiration? Your parents are both gone, right?"

That's information I got from Sloane, not Sully. He hasn't really talked about his parents, but Sloane turned out to be quite chatty once she ditched the attitude.

I look over at him and notice his jaw muscle ticking. His lips, normally full, are pressed into a tight line, and his eyes are aimed straight ahead.

"Is that a sore spot? Your parents?" I ask carefully.

He blows out a breath through pursed lips before he answers.

"Never fails to surprise me how much it is," he admits.

He darts a look at me, adjusts his grip on the steering wheel, and takes a cleansing breath.

"I never really talk about it. Not even with Isobel, although she lived through the same." He barks out a bitter laugh. "She lived through it twice."

Another glance at me and I give him a small, encouraging nod. Clearly this isn't an easy topic for him and I brace myself, remembering my visceral reaction when he first told me about the ordeal his sister and niece lived through.

"My father became an angry man. Maybe bitter is a more appropriate word. He came from a military family, had his hopes set on a military career—like his father before him—but was disqualified on medical grounds." His eyes briefly slide my way. "Bipolar, or manic depression, which is what it was called at the time. Grounds for disqualification in those days. He ended up a doorman at the Peery Hotel in downtown Salt Lake City and grew increasingly disappointed, which he started taking out on my mother. Repeatedly."

"Oh no..." I whisper, but he's not done yet.

"My mother—an old-fashioned, God-fearing woman—would then turn around and take her pain, anger, and frustration out on first Isobel, and later me."

"Aw shit, Sully," I mumble, as another layer peels away, giving me a deeper understanding of the man and his motivations.

I already figured his initial rejection of me was more about avoiding a relationship than anything to do with me. Given what he told me happened to his sister at the hands of a fellow veteran, I understood that motivation. What I'm now learning is that his initial resistance has much deeper roots.

"Yeah, so the answer is no. No family names from my side."

The knuckles of his hands curled around the steering wheel have turned white. When I cover the closest one with my hand, he loosens his grip, flips it palm up, and curls his fingers between mine.

"My mother's name was Carmella, which is a lot of name for a baby. But Carmi might work. It means garden, which I kind of like."

I hadn't thought hard about it, but as I'm voicing it out

loud, I really like the sound of it.

"Carmi," Sully tests the name in a rumbly voice I feel in my bones. "I gather your mother was a good woman?"

"The best," I respond with a sudden frog in my throat. "And gone from this world far too soon."

His hand presses mine.

"Carmi it is, then," he agrees, and my heart squeezes in the best possible way.

"Carmi Isobel Eckhart," I suggest, because while his parents don't deserve to be commemorated by name, surely his sister does.

He abruptly pulls his hand from mine and pulls off on the side of the highway. Then he turns to me, takes my face in his hands, and claims my mouth in a kiss that quite adequately conveys his appreciation. When he lifts his head to look at me, his blue eyes look lit from within.

"Love it."

~

Sully

"I love that too."

Pippa walks into the nursery and looks at the next sample paint patch I put on the wall.

We brought home some paint samples to match the linens and stuff she picked out for the nursery. This color is called Pale Sage and it's actually my favorite of the four samples.

"Too? You're going to have to decide on one. So far you seem to love them all equally."

"What's your favorite?" she bounces back at me.

Not a fan of the Cabbage Rose, not big on the Dutch Tulip, and the Autumn Glow looks like the inside of a diaper.

"This one." I point at the sage.

"Perfect."

That easy.

Something I noticed about her while shopping; she makes quick decisions and once she has, she sticks with it. I couldn't care less about color scheme, design, and stuff like that, but I can sort of envision how this room is going to look and I dig it.

"Now that we have that out of the way, Sloane just messaged me."

"You?"

What the hell? I'm the one who's been leaving messages and voicemails.

Frustrated, I toss the paintbrush at the tray sitting on the floor.

"Yes." Pippa sidesteps the tray and presses herself against my front, the swell of our baby between us. "She's on her way, and my guess is she hoped I could calm you down before she gets here," she says, sliding her arms around my waist and tilting her face up.

Fuck. I'm ready to take a strip off my niece, but this woman scrambles my brain every time she gets close. So, I kiss her upturned face instead.

"Is it working?" she asks when I let her up for air. A tiny, satisfied smirk on her swollen lips.

"No," I grumble. "Now I'm pissed I can't take you to bed like I want to, 'cause she's on her way."

She must've been around the corner because the next thing I know, her voice sounds from the living room.

"I'm home!"

I move to march in there, but Pippa holds on to me.

"Don't forget to listen," she says softly before letting me go.

The relief to see Sloane unharmed and in one piece goes a long way to banishing some of the mental visions of her lying injured in a ditch somewhere, or worse.

"Before you start," she says, her hand up, palm out, and I have to draw on my last reserves of patience not to react. "I was perfectly safe this whole time. Chappy is a police officer with the Kalispell PD."

"Who the fuck is Chappy?"

"Chapman Lubov. He's a friend from college, a year ahead of me. Anyway, as I was saying..." She sashays over to the fridge, diving in and pulling out a bottle of cranberry juice. "Chappy was a great help. He was able to get information I wouldn't have been able to get on my own."

"What kind of information?"

She pours a glass and takes it into the living room, plopping her ass down on the couch. I remain standing, my arms crossed over my chest as Pippa takes the other corner of the couch.

"I was digging around a little online—"

"Digging around," I echo. "You mean you were poking around in an investigation you have no business poking around in."

"Well, I do have a criminal justice degree," she says snootily.

"Not yet," I growl. Her graduation isn't until the end of the month. "And that's not the point. The point is that you don't work for law enforcement, this isn't your case, and even if it was you can't go hacking people's social media accounts. Are you nuts?"

"Are you telling me you've never hacked into someone's accounts, Uncle Sully? Bent the rules for the greater good?"

Goddammit.

"So what did you find?" Pippa asks, saving me from answering as she shoots me a warning glance.

Sloane turns away from me to face her.

"Okay, so you said you hadn't heard from this Marcie chick. I looked her up on Facebook to see if she left any clues on her profile, but it was set to private. Hacking her account was the only way to get information," she says, throwing a dirty look at me over her shoulder. "So I discovered she hadn't posted anything on her account in a couple of years, but I did find some older, interesting pictures of her posing with a trophy in front of a target. You know, one of those torso things with a bullseye on the chest and one on the head? Both of those were riddled with bullet holes. Anyway, it didn't say anything about where it was taken or what it was for, but when I enlarged the picture, I could barely make out a name in the bottom left-hand corner of the target. The Batavia Gun Range. Which, is located right outside Kalispell," she concludes proudly.

I reluctantly take a seat opposite the couch, intrigued despite my lingering anger. The look my niece throws me is one of triumph and the brat grins when I narrow my eyes at her.

"A gun range?" Pippa interrupts our stare down. "I didn't know she could shoot."

"Well, I couldn't be sure from just the pictures if she was actually the one who shot that target or earned the trophy. I didn't want to jump to conclusions and needed Chappy's help to get me inside the shooting range so I could talk to the manager and get confirmation," Sloane clarifies. "Anyway, I'd been playing telephone tag with Chappy when Ira messaged me to let me know the feds were looking for me. I figured it probably had something to do with the history they would've pulled up on the computers they confiscated. I was so close to getting the information, I decided to drive to Kalispell, see if I could chase down Chappy. To make an already long story short, I found him, he helped me get into Batavia, and I got the information I was looking for."

"Which is?" I prompt her, eliciting another cocky grin from my niece.

"Marcie was a three-time winner of the annual Flathead County Precision Rifle Shootout from 2009 through 2011."

Holy shit.

My eyes lock on Pippa, who looks shocked.

"Marcie? Are you sure?" she asks.

"Positive," Sloane says, leaning forward as she puts a hand on Pippa's arm. "I even recorded the whole conversation on my phone."

Call me a sexist, but I honestly would never have pegged a woman as the shooter in this case. I'm no profiler, but hunting these men down, shooting them in the back, it speaks more to exerting cold, calculated dominance. Something I automatically associated to a man. That said, it's not outside the realm and it definitely all adds up to look that way.

"The FBI needs to know this, Sloane," I tell her. "This could be their whole case right here and as a result you, and your friend, may find yourselves in some hot water."

"I realize that, but you know they wouldn't have listened to me, Uncle Sully," she directs at me, batting those familiar blue eyes at me. "You wouldn't have either."

She's right. I wouldn't have.

I'm still pissed at her, but damn, she makes me proud.

Twenty-Three

PIPPA

"Pippa, Honey…"

I'm in the zone and I love the way the muscles in his thighs bunch up under my hands. He's sitting with his back against the headboard and I know he's watching me. The small grunts he tries to swallow as I take him to the back of my throat, I can feel all the way down to my core.

"*Jesus*, woman…" he hisses when I almost let him slip from my lips, catching the plump head with my tongue before sucking him back in my mouth.

That breaks him, and the next moment he hooks his hands under my arms, pulls me up, and arranges me on his lap so I face the foot end of the bed.

"You promised it was my turn to play," I grumble.

"And now it's done," he growls as he firmly grabs my ever-expanding hips. "Lift, Pippa."

I lean forward, my hands braced on his bent knees, and raise my hips until I feel the blunt tip of his cock slide along my crease.

"Down, gorgeous," he whispers, his lips brushing the skin on my back.

My mouth drops open and my eyes close as he slowly fills me.

"Yesss."

~

"That puts a different spin on things."

I putz around in the kitchen because I'm too restless to sit, listening to Sully and his niece talk with Agent Wolff. He showed up about twenty minutes after Sloane called him, at her uncle's urging, and she's been answering all his questions, admitting freely she'd been digging and maybe doing a little hacking.

Wolff is good. Firm but not threatening, and the way he handles her, almost like she's a colleague giving a report rather than someone confessing to a crime.

Last night, as I have most nights recently, I fell asleep on the couch while Sully and Sloane were bent over the laptop he brought over from his office in the main house earlier in the day. From their conversation over breakfast this morning, it was clear he had her take him over every step of her research, and then spent half the night doing some of his own digging. I wasn't surprised to find out Cade Jackson is the person he chose to focus on. Truthfully, if I had to pick between Cade or Marcie as someone who might be involved, I'd pick Cade too.

It's not even nine, although I've been up for hours. The same restlessness had me wake up Sully before the sun came up. Of course, at the time, I had no idea he'd only come to bed an hour or two before. It didn't seem to hamper his enthusiasm though. A smile pulls at my lips, reliving the vivid memories of him moving inside me temporarily block out the discussion in the living room.

"Pippa?"

My head snaps up, when I hear Sully's voice, to find every eye fixed on me. Immediately, I feel the blood rush to my face as I focus on Sully, who is wearing a smirk. Bastard knows exactly where my mind had drifted.

"Sorry, I missed that..."

"We noticed," he returns smugly. "Wolff was just asking you something."

My eyes slide to the agent.

"I was simply curious whether—given this latest information—you might have given any more thought to where Marcie might've gone?"

I scoff a bit. "I've frankly been trying to wrap my head around the possibility someone I thought was a friend could be involved with any of this."

"Understandable," the agent sympathizes. "So is that what you believe? That she's involved?"

"I don't know, but the answer would've been a hell no only days ago, if that tells you anything," I share honestly as I move over to the couch where Sully pulls me down beside him. "I mean, at this point, all we know is she's passionate about the Fair Game mandate, she's some kind of sharpshooter, and she somehow disappeared last week. Unless I'm missing something?"

Sully's arm tucks me closer, giving me a sense of comfort as I listen to the agent.

"Actually, some new information has come to light..." Wolff starts, and the sympathetic look he sends me makes me feel uneasy. "...Which would indicate Ms. Watts may have been the one to place the rifle in your motorhome. That fingerprint we found on the loaded round? It matches

Marcie Watts's prints we were able to collect from her apartment. Is there any reason why she might try to implicate you?"

"What? No, there isn't."

My answer is immediate. This is nuts. My mind is scrambling to make sense of what he's suggesting, going over my interactions with Marcie since I met her last year.

It's not like she sought me out, ours was a chance encounter at rehab. We chatted, hit it off when we discovered mutual interests, and she introduced me to Fair Game. When I mentioned maybe wanting to set down roots here and expressed an interest in the vacant auto shop, she negotiated a great deal for me. There's nothing that might've given her reason to try and frame me, if that's in fact what she did.

"You know," Sully interrupts my thoughts as he addresses Agent Wolff. "You guys seem to focus all your energies in one single direction at a time. First, you were convinced Pippa was at the root of this."

"I wasn't," Wolff disagrees.

"Powell was and from what I can see he's in charge of this investigation. Despite what my niece uncovered; I hope you don't limit yourself to focusing only on Marcie."

"She fits the bill," the agent says defensively. "Besides, she's not the only person we're looking at, but she *is* the only one who's gone AWOL."

"Oh yeah? Tell me you're checking out Cade Jackson?" Sully pushes, slipping his arm from my shoulders as he sits forward, pointing a finger at Wolff for emphasis. "He actually has reason to implicate Pippa, not only because she rejected him but because she'd become competition. His family owns Jackson Automotive and I'm pretty sure he's the one who vandalized the Pit Stop.

"But what's more interesting is something I found out last night. Did you know the guy very publicly and very aggressively confronted Congresswoman Yokum on her stance on baiting at one of her campaign rallies two years ago? He tossed a bucket of rotting food onto the stage and called her a killer."

Whoa. That is news to me. To Sloane as well, judging from her sharp intake of breath. He never mentioned anything, then again, I didn't give him much of a chance this morning; I made sure his mind was on other things.

Wolff doesn't look in the least surprised though.

"Sheriff Ewing provided that information to us last night," he confirms.

"What is puzzling," Sully contemplates out loud. "Is that no charges were ever filed. He was hauled away by the cops and by all accounts should've been charged with assault or something, but instead he walked."

"Congresswoman Yokum apparently didn't want to press charges. Powell is actually meeting with her this morning to get some clarity on why that was," Wolff explains.

I'm only half listening and lean my head back, closing my eyes as I slowly breathe through another one of those damn fake contractions. As if on cue, the baby starts moving about as soon as it wanes. She obviously does not appreciate them either.

"Are you okay?" Sully asks beside me.

"Fine," I respond, rubbing a hand over my belly. "She's active, that's all."

Apparently, that's enough for Sully to call an end to this gathering. Wolff doesn't argue and gets to his feet, but he stops by the front door.

"Before I forget, we're done with your RV. You can pick

it up at our temporary digs at the game warden's station just east of town."

"That's where Marcie stores her trailer," I volunteer, remembering I dropped her off there once in the fall.

"Where?" the agent asks.

"At the station."

"There was no trailer there. Weird," he muses out loud. "Her car was still at the apartment and we didn't find any other vehicles in her name. Do you know what she would normally tow the trailer with?"

"I know she mentioned renting a tow vehicle before, and I think last fall she may have borrowed someone's truck. She was talking about trading her car in this summer for something with towing capacity."

He nods, looking a little distracted as he walks out.

Sully closes the door behind him.

"We should go pick it up."

Sloane claps her hands excitedly.

"Awesome. When are we going camping?"

"You're outta luck, kid," Sully says, bursting her bubble. "I'm taking Pippa outta here for a couple of days—think of it as our honeymoon—and someone needs to give Ira a hand at the garage."

"No fair," she complains, but then a grin steels over her face. "Then can I take it out for a few days when you guys get back?"

My anxiety ratchets up a notch at the thought.

Sully

Good to know Wayne Ewing finally got up off his ass and looked into Jackson.

I'd like Jackson to be guilty as all hell, but I can't dismiss the stuff Sloane pulled up on Marcie. Both are good candidates. Better than Pippa, thank God, which means the focus is no longer on her.

Only thing is, I can't quite figure out what Marcie's motivation would be to target Pippa. That part fits Jackson better. Limp-dicked momma's boy, who can't take no for an answer, so he takes it out on the woman who turns him down. *Coward*.

Boggles my mind though, it's one thing to be passionate about a cause, it's a whole different ballgame to start executing people. There has to be a better motivator for the murders than that. Something more that drives someone to become this bloodthirsty.

It's tempting to keep digging, but Pippa is out of the FBI's crosshairs and I promised to take her camping. I am worried, however, Sloane will continue her investigation.

"This Chappy guy, is he someone special?"

I look over at Sloane, sitting in the passenger seat.

She barks out a laugh. "God no. I mean, he's nice, and maybe he'd be interested in something more but I'm not."

Poor guy. Something tells me my niece didn't hesitate to use his interest in her to get what she wanted.

"Not cool, Sloane, bribing the guy with hope when there's none."

I glance over and catch her watching me from under her lashes, a small blush on her cheeks.

"It wasn't really like that. I never made any promises."

"Maybe not, but the guy potentially risked his career for you, which means at the very least you gave him the impression he had a chance, sweetheart. Please don't risk his, or your own, future by continuing to poke around in a federal investigation."

She turns to look out the side window, not saying anything but hopefully thinking on what I said.

Pippa is at home, having a nap. She was up early and got busy right away. A smile steals over my face thinking of my wake-up call at the crack of dawn. As a result, I didn't get a lot of shut-eye either, but I'll have to catch up on my sleep when we have Pippa's rig parked somewhere secluded and we don't have to worry about family interruptions or law enforcement knocking on the door.

We're in Pippa's truck on our way to the game warden's station to pick up the motorhome. Sloane will take the pickup to the garage and I can drive the rig home. This afternoon we can stock up and get it ready and tomorrow morning we'll head out.

I know we can't go too far, but there's a place we stumbled on last year on a search I'd like to take her to. It's only about ten miles from Libby; a small lake at the end of what was little more than two tire tracks veering off the forestry road for about half a mile. It'll be tough going—we did it on horseback—but it'll be worth it.

"What would be required to become a game warden?" Sloane asks as we turn onto the station parking lot.

Pippa's motorhome is parked behind the building and I pull the pickup in beside it before turning to my niece.

"I imagine your degree would be a good start, but it would also require a great deal of knowledge of fish and wildlife. It's not limited to policing in the great outdoors, it's in large part preservation as well."

From the corner of my eye, I see Woody Moses come out the station's rear door.

"Maybe you should ask him," I suggest, directing Sloane's attention to the approaching warden.

"Eckhart."

"Moses." I nod at him before turning to my niece, who is rounding the front of the pickup. "This is my niece, Sloane." The two shake hands. "She has a brand-new degree in criminal justice and is interested in the kind of work you do here," I add.

"I can speak for myself," she snipes at me before aiming a bright smile at Woody. "That said, yes, I would love to pick your brain at some point when you have a few minutes."

Woody grins. My niece knows how to turn on the charm when she wants to.

"I'm on my way out now, but why don't you leave your number with my office and I'll give you a call when I have some time."

With a nod for me he starts walking to his SUV parked on the other end.

"Before you go," I stop him. "Do you know where I can find the keys to the motorhome?"

He looks at the rig and then back at me. "She's more than welcome to leave it parked here. It's not in my way."

"Thanks, but we've got the space at the ranch. Besides, she's ready to get out of town for a bit."

He nods with a look of understanding. "Don't blame her." Then he jerks his head toward the rig. "Keys are behind the fuel tank door. See ya later."

Sloane is already behind the wheel of the pickup and is backing out, wiggling her fingers at me. I jerk my chin at her before heading around the rear of the motorhome. I retrieve the keys, get into the driver's seat, and start up the engine. As I maneuver out of the parking spot and head for the road, I notice the game warden's SUV still sitting in the same spot. Moses is on his phone behind the wheel and lifts his hand in greeting as I pass.

When I get home twenty minutes later, Pippa is sitting at the kitchen table, my laptop open in front of her. She smiles wide as I approach.

"How do you feel about dogs?"

Twenty-Four

PIPPA

"It's gorgeous."

No exaggeration either.

The lake is small, more like a sizable pond, but has a small waterfall coming down the rock face on the opposite side where the creek comes down the mountain. The rest of the basin is fairly densely surrounded by trees, with the exception of the small section where we've parked the rig.

I wasn't sure we'd make it here; the trail was only half a mile or so but extremely rough. Rocks, ruts, encroaching vegetation, and low-hanging branches, but Sully navigated us through. If I'm being honest, had I been by myself I probably would've backed right out again, which would've been a shame. I would've missed all this beauty.

"Want more?"

Sully lifts the camping kettle, which he repurposed as a teapot, from the grill over the campfire. That's what I woke up to twenty minutes ago, a campfire, a pot of tea, bacon sizzling in a cast-iron pan on the fire, and this phenomenal view.

"Please." I smile at him as he takes my mug from me. "You're spoiling me."

"Don't start praising me yet," he says with a grin. "It's breakfast, which happens to be the only thing I can cook. Guess who's cooking dinner again tonight?"

I don't mind. Camp cooking is fun. Days out here tend to be centered around the main meal of the day. I did most of the prep work at home yesterday and all the veggies are precut in containers in the fridge. I love making foil packets; they're easy to prep, easy to cook, are healthy, and create minimal waste or dishes.

I take a sip of the hot tea, sink back in my padded, over-sized camping chair, and look at the view. Even though we can't be more than maybe ten miles from Libby as the crow flies, the only sounds out here are sounds of nature featuring the falling water prominently.

Cold falling water, as I discovered last night when it seemed like a good idea to wash off what had been a hot day with a fresh dip under the gorgeous night sky. We'd arrived midafternoon, set up, and took a nice hike up to the top of the waterfall, from there we could see my rig parked on the other side of the lake. When we got back, we built a fire, had dinner, and when the logs had almost burned up, I suggested a swim. I'd been prepared for a bit of a chill in the cool mountain lake, but I've never experienced a full-body pucker like I did when I hit that water.

Luckily, it didn't last since Sully was right behind me and quickly saw to it I didn't stay cold long. We made our way over to the falls and made love against the rocks behind the curtain of water. I swear when we finally emerged, steam was rising from our bodies. We never bothered to dry off or get dressed and simply crawled into bed, wrapped up in each other.

"Here you go."

Sully hands me a plate with bacon and eggs, and two slices of toast he grilled over the fire. As is always the case, food cooked outside—especially over a wood fire—tastes a million times better. We eat breakfast in companionable silence, enjoying the view and each other's company.

"Are you up to a hike once I get these washed up?" Sully asks, taking the empty plate from my hands.

"Go," I urge him. "You cooked; I'll clean. Besides, I'm still recovering from yesterday's activities," I admit.

"Oh yeah?" he probes, wearing a smirk. He leans down, bracing his hands on my armrests, effectively boxing me in.

"Hmmm," I hum teasingly. "That hike really sapped my energy."

His response is a hard kiss on my mouth.

"You sure you don't wanna come?"

"Positive. Go. I'm gonna relax for a bit and I'll never grow tired of this view."

He brushes another kiss on my lips, this one sweet and gentle, before he straightens up and starts walking toward the trail. I'm all about this view too, his ass flexing underneath the worn jeans with every stride of his long legs.

I'm starting to love all these sides of him. The inside and the outside views. Turns out, maybe I wasn't so wrong taking a chance on him last New Year's Eve. Hell, I'd been falling for him even before that night. He's a good man and it shines through. Probably why I was so confused with his strong rejection and subsequent ghosting, and why—despite a little early apprehension—it wasn't too hard to trust him again.

Love.

Such a small word for a life-altering emotion. Once you open yourself up to the possibility your perception changes: your heart feels lighter, the air fresher, the sky brighter.

I let breakfast digest and sit for a few minutes, enjoying the quiet before finally hoisting myself out of the chair. I fetch the dishpan and soap from the motorhome and when back outside, drop the dishes in a plastic tub, squirt a little soap in it, and grab the now empty kettle to fill with lake water. Then I throw another log on the fire, put the water on to boil, and start carrying in the perishables to stick back in the fridge.

When I head back outside, I notice steam is coming from the kettle. Using a towel so I don't burn my hand on the handle, I take it off the fire, and bend over to pour the hot water in the tub I set on the ground.

Right then I hear a dull crack, like the snap of a branch, and I straighten up to look behind me. Another crack sounds at the same time I hear a metal ping off the side of my rig. I immediately drop down to the ground.

I can't fucking believe someone is shooting at me...again.

Beside me dirt spits up simultaneously to yet another crack, and I know I'm not safe where I am. On hands and knees, I scramble underneath the rig. I'm probably safe from bullets here but I don't like the idea of making myself a sitting duck. How long before whoever the fuck is shooting comes looking for me?

I'm not sure where the shots are coming from, but they can't be that far.

Would Sully have heard or is he out of earshot? Sound has a weird way of traveling through these mountains. He could be a few hundred feet away in a gully and not have heard it. I can't count on him to get me out of this.

Sully pulled the rig tight to the tree line on the driver's side in the shade, which means if I scoot through to the other side, I'll have the motorhome between me and whoever the hell is shooting.

Marcie? I can't wrap my head around that possibility. Why? What have I done to her? Or is it someone else?

I'm not going to get the answers hanging out under here. I have to assume the shooter will come looking for me and I'm wasting time. My guess is they'll count on me hiding instead of moving, so I'm going to try and get under the cover of the trees, and make my way to the other side of the lake.

What scares me to death is Sully coming back and walking in on someone brandishing a weapon. He left on the same trail we took yesterday, so I'm hoping if I can get to the top of the waterfall, I'll be able to intercept him there. If anything, I'll be on high ground and should be able to keep an eye on the campsite and maybe warn him.

Those thoughts propel me out from under the motorhome, where I scramble to my feet and dart into the cover of the trees. I stop, sheltering behind a tree while I listen for any movement, but the only thing I hear is my own rasping breath and pounding heart. I haven't heard a shot after the third one, which may mean the shooter is on the move.

I need to keep going. I'm afraid if I don't, fear may paralyze me.

Temperatures are already creeping up and it doesn't take long for me to break out in a sweat. It's tough going over the uneven surface and through the occasional thick underbrush, while trying to be as quiet as I can. Don't want to make a racket announcing my location to the shooter.

Not quite a year ago I was in a similar situation, but

back then I was running for my life. This time I'm not only running for my own, but my baby's and Sully's as well.

I stop abruptly when I hear a faint rustle like something is moving. I tilt my head slightly, waiting to see if I can hear it again. If I run into a mountain lion or a bear—or God forbid, a cub—out here, I'm in big trouble. Normally I carry a can of bear spray when I venture out, but it's in the motorhome, along with anything I might've used for a weapon.

When it stays quiet, I start walking again. A little more cautiously though, with my awareness heightened. Which is how I catch a hint of movement from the corner of my eye.

Before I can turn toward it, I'm jerked back with a large hand clamped over my mouth, and my heart stops.

∾

Sully

When I hear the second crack, I know what I am hearing and my eyes are scanning the landscape. By the third shot I have an approximate location.

There, on the east side of the lake, the shots are fired from that outcropping of rocks. My eyes immediately dart to the campsite where I just see Pippa crawl under the motorhome. *Good girl.*

I'm at the top of the waterfall on high ground, where I was hoping to get cell reception, so I could check in with my niece. Instead, I'm dialing Jonas as I'm on the move.

"Shots fired. We're at Flower Lake, came in on the trail we—"

"I know where. Status?"

I can tell from his breathing he's running.

"Both alive but separated. Got a bead on the shooter, going after him. Suspect he left his vehicle farther back on the trail and walked in."

"...want you...until...half an hour...not engage..."

I'm losing signal and only pick up a few of Jonas's words, but I get the gist of his message as I tuck away my phone.

My heart is beating in my throat and everything in me wants to go after the threat. An automatic response honed by years of training and fieldwork. I'm armed, I always am, but instead of hightailing it after him, I retrace my steps to the path I came up on the opposite side of the lake. The one leading back to Pippa.

Speed is of the essence. I need to get back to the campsite before the shooter can. Was he watching? Lying in wait until I left? Maybe he doesn't know I'm out here and is only expecting Pippa. Because it's clear to me this isn't an accident or a coincidence. Someone is after my wife. But why? And how did they find us?

I hear her before I have a visual. Should've known she wouldn't hide under that rig for long. My wife has a take-charge personality, although what the hell she thinks she's doing traipsing through the damn woods I don't know. Grinding my teeth, I let her pass by my position. I don't want to startle her and alert whoever is out there.

I manage to loop around and approach her from behind. To prevent her from crying out, I cover her mouth with my hand and lock an arm around her chest. But before I can whisper in her ear to let her know it's me, she steals my breath in an entirely new way.

"*Fuck*...it's me," I manage in a strangled whisper as her bruising clasp tightens around my junk.

It's almost worse when she lets go, the blood immediately surging back to the tender area. I turn my back, bending over and bracing my hands on my knees as I breathe through the pain.

"Sorry. I came looking for you, I was worried. Someone is shooting," she mumbles behind me, instinctively keeping her voice low. Thank God.

Right. The shooter is still out there.

The fact she was out here in the open, putting herself at risk because she was worried about me—armed, trained, and ex special ops—says a lot about her character, and the size of her heart. As much as it warms me, it pisses me off and requires a serious talk, but now is not the time.

I reach for Pippa's hand, taking a firm hold. "Stay behind me."

My plan is to get back to the RV, where we have a few more options for shelter and methods of defense available to us. Problem is, the shooter may well have gotten there first, which means we have to approach carefully. Anyone other than Pippa, I would stash out here somewhere while I deal with the threat, but I'm convinced she won't stay put. Bringing her with me is probably safer.

We stay off the trail and when we get close to the campsite, I turn my head and put my finger to my lips, reminding her to be quiet. There is no movement I can discern from here, but that doesn't necessarily mean anything.

Our approach is slow, cautious, and every so often we stop to listen. When we reach the trees behind the motorhome, I'm half convinced whoever was here is already gone.

Crack.

A piece of bark hits my cheek when a bullet strikes the tree trunk six inches from my face. I drop down immediately, pulling Pippa down with me and behind the tree.

I have to let go of her hand to prop myself up and aim in the general direction I think the shot came from, firing off a few rounds. I guess I surprised the shooter because it takes him a moment to react and return fire. I have to squint against the splinters flying as he hits the tree trunk again, but I'm able to pinpoint his location.

He's about seventy-five yards in front of us near where the trail hits the clearing. The motorhome is about ten feet to our left, I'll feel a whole fucking lot better if I can get Pippa underneath. Then I have my hands free to deal with that sonofabitch taking potshots.

"Need to get you to cover. I'm going to distract him while you make your way under the rig," I tell her in a low voice. "Stay as close to the ground as you can and don't stop for anything. The team is ten minutes out."

"What about you?"

"I'll be right behind you," I promise.

But the moment she starts moving toward the RV, I head in the opposite direction, firing off a couple of shots as I go and drawing return fire. Good, if it's coming to me, it's not going to her.

My Sig holds ten rounds and I've already wasted half of them on a target I know is too far for me to hit under the circumstances. I'd like to preserve as many as I can. A quick glance over my shoulder shows Pippa already halfway underneath the vehicle. I immediately go down on my belly and follow in her direction.

The adrenaline is pumping and I need both my hands to move so speed is my only weapon. I ignore the impact of a round only inches in front of me before I'm able to dive underneath the RV.

"Are you okay?"

Her eyes are wide in her pale face, but she seems calm and collected. Fuck, this woman knows how to roll with the punches.

"I'm fine. Shhh. I want to hear him coming."

My vantage point under here is limited and I don't know from what side he'll be coming, so we take opposite ends where we wait and listen. There has been no movement until about ten or so minutes later when we hear engines approach.

Pippa crawls over to my side and both of us watch as Jonas's truck pulls into the clearing, followed closely by the game warden's SUV.

The cavalry has arrived.

Twenty-Five

SULLY

"Dead?"

My eyes immediately seek out Pippa, who is sitting on the steps into the RV, her face drawn as she stares out on the lake. So much for a quiet few days away. I hate this place is permanently stained by an asshole with a rifle. This news would make it even more so.

"Gunshot wound to the head. Stippling present. Glock 42 in the victim's hand."

I turn back to Jonas. "Suicide?"

"Or made to look like it. It was a fresh scene."

"How do you know all this?"

"Happened to be in Wayne's office when the call came in this morning," he explains. "I'm sure the feds are still out there processing that scene and Ewing is en route here, but Woody was out on a poaching call just down the road from here and followed us."

I already showed the game warden the tree trunk where one of the slugs lodged, inches from my face. Jonas arrived with James and Fletch, who are both helping look for the other rounds, with Pippa looking on. Of course, Fletch had to make sure she was all right first.

This news is going to come as a blow to her, and what kills me is it doesn't look like we're any closer to ending this fucking mess. Especially now the person topping the short list of possible suspects was found in her trailer, fifteen miles north of town, with a bullet in her head.

Which leaves me to wonder; who the fuck was shooting at us?

"Sully? What's wrong?"

I catch sight of Pippa getting to her feet, a worried look focused on me. I move toward her, urging her up the steps and inside, where she has some privacy when I break the news to her.

As is becoming her habit, Pippa surprises me again. No tears, but a pained look on her face when I tell her what I know.

"I don't know why but I had a feeling things wouldn't end well for her," she says, shaking her head before she continues firmly. "However, I don't buy for a minute she'd hide out somewhere for over a week to then suddenly decide to kill herself. That's bullshit."

I don't disagree with her. Suicide seems a little too convenient. Perhaps someone's attempt to tie off loose ends. Maybe the same person thought Pippa was a loose end as well and was out here trying to take care of her. Were they hoping to make it look like Marcie shot Pippa and then killed herself? Maybe hoping by the time the bodies were discovered it would be too difficult to pinpoint exact time of death and, therefore, the time line?

Which brings me to my earlier question; how the hell did the shooter find us? I still don't have an answer.

"Eckhart?" I turn my head to find the sheriff sticking his head in the door. "Wouldn't mind a word."

When he starts climbing into the rig, I get to my feet right away. It's cozy with only Pippa and me, but with Ewing as a third it's definitely a crowd.

"We'll come out," I inform him.

I wait for him to back out and turn to Pippa holding out my hand.

"You okay? There'll be more questions."

Her deep brown eyes lift up to me and I see pain, but also resolve.

"Let's get it done," she says, putting her hand in mine so I can pull her up.

I take the time to wrap her in a hug—those guys out there can wait—and for a moment I feel her cling to me like I'm the only thing keeping her standing, but then she lets go, straightens her back, and precedes me outside.

It's already close to the dinner hour by the time we pull up to the cabin. Once again, Pippa's motorhome was taken, this time to retrieve one of the bullets lodged in the exterior paneling, so we hitched a ride home with the team. After a long day of questioning from all branches of law enforcement—the feds showed up shortly after Sheriff Ewing was done with us—we're finally home.

Sloane, who'd heard about what happened through the grapevine, comes barreling from the cabin next door. After we're able to assure her we're both unscathed she returns next door, leaving us alone.

"Hungry?" I ask Pippa, who is on the couch, her feet pulled up under her.

"Hungry is a big word, but I'll eat. For this one, if anything," she adds, rubbing a hand over her stomach. "But can we do something easy? I don't feel up to cooking."

I open the fridge and as I'd hoped, Ama did not disappoint; a tinfoil covered oven dish is sitting on the top shelf, with cooking instructions on a sticky note attached. I lift a corner of the foil.

"How does baked ziti sound?"

"Divine."

Pippa takes a call from her sister, while I shove the dish in the oven to heat. Then I wander into what is supposed to become the nursery, where the faint smell of paint draws me, and find the reason why Bo didn't show up with the rest of the team. I suspect Ama may have had a hand in this as well.

The walls are painted the sage green color Pippa and I agreed on. The crib, changing table, and the dresser have all been assembled, and a brand-new light fixture hangs from the ceiling. The latter, I'm sure, Ama's doing since I don't see the mini-chandelier to be Bo's contribution.

I can't fucking believe this is my house. I'm standing in a nursery, looking at a crib my baby will be sleeping in soon. Suddenly light-headed, I sink my ass on the floor, letting my head catch up with the sudden wave of delayed panic.

"Sully, are you..." I hear Pippa walk into the room. "Oh, my God, it's so pretty. Look at that chandelier... Sully? Are you okay?"

She crouches beside me, her hand on my shoulder, and her expression one of concern.

"It only now occurred to me; I could've lost all of this today. You, the baby..." I gesture my hand around the room. "This. It could've become a shrine."

"Honey, we're fine. Both of us."

"I know, I just need a minute."

She gives me that by sinking down on the floor beside me, folding her legs in an impossible pretzel—like she's some kind of contortionist—and putting a hand on my knee.

Invading my space.

And I'm so fucking thankful.

~

Pippa

I can almost hear the wheels turning.

Wish I knew what has him sitting on the floor of the nursery looking so forlorn all of a sudden, but I resist the urge to question him. He looks like he's still working out the answer to that for himself.

He's proven himself to be here for me when I needed it on several occasions now, the least I can do is show my support silently. I can wait.

"My parents didn't exactly provide us with a safe upbringing," he starts abruptly.

"Sure doesn't seem that way," I agree softly, remembering the picture he painted of his childhood only a few days ago, although it feels a lot longer.

"It scares me..."

The pause that follows is so long I wonder if that's all he's willing to share. I'm about to prompt him when he starts talking again.

"The weight of responsibility. I fucked up today, almost lost both of you as a result. I'm not sure if I'm cut out for this." He turns to me and I can see the struggle in his eyes. "Don't get me wrong, I'm not backing out. I'll fucking work my ass off to be a good father, a decent husband, but I've had no example. I'll be flying by the seat of my pants."

"I love you." The words tumble from my mouth unprovoked but they feel necessary. "I had a good example and still managed to fuck up my marriage. I've been tested and failed; you haven't even been tested yet. Already you're doing better than I am."

I know I'm rambling but I don't like seeing him so troubled. I've started to rely on him as my stalwart, my rock.

"So I'm not sure I'm cut out for this either, but I'm here, with you." I bump his shoulder with mine. "And I know I'm a better person for it."

He bumps my shoulder back, a small twitch at the corner of his mouth.

"You love me."

Not exactly a question, it's more of a statement, so I don't feel compelled to respond. I hopped over that fence, just like I was the one to put my heart on the line last New Year's Eve, but I'm not about to do it again unless I know he won't leave me hanging.

He reaches out, gently stroking the backs of his fingers down my cheek before brushing the pad of his thumb along my bottom lip, following his own movements with keen interest. Then his eyes come up to meet mine, the words that follow already visible in their depths.

"I love you back." He shakes his head, lowering his eyes. "Only people I ever occasionally heard those words from, or spoke them to, are Isobel and Sloane. Hearing them from you and giving them back feels unfamiliar, but right." Then he looks up. "Our daughter is going to hear them a lot."

My nose stings, but I'm not going to get sloppy. Instead, I lean in, curve a hand along his stubbled jaw, and press my mouth to his.

"She's already a lucky girl," I mumble against his lips.

Sitting here on the nursery floor, with my arms around a good man, it's hard to believe my friend is dead and someone is out to hurt me. This feels like a sanctuary of sorts; a place sheltered from a world gone crazy out there.

Unfortunately, reality strikes with the incessant beep of the oven timer, bursting our little bubble.

Sully gets to his feet, helping me up, and goes to take care of dinner. I follow him to the kitchen and maneuver around him to set the table. It's surprising how easily we move about in the small space, instinctively aware at all times where the other is.

We don't talk much during dinner and today's events start replaying in my mind. The shots, the fear, the urge to get to Sully, his team arriving with law enforcement, and the sudden disappearance of the shooter. Gone, no trace of him or her. And then the devastating news Marcie was murdered. The suggestion she may have taken her own life out of some kind of remorse, which is a load of bull.

I was shocked to find out Cade Jackson was in FBI custody at the time of the shooting. In fact, he'd been held over in the local jail since last night. Agent Wolff mentioned they were questioning him about the murders and his connection to the Yokum family. He finally confessed to the two incidents of vandalism at the garage, which he justified as protecting family investments, even though Wolff suspects that what ignited those actions was my rejection of him. Your guess is as good as mine, maybe he had visions of a second Jackson's Automotive. Who the hell knows?

But if not Cade, then who? I'm not sure who else the FBI has on their suspect list. What would they want with me? That's the part I don't get. Did I do something? See something? I've been racking my brain since Wolff and

281

Powell questioned me earlier. They wanted to know if Marcie had maybe shared something with me she didn't want anyone else to know, but that was assuming she'd done the shooting, which we already know couldn't have been the case since she was already dead. Besides, I don't know anything.

"How did he, or she, find us?" I ask out loud.

Sully doesn't need clarification; he immediately knows what I'm talking about, which tells me he was mulling things over as well.

"Tracker. While you were answering questions for the feds, Fletch and I dove under the rig to look. It was stuck to the back of the black tank. Another reason why the FBI decided to take your camper in again."

"Why?" The whole thing simply boggles my mind. "I mean, I'm not sure what I've done, or done wrong? Why kill Marcie or focus on me?" Frustrated, I get up from the table and start pacing. "Those agents were hammering on that again yesterday, like there has to be a reason."

Sully shoves back from the table, folding his arms behind his head as he regards me calmly.

"There does have to be a reason," he confirms to my annoyance. "But that doesn't mean you're supposed to know what it is. Wanna know what I think? I think it was Marcie who knew something. The way you describe her reaction to the Yokum name suggests she realized something the moment she heard it."

"Maybe so, but it's not like she shared that with me."

"You know that, I know that, but the shooter may not know that," he clarifies.

"Which could be why he's after me," I conclude.

"That would be my guess."

I start clearing away dishes, but when I lean over, Sully pulls me down on his lap.

"Are you okay?" he asks, way too gently.

His arms tighten around me when I try to get up. I need to walk, wash dishes, do something—anything—to keep myself busy, before the sudden wave of grief for my friend drowns me. But Sully doesn't let go.

"Let it go, Honey." Again with the soft, caring voice, and I shake my head as if to ward off its effects. "All of it," he persists. "Let it go."

The first tear is one of frustration. The ones that follow are all for Marcie.

By the time my tears dry up, my eyes are gritty and swollen and I'm so exhausted I don't even blink when I feel Sully carry me to bed.

Twenty-Six

"You have got to be kidding me."

I barely managed to stop the by-now-familiar dark SUV the feds are driving before it was able to head over to my cabin.

Pippa is working out some of her grief and frustration in the kitchen, and I've discovered it's best to give her the space to do that. I made myself scarce and went to check in the barn to see how Sunny and her foal are doing. I was just on my way to look in at the office before heading back when I saw the SUV drive up.

Wolff rolls down his window and leans an elbow out.

"Seriously, Wolff? What do you want with her now?"

"Easy. I'm simply the delivery guy today," he says, jerking his thumb behind him. "I've got both your computers in the back."

I peer in and over his shoulder to the back seat.

"Unload them here," I suggest. "No offense to you, but my wife needs a break from this case, so unless you're here to tell her you've caught the son of a bitch, I don't want her catching sight of your ugly mug."

"Fair enough," he says as he gets out of the vehicle and opens the back door. "Porch?"

"That would be easiest."

I take the first computer he pulls out from him and carry it to the porch steps. I'll haul mine back to the cabin later, and load Pippa's into my truck. Maybe we can drop that off at the garage later this afternoon.

"What's this?"

Jonas walks out on the porch with a bottle of scotch, a couple of tumblers, and his father in tow.

"Computers the feds took," I explain as Wolff sets the second one on the porch. "Little early for that, no?" I point at the bottle.

"Actually, it's the anniversary of my mother's death. Dad and I are having a drink and a cigar on the porch."

"I'm sorry," I automatically respond, but Jonas waves me off.

"Wolff, you on the clock?"

"I'm always on the clock," the younger man says with a lopsided grin.

"You take breaks to eat, don't you?" Jonas persists. "Take a load off and have a drink, both of you."

He doesn't wait for a response and sets the bottle and glasses on the porch railing before he disappears inside, only to reappear moments later with more glasses and a box of cigars. In the meantime, I helped Thomas drag over his favorite rocking chair. Wolff has taken a seat on the steps.

"Here's to my Mary," Thomas says, right after Jonas hands out glasses.

"To Mary," I echo.

Never actually met her but I feel I know her from Thomas's stories alone.

"So...you done harassing our girl now? Seeing as she almost got killed by the *real* shooter," the old man fires at Wolff, who blinks a few times at the unexpected frontal attack.

Jonas groans and I suppress a grin. Trust Thomas to lay claim to Pippa, he's done so with every other female.

"She's not a suspect," Wolff concedes.

"'Bout fuckin' time you yahoos figured that out."

"Dad," Jonas intervenes. "I don't think Wolff was ever on board with that idea."

"Well, at least that's something. So, who do you have in your crosshairs now?" Thomas pries. "I hear there's a fifth victim? Pippa's friend?"

"We haven't confirmed her death is related yet," Wolff defers.

Probably a standard response when you're trying to avoid an answer. I can't blame the guy; Jonas's old man seems determined to score points.

"I've been meaning to ask you," the agent turns decisively to Jonas. "You were the first one to arrive on scene, correct?"

"We were."

"Do you remember passing any vehicles on the way up to the lake?"

That's right; the shooter got away somehow. For him to get back to the main road he'd have to take the forestry road Jonas came up, but unfortunately it has a few trails branching off someone could duck into and hide a vehicle.

"No. Not on the forestry road anyway," Jonas specifies. "Did you ask Moses? The game warden? He was right behind us."

"Yeah, yours was the only vehicle he encountered after the call went out," Wolff answers before turning to me. "And you never saw or heard a vehicle, did you?"

Not the first time I'm asked that question but I understand the need to repeat it. People sometimes recall things when they've had a chance to process events. Unfortunately, my response is the same as it was yesterday.

"No. And between the time the last shot was fired and the cavalry showed up was only ten minutes. Not a lot of time to disappear. What are you thinking?"

I take a fortifying sip of my scotch and watch as the agent visibly considers how much to share.

"We found the location where we think the first shots came from. Our forensics team found only a few tracks but couldn't trace it back to a trail he might have taken coming in, or going out, for that matter. Whoever it is seems very familiar with the terrain."

"So are we," Jonas offers.

Wolff looks at him from over the rim of his glass. "I know." He says nothing more as he takes a sip.

"Are you asking for our help?" I suggest.

The agent's eyes turn to me. "As you know, I'm not in charge of this case and Powell has made it clear he doesn't trust any local involvement."

True enough. Powell got pissed when our guys handed him the slug they'd recovered from the tree and he was adamant we not touch anything else.

"All I'm interested in is getting my hands on the shooter, by whatever means at our disposal, but..." Wolff shrugs his shoulders. "Like I said; I'm not in a position to make that call..."

He leaves that statement open-ended as he takes another sip. Jonas fills it in for him.

"You want us to have a look."

"Nothing I could do to stop you."

"This going to blow back on us when Powell clues in?" Jonas wants to know. "Because you're a decent enough guy and all, but I'm not sure I wanna piss off an agency that regularly pays my bills."

"No blowback. Why? It's not a restricted area, no active investigation there since Powell pulled everyone out of there last night. You wouldn't be breaking any rules."

"And should we find something?" I inquire.

"Just point me in the right direction, I'll take it from there."

Thomas draws the attention by slamming his tumbler down on the porch railing.

"No more booze for you guys," he announces, grabbing the scotch and pouring himself another few fingers. "Sounds like you've got a job to do. I'll hold down the fort here."

Jonas plucks the bottle from his father's hands. "Then you best stop guzzling the stuff too. You drink like it's lemonade."

"You know what?" the old man continues, undeterred as he wags a finger in Wolff's direction. "You're not as big of an ass as I thought. Why don't you ditch that government job and come work for my son? You can ride, right?"

Jonas shakes his head and turns to me.

"Right. Sully? Wanna go grab the team? James and Fletch are in the breeding barn."

I nod, and as I walk away, I hear Thomas pipe up again.

"Of course if you're not man enough..."

Jesus, the old guy is a card.

Pippa

"Fletch is sticking around."

I tilt my head back, catching a glint of his blues above the growing stubble on his jaw. I reach out and brush it with my fingers.

"Are you growing a beard like Fletch?"

He shakes his head slightly. "I don't know. Are you even listening?"

"I'm listening. You're going back out there to see if you can find tracks that might lead you to the shooter. I like it." I smile up at him. "The beard, I mean. But I'll miss that dimple."

I dip the tip of my finger into the small divot next to his mouth, which becomes more pronounced as he cracks a smile.

"So noted," he mumbles, bending down to brush my lips. "Don't go running off on your own somewhere without letting Fletch know. He's got a radio too, should you need to get in touch with me—cell signal will be spotty —but I should be back before dark."

"I won't," I promise.

I'm not a coward but until this bastard is caught, I have no desire to make myself—but more so my unborn daughter—an easy target again.

He kisses my forehead and then I watch him walk off to join his teammates assembling in front of the main house, before I head back inside.

Sully relayed the conversation the guys had with Agent Wolff, who'd apparently stopped by earlier to drop off the computers. I know what the plan is. They're going back to the lake to see if they can retrace the steps of the shooter. Apparently, the agents are not having much success tracking this guy down. Clearly Powell and Wolff have different ideas on how to proceed, but Wolff's hands are tied since Powell is in charge. It was a smart move on his part to plant a seed for HMT to pursue.

To be honest, I've been racking my brain as well this morning. I've gone through everyone I know with Fair Game—which is a very short list once you eliminate Marcie and Cade—and I'm starting to think whoever is doing this has nothing to do with the organization. Fair Game isn't local to the Libby area, these are volunteers from all over the state with a common goal. It's not some armed, militant group doling out their own form of justice. Heck, all we do is call any possible sightings of baiting in for law enforcement to further look into.

Sure, I could be wrong. I would never have guessed Marcie to be a sharpshooter, but I was right she couldn't have had anything to do with the murders. Still, I knew her better than any of the others, so who's to say there isn't one of them hiding a blood-thirsty alter ego I'm not seeing.

After transferring a load of laundry from the washer to the dryer, I sit back down at the kitchen table and open my laptop, which had been locked in the motorhome.

All I was doing earlier was popping names of group members I know into Google search to see what—if anything—popped up. There has to be a better way than randomly running names through a search, but it's all I can think of to do since I don't have the skills to do any in-depth snooping like Sloane and her uncle.

Somehow my gut says Marcie is the key. If she knew

something, if she had information on someone, why not notify law enforcement?

Unless...

I pull the laptop closer and type 'bear baiting' and add a name in the search bar before hitting enter.

Three pages with hits, mostly listings, a few local news updates, some social media links, but on the second page I find a five-year-old article I can't quite place at first.

It's a gruesome story about a woman, a cyclist, who was part of a group of cyclists riding a portion of the Continental Divide Bike Trail that runs from Banff in Canada, all the way down to the US/Mexico border. According to the article, the group was looking for a place to camp overnight not far from Eureka, when they happened on a couple of bears eating from a pile of garbage someone left behind. The group tried to get away when one of the bears attacked, pulling Elizabeth Kiley from her bike, and savagely mauling her. She was dead before anyone had a chance to intervene.

This happened on land reportedly belonging to one Janet Yokum, the congresswoman.

But it's one of the names mentioned in the last paragraph that jumps out at me. Elizabeth Kiley left behind parents and a half brother.

Oh my God, all of it makes sense. Motive, means, and opportunity. *Wow.*

If Marcie knew about this story, I can see why she might've reacted strongly when I mentioned Congresswoman Yokum. I always suspected there was something going on between them, is this why she disappeared? I wonder if Sloane found anything, I bet she never stopped looking.

Grabbing my phone, I dial the number for the garage. It

rings and rings, and I'm about to hang up and try on her cell phone when Ira answers.

"Pit Stop."

"Ira, it's Pippa, is Sloane there?"

"Nah, she said she had to leave. She had a meeting."

"A meeting?"

"Yeah."

As far as I know, Sloane doesn't know anyone here other than people here at the ranch and Ira. Although she did mention...

"Ira? Who is she meeting?"

Twenty-Seven

SULLY

We opted to leave the horses and do some old-fashioned tracking on foot, which has been a while.

One of the benefits of doing this on horseback is that your vantage point is higher, and therefore the ability to scan a larger area faster than the more myopic view from the ground. It also means overall progress tends to be slower, but there's less chance we miss anything.

Still, we've not been on the ground for fifteen minutes when James calls out.

"I've got something."

He's about two-hundred feet from the location we suspect the shooter was firing from. We spread out from that point but now all congregate around James. He's pointing at what looks like a toe print—only the upper ridge of a shoe sole—in this case of a boot. The deep groove visible in the soft dirt right beside a boulder looks like the tread of a hiking boot. The toe is aimed downhill.

We're like a well-oiled machine and, without discussion,

recalibrate using this spot as a center to spread out from. I spot the next track, about twenty feet downhill. The snapped branch of a sapling, low to the ground with its young leaves pressed into the dirt by what appears to be another partial footprint.

The same routine follows; we use the track as the new center to continue our search from. Ten minutes later we hit on a trail, no more than two tire-grooves cutting through the forest.

"It doesn't make sense," I remark. "We're maybe two-hundred yards from the campsite and I would've heard a vehicle out here, but I didn't. Not until I heard you guys driving up."

"Electric car? Hybrid?" Bo offers.

"You won't find many of those out here," James counters.

It's quiet as we start moving down the trail. I'm sure we're all trying to think of people we know who drive hybrids. Especially hybrids that can handle this terrain. Following the dual tracks for a quarter of a mile, we hit the main forestry road we came in on, and suddenly it comes to me with the impact of a lightning strike.

"Montana Fish, Wildlife, and Parks uses hybrids. Toyota Highlanders."

I remember seeing one just yesterday.

Fucking son of a bitch," Jonas explodes.

"You're shitting me," James contributes. "That's why the guy was right behind us."

Bo simply nods his head. "Makes sense to me. Definitely has the skills and plenty of opportunity, but what about motivation?"

"Not sure, but I'll be damned if it doesn't feel right, and I'm saying that after not even considering him a possibility."

"Fucking Woody Moses," Jonas mumbles, shaking his head. "We've known the guy for years. Hell, we've worked with him plenty of times."

"You've gotta call Wolff," I urge him. "And Ewing...I don't think Moses is on anyone's radar. He's fucking part of the task force."

I also have to get in touch with Pippa right now, because Woody could walk right up to her and she wouldn't blink an eye.

"I'll let Fletch know," I announce, checking my phone for bars.

But before either of us have a chance to call out, my phone vibrates in my hand with an incoming call.

~

Pippa

"Where the hell are you going?"

I ignore Fletch yelling behind me as I fit myself behind the wheel of my pickup. I'd done my bit, the moment I found out Sloane had gone off to meet up with Woody Moses I ran to the barn to find Fletch. He heard my story, told me to stay put while he made some calls, and then disappeared inside the main house.

Dammit. I tried several times but Sloane wasn't answering her phone and I need to get to her. I'm not going to wait around and do nothing when she has no idea the kind of danger she is walking into. Ira said she was supposed to meet him at the game warden station and had only just left. I'm about ten minutes from the garage and she's minutes ahead of me, but I'm hoping maybe she stopped somewhere in town, or was held up somewhere so I can intercept her.

The passenger door is suddenly wrangled open when I start backing away from the cabin. Fletch sticks in his angry face.

"Are you fucking insane?" he barks.

"Get in or get out, Fletch. Either way, I'm going."

I give him a few seconds to decide, even though I already know which way he's going to go.

"Fucking crazy reckless women in your family," he mutters, as he climbs in. "I swear you're as bad as your sister."

"What did Sully say?" I ask, pointedly ignoring his complaints as I drive away from the ranch.

"They'd come to the same conclusion you did but via a different path. They're on their way to the warden's station."

"Should we call the sheriff? The FBI?"

"The team will take care of that," he says before falling silent.

But a few minutes later he pipes up again when I pass a slow-moving truck on the highway, narrowly squeezing back in my lane before hitting oncoming traffic. Almost literally.

"Why don't you let me drive before you fucking kill us both?"

"No time to lose," I tell him, as my heart still beats in my throat.

That was a close call.

It's a good thing my doctor can't see me now, or she'd have me strapped to a hospital bed so fast I wouldn't know what hit me. What's worse, she'd have Sully backing her up all the way. I'm sure my blood pressure is through the roof, so I try to do some deep breathing as I drive into town.

"Keep your eyes peeled for a white, older Honda Accord," I tell Fletch. "Hopefully she stopped off somewhere."

We look but see nothing as we drive through town and out on the other side. The station is along the Kootenay River, a few minutes out of town. We're about to come up on it when Fletch's phone rings.

"Tell me you're fucking driving Pippa's truck."

I have no trouble hearing Sully and my eyes immediately flit up to the rearview mirror. The truck the team piled into earlier is right on my tail.

"Brother, I'm shotgun, and trust me I tried to—"

"Fucking hell, put me on speaker."

I'm about to tell him there's no need, I can hear every yelled word, but I figure it's best not to poke the bear. Instead, I flick on my blinker, indicating my left turn, right as I hear Sully's voice full strength, swearing profusely.

"Goddammit, Pippa, keep driving. Don't you dare think of..."

There's an opening in oncoming traffic and I make quick use of it. No way I'm going to drive by, especially now I can see Ira's old pickup parked beside Sloane's Honda, right outside the station. I noticed when we drove by the Pit Stop the 'Open' sign wasn't lit, but I thought maybe Ira already had left for the day. Clearly, he heard the worry in my voice when he told me Woody's name and decided to come and investigate himself.

"...Turning in there. Fuck me, woman. The feds are right behind us, turn the fuck around!"

"Watch your language in front of the baby," I snap at his litany of curses.

Still, I pull through to the farthest corner of the parking lot, where I back into a spot so I'm facing the back of the building. The only other vehicle, aside from Ira's truck and Sloane's Honda, is the SUV with the Montana Fish, Wildlife, and Parks logo on the side. Woody's cruiser.

I watch as Sully jumps out of the rear of the truck, a gun at the ready. Immediately a shot is fired from inside and I scream when I see Sully hit the deck.

"He's fine," Fletch says, drawing his own weapon from an ankle holster as he indicates Sully, who is crawling behind the truck. "You need to get down, Pippa."

He swings open the door and slides out of the truck, using it as cover.

I try to duck down but I don't have a lot of wiggle room; already I have the seat back as far as possible. I've been driving with nothing more than the tips of my toes on the pedals. As best I can, I lean over the center console and rest my upper body on the passenger seat. My stomach is in the way though.

"This is the bes—" I start saying when a loud yell cuts me off.

"Moses!"

I peek over the dashboard, seeing the two FBI agents shielding themselves behind their vehicle. With them is Sheriff Ewing, his hat easily recognizable. He's the one with the megaphone, which initially surprises me, but now that I think about it, it makes sense. Those two have worked together for years, there's already rapport built so Woody is more likely to respond to him.

"Go fuck yourself, Ewing!"

"Can't do that, my friend. I *might* consider it if you let your hostages go."

While Ewing is keeping Woody distracted, I notice Sully

and Bo crouching low behind the vehicles and moving toward this end of the building.

"And let you mow me down after? No fucking way."

As Woody yells, Bo and Sully duck around the corner and out of sight. When I look toward the other side, I notice both agents have disappeared from sight as well.

"How are you seeing this end, Woody?" Ewing asks.

Something I'd like to know as well, because not only is the man presumably holding Sloane and Ira hostage—and I hope to God they're both still in one piece—but now Sully is putting himself in harm's way as well.

"How can we resolve this situation?" he adds.

"With Congresswoman Yokum right here, admitting responsibility for the death of my sister. I want to hear her admit she knew of her son's illegal bear baiting on her property. You deliver her to me, and I'll let these two go."

"Holy shit," I mutter.

"Crazy fuck," is his reply.

"He's got to know that's never going to happen." When Fletch doesn't answer, I prompt him, "Right?"

"Let the boys do their thing," he finally says.

It's the equivalent of a pat on the head, which doesn't make me feel any better.

Sully

I hope to God Ewing has him sufficiently distracted, because climbing through this window isn't exactly quiet.

At least not for me. Bo is like a giant cat, moving on

surprisingly light feet for the solid man he is. I'm not quite so limber and light-footed, not anymore.

The moment my feet land on the linoleum floor in the small office we find ourselves in, Bo motions for quiet. I freeze and listen to Woody ranting on the other side of this door. The man I know doesn't waste words and has a calm, quiet demeanor, but this guy yelling his outrageous demands is someone I don't recognize.

And somewhere out there with him is my niece. If he's hurt her in any way, if she is injured or worse, I am going to rip him apart, limb by limb.

"What would your sister say, Woody?"

Shit. That's Sloane talking.

Bo turns to me, his eyebrows raised in question and I nod a confirmation. Goddammit, Sloane, be careful. It shouldn't surprise me my nosy niece dug up that bit of information but since it's what appears to be the man's motivation, she may be juggling nitroglycerine.

"Shut up," he barks.

From outside I can hear Ewing over the megaphone. I can't make out what he says, but it's Sloane demanding Woody's attention in here.

"What about your mom?"

"I said, shut up!"

"I'm sorry you lost her as well. Is that what made you—"

"Grief killed her."

He sounds unhinged, his voice high-pitched and almost hysterical. Both Bo and I move closer to the door. With hand signals we communicate how we're going to proceed. From what I can tell, Sloane is to the left of the door and Woody to the right. The problem with that is this door opens out and from left to right, which means we'll be able to see my niece, but won't have an eye on Moses until the very last minute.

Bo carefully pushes the door open a crack. A sliver just big enough for me to be able to see Sloane. She's sitting on the ground, about six feet from the door, with her back against the wall. From the way her body seizes up, I guess she's aware of the door opening but to her credit she doesn't look, keeping her eyes fixed on something to my right.

They're in the reception area, an open space you walk into when you enter the station. From my recollection, there are a few stands with flyers to my right and I can see a corner of the reception desk through the crack. I don't have a visual for Ira though, and I haven't heard him speak at all.

The silence on the other side is becoming a little unnerving, but when I reach out a hand to push the door open farther, Sloane must've seen the move and gives her head a sharp little shake.

"Grief killed her," Moses suddenly repeats as he starts talking again. "And yet that woman still doesn't take responsibility, still gets herself elected to Congress. She needs to pay for what she did, they all needed to pay."

"What about Marcie?" Sloane probes, at the same time a loud crash sounds.

I react immediately, kick open the door, and catch Woody turning his gun toward Agent Powell, who is standing in a doorway on the opposite side of the reception area. Before either can start shooting, Sloane makes use of the moment of hesitation to launch herself across the room, taking out Woody's legs and knocking him to the floor. I don't think and rush in, dropping my full weight on the man's upper body as I reach for his hand still clutching the gun.

I'm aware of the others crowding in around me until I hear Bo behind me.

"Weapon secure, you can let go. We've got him."

I lift myself off the guy, grab Sloane's arm, and pull her back with me. As soon as we get to our feet, I scan her tip to toe for injuries.

"You hurt? Sloane?"

Her head is turned away, her eyes fixed on a pair of work boots sticking out from behind the reception desk.

Shit. Ira.

"Stay," I order her as I hurry over to him.

He's lying face down in a puddle of blood and I drop down on my knees beside him, reaching out to feel for a pulse.

"Bo! Need a medic here!"

Twenty-Eight

Pippa

An army couldn't have stopped me when I heard Sully's voice yell for a medic.

Fletch tried to hold me back, but I was determined and plowed past everyone I encountered. I barely glanced at Woody in cuffs in my rush to get inside. The first thing I noticed was the blood when I rushed over to the desk.

Then it had been Ira, facedown on the ground.

This morning, sitting up in bed with dawn's watery light making its way in through the window, I'm still seeing Sully's prone figure, blood pooling under his body.

A warm hand slides up my spine, anchoring me to reality.

"Another one?"

Sully's sleepy rasp brings me such intense, physical relief, a single dry sob escapes my lips.

It's been a week since it happened and I've had the same nightmare almost every night. The only thing that seems unpredictable is the victim. I've seen Sloane behind the desk, even myself with a baby in my arms, but this is the third time I found Sully lying in a pool of blood.

"Yeah."

"Come lie down for a bit."

Tempting, but when I glance over at the alarm clock on the nightstand, I notice it's five thirty already. I have an oil change and tire rotation coming in at seven and I don't like feeling rushed.

"I should hop in the shower. First customer at seven this morning."

By a stroke of luck I received my work permit, or EAD, this past Monday. Thanks to Jonas pulling strings, otherwise I could've been waiting another month or two, if not longer. Permit or not, I would've worked anyway, doing whatever it takes to keep the business running. I really don't think after these past months anyone in local law enforcement would have the heart to bother me, but it feels better not to have to tempt the fates.

"That early?" Sully observes.

I lean back and brush a kiss on his mouth before getting to my feet.

"It's the only time the guy had available," I explain as I pad to the bathroom. "I wasn't about to argue, business is business."

I have to admit, it's picked up a bit since the FBI arrested Woody Moses last week, but it's still slow going and I have to grab what I can get. Especially now Ira is going to be out of commission for however long he needs.

That was such a relief, finding out he would live, and once he is recovered, I plan on giving him a piece of my mind for barreling into a dangerous situation. He apparently hadn't hesitated after I mentioned on the phone I suspected Woody might be involved with the murders. He closed the garage, hopped in his truck, and went barging into the game warden's station.

Of course, I'm sure he'll point out I'd been ready to do the exact same thing, but I'm not the one who ended up with a hole in my shoulder from a bullet and a skull fracture from where my head hit the corner of the desk going down. Turns out we were both willing to do whatever it took for Sloane.

I'd have a word or two for Sloane as well, but Sully already crawled up one side of her and down the other after finding out she'd decided to confront Woody on her own.

As I suspected, her curiosity got the better of her and she never stopped digging around. Sloane had been talking to Marcie's assistant at the office, finding out from her that Marcie received fairly regular visits from the game warden. According to the assistant, she swore high and low they were only friends, but the assistant suspected there'd been more going on.

That made Sloane suspicious, because even if they'd just been friends, Woody Moses had not acted as someone worried when she went missing or torn up when she turned up dead.

Of course, what she should've done is contact law enforcement or at the very least let her uncle know, but the girl is so eager to prove herself, and so damn fearless, she wanted to make sure she was on the right track first. Trust me, she feels guilty about Ira. Sully made sure of that. She's spent most afternoons this past week by his bedside after working mornings at the garage with me.

It's been a long week, but I'm happy to be working again. Although, I'm not sure how long I'll be able to, my stomach is getting in the way and I'm easily tired. I'll have to hang in for a bit at least, or I'm going to have to close the garage. Ira won't be back for a month at the very least, although he swears he'll be good to go in a week.

I get ready in record time and when I walk into the kitchen, Sully is already there, pouring me a cup of decaf coffee. Such a good guy, he's taken to drinking decaf right along with me, claiming it doesn't make a difference to him, but I'm pretty sure the moment I'm gone he'll race to the main house for a good hit of caffeine.

"Thank you."

"I'm thinking maybe you should talk to someone about those nightmares," Sully says as he pops some bread in the toaster.

"I'm fine," I dismiss him.

"Obviously not if they have you yell or shoot up in the middle of the night on a daily basis," he pushes.

"They'll pass."

He drops the butter he just pulled from the fridge on the counter and swings around to face me, grabbing my shoulders.

"Fillippa, in the past ten months you've been through one ordeal after another. You look to have bounced back effortlessly, which is worrisome to me because I know it isn't that easy. There's a reason why you have nightmares nightly."

I shake my head and am about to voice a protest when he gives my shoulders a squeeze.

"You think you have it under control, you think it'll all simply pass with time, but I know a little about being traumatized by events, and I've learned the hard way that is an illusion. It'll hit you like a ton of bricks when you aren't prepared for it. You absorb stress but you don't process it. It's not healthy for you, or for the baby."

Low blow. Accurate, but it feels below the belt.

The hard part is, I know he's right. I bulldoze through life, shoving anything and everything I can't control in a box, where it will hopefully remain, collecting dust. I'm afraid if even one corner of the lid is lifted, there is no way to hold back the nuclear meltdown I envision following.

"It's the only way I know how," I whisper. "Without disintegrating."

His gentle smile and soft stroke over my cheek are almost my undoing.

"That was before you had someone to keep you standing. Not gonna let you fall apart, Honey. Trust me."

Trust me.

I almost argue I do trust him, but how true is it really? Sure, I trust him when he says he loves me. I don't doubt for a minute he'll protect me from physical harm. I even believe he has my best interests at heart. But what he's asking me to do is make myself as vulnerable as I possibly can—strip myself down to the very fibers of my soul—and trust him not to let me fall or hurt me when I'm unable to protect myself.

He's asking me to trust him *more* than I trust myself.

"I love you."

Another low blow, as I look into those clear blue eyes and see the truth of his feelings reflected. How can I resist his confidence?

I do a face plant against his chest as his arms encircle me. Even with my eyes closed I can see the victorious smirk on his face.

"Fine," I mumble ungraciously into his shirt.

~

"Wolff, what are you doing here?"

I watch the agent walk toward me through the mud.

We have a pressurized water system in the fields closest to the ranch house, but some of these back fields still have to make do with an old tub we fill daily. The ground always gets sloppy around the water tubs.

I'm surprised he came all the way up here; I assume to look for me.

"It's Lucas," he starts, shaking the clumps of mud off his dress shoes. "And I wanted to give you an update before I head back to the office in Kalispell."

"You guys are done already?"

A week hardly seems long enough to wrap up the investigation into now five murders and one attempted murder.

"No, Powell and his team will probably be here for a few more days, but I've been called back on another case."

The tub is almost full so I walk over to the water tank on the back of the truck and close the valve before rolling up the hose. Wolff follows me.

"Must be frustrating, not to be able to see it through to the end," I observe.

He winces at my words. "Par for the course," he mutters. "Seems to be my curse. I'm not as ambitious as most. Just not cut out to climb over others to get ahead. I'm more of a team player."

I can see that. Despite a few run-ins, the guy has been fair and not averse to collaborating.

"Well, I appreciate you stopping by. So, what do you have in terms of an update? I gather one would not be forthcoming from Powell?" I add as an afterthought.

It makes Wolff chuckle.

"Don't hold your breath. As for an update; Moses was transported to Kalispell yesterday. He basically confessed. To be honest, I think in his mind he'd either get away with it or die trying. I think the fact he was caught shocked him."

"Isn't that often the case when someone is law enforcement? They think they can commit the perfect crime?" I comment.

"True. Anyway, you know the story about how his sister died. He had a beef with Congresswoman Yokum and her son for years, looking to get some kind of admission of wrongdoing on their part, but that never happened. It's too late to go back and figure out what exactly happened but in Moses's view, his sister's death was never the accident it was labeled as. In his mind the congresswoman's political influence buried the case. Then two years ago he heard about the incident where Jackson tossed garbage at Yokum. That was at a campaign event where she was once again flying her pro-baiting banner high, and it tripped him. He reinvented himself as some kind of avenging angel meting justice on illegal baiting."

"Doesn't exactly sound like the actions of a rational man," I point out.

"Not in the least. If anything should tell you that, it's what happened to Marcie. Those two had an on-again-off-again relationship for a couple of years. I don't think she had a clue how deep Moses was into her cause though."

I duck into the cab of the truck, grab a couple of bottles of water from the cooler wedged between the seats, and toss one at Wolff.

"But she freaked out when Pippa mentioned the Yokum name, she must've known about his hatred for the family. My guess is she confronted him?"

"She did, or at least she questioned him, he panicked and lashed out. He hit her, then realized he had to keep her quiet, so he taped her up, stuck her in her own trailer, and he pulled it up the mountain." He pauses to take a deep drink from his bottle before finishing with, "Bastard planted that rifle with the slug with Marcie's fingerprint, trying to make it look like maybe she had tried to set Pippa up. Then kept her captive for a week and a half before he could finally bring himself to kill her, making it look like a suicide."

"Why come after Pippa though?" I want to know. "It's not like she knew anything."

"Maybe he suspected Marcie would've let something slip to Pippa. Maybe Marcie told him she talked to Pippa, hoping it might keep him from killing her. Who knows?" Wolff shrugs. "Could've been anything. I'm pretty sure the guy wasn't exactly thinking straight."

Good point. He was clearly off his rocker. Trying to find logic in the thinking of a serial killer is not something that's easy for the average person to do, that kind of warped insight is best left to professionals.

"I'm sure Pippa will be relieved to hear it's not something she did. Or did you talk to her already?"

"No, thought I'd leave that to you. I didn't want to chance causing her any more anxiety than we already have."

Yeah, Lucas Wolff is a decent guy, who sometimes has a shitty job to do, which reminds me of something Thomas said to him the other day.

"Fair enough. You ever think of leaving the Bureau?"

Wolff takes another drink, his eyes on the view of the herd against the backdrop of the mountains.

"More frequently these past few years. It's tough though, I always thought this would be my career until I retire."

314

"A little young to be talking retirement, aren't you?"

"Recently turned thirty," he admits with a sheepish grin.

"Well, maybe you should consider how those next twenty-five or so years are going to look if you're already unhappy."

He slaps some imaginary dirt off his pant leg, his eyes down.

"Point taken," he mumbles, before holding out his hand for me to take. "I should head out, but I'll keep what you said in mind. Best of luck to you and your wife."

I watch as he saunters with his lanky, easy gait to the SUV parked behind the water truck.

Maybe Lucas Wolff would be a good candidate for that revitalization of our team Jonas was hinting at.

He'd be the kind of man we'd want.

Twenty-Nine

PIPPA

"You look sharp today."

We look up when Lindsey Tippen walks into the exam room.

"Funeral," Sully explains, his hand on my shoulder squeezing lightly.

The doctor's face drops immediately.

"Oh no, I'm sorry."

"She was a friend," I explain. "And one of the victims of Woody Moses."

I know she would've heard the game warden's name. The lurid story of a law enforcement officer gone rogue has already done the rounds and even hit major news outlets these past weeks.

It's been almost a month since she was discovered but it's taken this long for the FBI to release her body. The funeral is supposed to be small, arranged by her assistant by proxy of Marcie's brother. He's flying in from Panama, where he's lived the past twenty or so years. Since Marcie wasn't particularly religious, the service will be held at Pearson Funeral Home in town. No muss, no fuss, which wouldn't have suited her anyway.

"The real estate agent," Lindsey confirms as she gestures for me to get up on the table. "I'm sorry, I didn't realize she was a friend."

She lifts my top and gently palpates my abdomen.

"Feels right on target. Still getting Braxton-Hicks?"

"Every so often. They don't take my breath away like they did in the beginning."

She smiles. "That's why they call them practice contractions."

She produces the doppler and searches for the baby's heartbeat. I inadvertently hold my breath until I hear the rapid thump signaling she's still there.

"She sounds good. How have you been feeling? Blood pressure is better."

"I'm good. Work is getting difficult but my mechanic is back this week, so between us we manage."

Ira got a clean bill of health from his doctor and I breathed a sigh of relief when he showed up Monday morning. With more work coming in, I'm wondering if I shouldn't start looking at hiring someone else, at least part time. I'm limited in what I can do at this point and that's only going to get tougher as this baby grows, but I'm determined to hang in as long as I can.

"When do you plan to stop?"

She pulls up an eyebrow when I hesitate but Sully jumps in.

"She wants to work until she goes into labor," he shares grumpily.

This has been a bone of contention, but I have poured all my earthly possessions into the garage. It's my means of

318

living, my retirement fund, my security blanket, and my pride. I need to make it a success, if anything, to prove to myself I can do it.

The other night Sully pulled up all his banking information on the computer and showed me his accounts and all of his investments. He wanted me to see he was more than capable of looking after me and our baby. That was a bit of a shocker. I knew he wasn't hurting, but he's actually in great financial shape.

"At this point, there's no medical reason why you couldn't," Lindsey says with a shrug.

"You're a great help," Sully points out with a hefty dose of sarcasm that has the doctor smiling.

"You didn't give me a chance to finish. What I was going to say is that you, Pippa, will regret not taking some time to yourself before this little one comes. Once she's here, you can forget about ever having any time to yourself again. You can bank on that."

Those words are still playing through my head during Marcie's service and the small reception afterward. I love my job, I enjoy taking things apart and putting them back together, better. It gives me great satisfaction to turn the key in the ignition and hear the smooth purr of the engine.

"You must be Pippa. Marcie mentioned you."

The voice pulls me from the thoughts I've been hiding behind the past half hour.

I turn around to find the tall, lanky man I pegged as the brother standing behind me. I hate to admit to him Marcie never mentioned his name. I'm not sure why, but I slap on a smile and hope to fake my way through.

"It's Nate Watts," he clarifies, obviously not fooled by my ruse as he offers his hand.

"I'm sorry to meet you under these circumstances. I'm

so sorry for your loss." I quickly indicate Sully by my side. "This is my husband, Sully Eckhart."

The two men appear to size each other up.

"My condolences," Sully mutters.

"Appreciate it." Nate turns back to me. "I know my sister probably didn't talk about me. I work in an industry that is built on secrecy. Marcie took that very seriously, as my big sister she always worried about me."

My immediate instinct is to start guessing what industry that might be, but instead I force myself to nod my understanding.

"Pippa!"

My name is called again, but this time my spine goes ramrod straight when I recognize the voice.

"You've gotta be shitting me," Sully grumbles, pulling me behind him.

I keep my eyes on Nate, who appears to be weighing the situation, when Cade Jackson walks up. I knew he was released awaiting a hearing, but I didn't think he'd have the balls to show up here.

"I only want to apologize, I didn't mean—"

"Stop right there," Sully intervenes, aiming a finger at the man while holding me back with his other arm. "You have nothing to say to her."

"I have a few things to say to him," I snap, barely able to hang on to my sudden rage.

Every struggle, every frustration, and every loss suddenly narrows into a laser-sharp focus on Cade Jackson.

"How dare you show up at Marcie's funeral," I spit out, but before I can follow my urge and tear his head off, Nate steps in.

"Who is this guy?" he asks Sully, who explains in a few

sentences. "And you choose my sister's funeral for this?" he directs at Cade with palpable authority.

In less than two minutes, Nate has Cade firmly by the arm and marches him toward the door.

It's twenty minutes later, after we've taken our leave, I make a comment to Sully as he helps me into the truck.

"Marcie's brother seems a take-charge type of guy. I wonder what he does that's so secret."

Sully ducks his head in the door and kisses my mouth before he whispers in my ear.

"Government."

~

Sully

I'm pretty sure the guy is CIA.

He probably has an elaborate cover; it sounds like he's been in Panama for a while. Quite a few points of interest in Panama, not the least of which the border it shares with Colombia. But also the Panama Canal, a major traffic route to legal as well as illegal goods.

An interesting line of work; I'll admit, at times, I fantasized about when I was younger and a lot more idealistic. But it's a lonely existence, one that would not have allowed me to meet and fall in love with this woman.

I get in behind the wheel, start the engine, and grab for Pippa's hand.

I know she's probably ready for a nap, after the doctor's visit and the funeral, but I have one more stop I'd like to make before I take her home.

"Why are we stopping at the rescue?" she asks when I turn down the long driveway.

"You'll see."

I talked to Lucy a couple of weeks ago after Pippa had woken up after yet another nightmare. She did set up an appointment with a therapist associated with the hospital, but she won't be able to get in to see them until sometime next month. In the meantime, I thought Lucy might be able to help.

I got her message a couple of days ago and went to look when Pippa was at the Pit Stop yesterday, but decided to wait until after the funeral to bring her here.

Lucy is expecting us, and her dogs come running up to the truck when I park in front of the house. She's just coming out the storm door when I round the truck to help Pippa down.

"What's going on?" she asks suspiciously as she bends down to greet the dogs.

Then she straightens and looks toward Lucy, who is standing at the top of the stairs, holding the leash of a pretty, six-month old chocolate lab sitting on the step beside her.

"Oh my God, you have a new puppy," she exclaims, rushing up the steps where she sits herself down at face level with the animal.

"Oh, a little girl. Aren't you the sweetest thing? Does she have a name?" she asks Lucy, who flashes one of her rare grins.

"Not yet."

"Where'd you get her?"

"Got her through K9 Care Montana. She's blind in one eye and was a program reject," Lucy explains.

Pippa clamps her hands over the dog's ears and presses its face to her chest.

"Don't call her a reject," she chides her friend, who shakes her head. "She's a sweetie."

"You like her?"

That question comes from me and she turns her head as if she'd forgotten I was here. Upstaged by a dog, who seems to be loving the attention showered on her.

"What's not to like? She's precious."

I meet Lucy's eyes and give her a nod.

"She's yours, if you want her," Lucy announces.

"You're kidding."

Pippa shoots to her feet, shock on her face, which is quickly replaced with a smile so bright, she's literally beaming.

"Are you for real?"

"Dead serious. She's housebroken, good with other animals, loves people, and would make a great buddy for your baby to grow up with."

Cue the tears, which I knew would be forthcoming. Pippa is not supposed to be a crier, but her tears are at the surface these days. I've learned more about female hormones and a woman's anatomy in the past almost two months than I had in the previous forty-four years.

"Thank you so much. I love you," she sobs, throwing herself at Lucy, who seems more than a tad uncomfortable with the show of affection.

"Hey, you should be thanking your husband," she says, peeling Pippa's arms from her neck. "It was his idea."

Next thing I know she's in my arms, sobbing her gratitude.

"I love you so much."

"Fillippa, stop crying," I try to tell her in a firm voice after a few minutes.

"I'm trying," she snaps, rubbing her face on my shirt.

Not the first time I've walked around in a wet shirt in recent days.

I try to distract her. "She still needs a name."

Pippa turns back to the puppy with a smile on her face.

"She's such a sweetie."

"She is, but what do you want to call her?"

"Sweetie." She throws me a glance over her shoulder. "That's her name; Sweetie."

I squeeze the back of my neck and close my eyes.

"What? It's a perfect name for her," she insists.

Lucy starts chuckling and I toss her a dirty look before I turn back to Pippa, who is looking at me like I hung the moon.

Fuck.

"Sweetie it is," I confirm reluctantly.

I'll never hear the end of it from the guys.

Thirty

SULLY

She's beautiful.

Long brown hair wild around her flushed face, big brown eyes shiny and alive in her reflection as her full breasts bounce each time I power inside her. She's close, her mouth —still slick and swollen from the kisses I woke her up with —parted in anticipation.

Braced with her hands on the vanity, I notice her arms start to wobble. So, I wrap my forearm around her chest, avoiding the swell of her belly, and keep her steady while slipping my other hand between her legs.

"Let go, Honey," I whisper with my lips against the shell of her ear, as I work her clit. "Fly apart for me."

The moment I feel her pussy contract around my cock, I throw my head back and let the last thread of control go, emptying myself inside her.

"Let's go, Sweetie."

I left Pippa to finish getting ready while I take the dog for a walk.

Max, Jonas's dog, was already roaming around the cabin, waiting for his new buddy to make an appearance. As he does most mornings, he follows along while I still keep Sweetie on a leash. I can tell she's eager to take off with him, but she's still learning where her boundaries are. I'm worried if I let her go before she responds to commands, she and Max are going to run off and I'll never see her back. That would kill Pippa, who's already bonded to this dog.

Who am I kidding? I'm as attached to Sweetie as she is.

As much as she's already grown since we got her, she's still very much a pup, sniffing every blade of grass or tree trunk we encounter. I'm not always the most patient man, but I'm forced to be with her. Guess it's good training for when our daughter arrives. Less than two months to go.

The dog does her business at her preferred spots on our regular morning loop, but starts barking when we approach the rear of the ranch house. Ama is already on the back patio, issuing orders to some of the guys hauling tables and chairs from a delivery trucked parked around the side.

I couldn't have stopped her if I tried. Ama's determination is legendary and she is hell-bent on throwing Pippa the perfect, most elaborate baby shower ever.

But it was my wife who insisted it be a co-ed event to the loud groans of most of the guys, myself included. I'd rather have a prostate exam than have to sit through a baby shower, but when Pippa turns those big, pleading eyes on me, I give her whatever the hell she wants.

The whole thing has now turned into some kind of hybrid, baby-shower cookout, with pink fucking balloons and the smell of smoking mesquite brisket. Even the cooler of beer has a pink ribbon and is sitting beside a decorated table stacked with gifts. One glimpse at the excruciatingly pink display will eliminate any ambiguity as to the baby's sex.

"Come on, Sweetie," I order the dog. "Let's go see if your mom is ready."

"Damn, brother..." Bo claps me on the shoulder, chuckling.

I'm so distracted with the decorations I never noticed him walk up behind me.

"I watched Jonas fall," he continues. "And Fletch succumbed not long after, but you, my friend, have blown the record in domestication."

"Fuck off, Bo. Just you wait."

He shakes his head before stating firmly, "Never."

"Famous last words," I toss at him over my shoulder before giving the dog's leash a tug. "Let's go, Sweetie."

Behind me Bo echoes, "Sweetie," and bursts out laughing.

Asshole.

An hour and a half later, I'm sitting at one of the tables with Thomas, having my first beer—I'm sure I'll have plenty more before the day is done—when Fletch walks over with Hunter, plunking the baby in my arms before walking away.

"What the hell?" I yell after him.

"Practice," he fires over his shoulder as he disappears inside.

I look over at Pippa, hoping she'll rescue me, but she's sitting with her sister, Alex, Lucy, Ama, and her daughter Una, all laughing hard at something. I don't have the heart to interrupt them. Pippa has been seeing her therapist, who is helping her embrace joy again. She still struggles with nightmares but they don't happen as often anymore, and she's working on regaining some of that fearless zest for life.

Hunter squirms in my arms, clearly uncomfortable as he starts to make a cry face.

"Hold him up against your shoulder. The kid wants to look at something other than your ugly mug," Thomas educates me.

I do as he suggests, propping the baby against my shoulder with one hand covering his diapered butt. The old man's right, the sounds coming from the baby are happy little squeals and gurgles. I glance over at my wife again, this time catching her eyes on me, a smile on her face that makes me feel like the luckiest fucker on the face of the earth.

This is good, her enjoying time with family and friends without reservation.

Talking about family, where the hell are Sloane and Isobel? Sloane was driving to Kalispell this morning to pick her mom up from the airport. Isobel is flying in for the shower, but Steve was at some conference this weekend. Lucky bastard.

"Well, y'all can color me surprised," I hear Thomas mumble.

When I turn to see what he's referring to, I just catch a glimpse of my niece getting out of her car in front of the cabins. I'm not aware I jerk to my feet until Hunter starts crying at the abrupt movement, I'm too busy staring at my niece dressed in a Lincoln County Sheriff's Office uniform.

"Gimme that baby before ya drop him," Thomas grumbles, plucking Hunter off me.

My eyes locked on her, I march over to where my sister is getting out of the passenger side.

"What the hell, Sloane?"

"That's what I said," Isobel agrees.

"Well, I thought it would be a nice surprise!" Sloane complains, throwing her hands in the air. "I thought you'd be happy I found a direction."

"A little advance notice you not only decided to move here but secured yourself a dangerous job would've been nice," my sister snaps.

"Whatever, I can't seem to do anything right."

"Can someone please get me up to fucking speed here?" I jump in, running out of patience.

"Fine," Sloane says, rolling her eyes. "Sheriff Ewing stopped by at the Pit Stop last week to get an engine light on his cruiser checked out. He asked if I was interested in law enforcement, given my interest in the investigation into the murders. I told him I was, and he mentioned the sheriff's department was looking for new recruits. I picked up my uniform this morning and training starts on Monday," she rattles off.

"And you didn't mention anything, because?" I prompt her.

"Because, I wanted Mom to be the first to know," she explains, suddenly emotional.

"Oh, honey," Isobel coos, pulling Sloane in an embrace.

I can't keep up with these women and spin around, throwing my arms up in the air, exasperated.

Only to be faced with a smiling Pippa, who must've seen me come out here.

"What am I missing?"

Pippa

I bump Sully's shoulder with mine.

"Lighten up, Eckhart. There's gonna be cake."

He's still glaring at his niece, who decided to go change before we sat down to eat, but when I whisper in his ear his clear blue eyes zoom in on me.

"You're trying to manipulate me with cake?" he asks, a half-smirk on his lips.

I shrug. "Cake always gets me in a better mood."

"Honey, you want a guy in a better mood you offer grilled meat or sex," Sully comments.

"Amen to that," Thomas contributes, causing my sister to burst out laughing.

"Good God," Ama mutters. "You old fart, you probably can't remember what sex was like it's been so damn long, and grilled meat is not good for your heart."

"Sweetheart, I've probably forgotten more than you'll ever know," Thomas returns with a big grin on his face.

"Please," Sloane pleads, her hands over her ears. "You're traumatizing me."

A wave of laughter breaks out in response, making her look even more mortified.

"Ignore them," Ama and James's daughter, Una, suggests. "They're all delusional. Come on, let's go check out the foals."

She hooks an arm through Sloane's, and drags her off in the direction of the barn. I watch them walk away; four years apart, a different ethnic background, one with blond, the other raven-black hair, but they sure have an attitude in common.

"That's what you can look forward to," Ama directs at Sully and me with a little too much merriment.

"You've got it, sister," Isobel agrees with Ama, raising

her glass before she turns to her brother with an evil smile. "And I can't wait."

"All right, where are those gifts?" Alex says after the girls come back from the barn.

She walks over to the table decorated in pink balloons and covered with presents. I find this part a little embarrassing, but with a wink from my sister—who had to go through the same thing only a few months ago—and Sully's reassuring hand rubbing the small of my back, I start unwrapping gifts.

Clothes, a high chair, a Diaper Genie, books, toys, an extra base for the car seat so both Sully and I have one in our trucks, a super cool leather diaper bag from Ama, and finally a pair of pink cowboy boots and a little pink Stetson from Thomas. That man brings me to tears.

I'm about to excuse myself to splash some cold water on my face when Sully slides a small box onto the table in front of me. Suddenly my heart is hammering in my throat. Ridiculous, since we're already married, but there's something weighted about the way he's looking at me.

"What's that?"

"You were unconscious, looked like hell, weighed no more than a bag of bones, and still there was something about you that both pulled me in and scared me shitless."

I open my mouth a few times, but never get a chance to react because Thomas jumps in for me.

"Son, I suggest you get to the good stuff 'cause it don't look like you're making headway."

"Gettin' to it, old man," Sully retorts.

"Wasting what little time I have left, young buck."

Sully shakes his head but doesn't bother firing back, giving Thomas the last word. Then he turns back to me, taking my hand and kissing the palm before he continues.

"I may have been in denial, but even while I was doing my best to avoid you, I realized the kind of impact you could have on my life. Resistance was futile." He grins at me and shakes his head. "Fuck, Honey, you're gonna have to stop this crying."

I give his shoulder a shove.

"Then quit being nice to me," I whine to everyone's hilarity.

My sister laughs hardest—traitor—but when I glare at her I notice mine aren't the only eyes not dry.

"Swear I'm almost done," he says, picking up the small box. My eyes are locked to the pretty diamond band he plucks out between thumb and forefinger. "It's a little too late for a proposal, but I'd like to think we would've made our way to this point regardless." He slides it on my finger. "This is a promise I make in front of our friends and family; you own me and I'll spend the rest of my life striving to deserve you."

It's not until later when we walk back to the cabin, I realize I've been so overwhelmed I never thanked him. I step around him and block his way, putting my hands on his chest as I tilt my head back.

"I love you, Sullivan Eckhart. You are the absolute best mistake I ever made."

Epilogue

PIPPA

"What the hell are you talking about?"

Lucy swings around, eyeing me suspiciously as I sink down on the bale of hay outside the stall door, barely able to catch my breath.

I've been keeping her company while she mucks out the barn. I drove here after Sully and Jonas left for Eureka, where they're supposed to be looking at some new horses. Actually, I was on my way to the Pit Stop but I figure word would get back to my husband I'd gone in to work and he would not hesitate to make his displeasure known.

I'm supposed to be taking it easy. I handed off the day-to-day running of the garage to Ira last week. We managed to obtain the sheriff's department's new fleet contract and we are no longer hurting for work. In fact, in the past few weeks we've hired a second mechanic and a part-time admin to replace Sloane.

I miss it though, miss having a purpose, which is what

landed me here. I was restless, which maybe should've been a sign.

"Like I said, I think my water just broke."

"The fuck it did," Lucy says, taking a few steps back like I'm suddenly contagious.

"Yup. I'm pretty sure...*holy shit*," I mutter a curse when another contraction hits me with the force of a tidal wave.

I'd woken up with some vague pain low in my back, but it was so different from the Braxton-Hicks I've become accustomed to, I never took it for labor. Hard to know what is what these days, everything feels tight and achy, but there's no mistaking these nor the clammy wetness sticking my yoga pants to my legs.

"What do I do?" Lucy mutters, uncommonly flustered.

I wait for the wave to ease before I answer.

"Help me up. I have to call Sully. I guess this is happening now."

He's going to be pissed I didn't mention the back pain this morning. He asked how I was feeling and offered to stay back and let someone else go with Jonas, but I assured him I was fine and he should go. This was only a few-hours' trip to Eureka. Luckily, it'll only take him an hour to get back to Libby. Plenty of time.

The thought has no sooner formed when another wave knocks the air from my lungs.

Maybe not so much time.

I'm only vaguely aware of Lucy talking to someone, I assume on the phone. I can't tell because my eyes are closed, the only thing I can focus on is getting to the other side of this contraction. Only to find myself at the start of another one.

I'm not sure how long I'm lost in this storm of contractions, but at some point, Lucy tries to pull me to my feet,

338

except my legs won't hold me. A groan is forced from deep inside my body when I sink back down on the bale of hay.

"Maybe I can get you in the wheelbarrow," Lucy suggests. "Get you to the truck."

If I weren't so overwhelmed, all of this would have struck me as funny. Like hell I'm getting in a wheelbarrow, even though the last place I'd imagined delivering this baby in was a barn.

"Sully?" I manage to ask her during a brief respite between contractions.

"On his way back. He'll be going straight to the hospital and told me to call for an ambulance. Unfortunately, there was a multiple car accident north of town so I don't know when they'll be able to get here. Which is why I called Bo to come help us get to Libby. He'll be here any minute."

I nod. *Good.* Bo is good. He'll know what to do, he was a surgical nurse and a medic.

What feels only moments later, but is likely a lot longer, I am lifted in a pair of strong arms. I groan, because it doesn't feel good. Pressure has been building between my legs and I simply want to be left alone.

"Hang in there, Pippa," Bo's deep voice rumbles above me. Then he follows it up with instructions for Lucy, "Call Sully. Don't think we'll make the hospital. Tell him to floor it here."

Oh shit.

~

Sully

"What the hell are you talking about?"

As if my anxiety wasn't ramped up enough after that first call.

I knew I shouldn't have gone. There'd been something about the way she looked this morning that raised a flag, but after her assurances she was perfectly fine, I went. *Dammit.*

"Don't bite my head off," Lucy snaps back. "I'm only the goddamn messenger here. Bo says there's no time. Baby's coming so get your ass over here."

We're coming up on Libby and I turn to Jonas, who insisted on driving.

"Go faster."

"Going as fast as I can without killing us or anyone else, my friend."

To Lucy I say, "Let me talk to Pippa."

"Don't think she's in any condition to chat now, Sully."

"Humor me," I grind out, getting increasingly close to losing my shit.

"Fine, I'm putting the phone to her ear."

I hear rustling first, followed by the sound of heavy breathing.

"Hey, Honey."

"Sully..."

It's no more than a whisper but enough to let me know she's listening.

"I won't be long, sweetheart. We're just driving through Libby now. I love you. Hang in there."

She starts saying something but it turns into a deep groan.

"Luce, grab me some towels and I need you to put a pot of water on to boil." I hear Bo say in the background. Then Lucy is back on the line.

"Gotta go. Hurry," she urges before ending the call.

Longest fucking ten minutes of my life and I'm already halfway out of the truck when Jonas rolls up to the farmhouse.

I can hear her before I'm through the door, her deep primordial groan its own force of nature as the hair on my arms stand on end.

She's on the couch, her back resting against Lucy, who is behind her, helping her pull her knees back. For a moment I'm frozen in the doorway as I watch Bo kneeling on the floor in front of her. A hand in the small of my back shoves me inside.

"I'll be out here," Jonas rumbles behind me.

"Just in the nick of time," Bo says when I approach, bending down to kiss Pippa's forehead, but I doubt she knows I'm here. "Get down here," he orders, making room for me.

Jesus, oh Jesus, I'm going to be sick. That's a head. Right there, between her legs.

Bo's large shovel hand is cradling it.

"Suck it back and slide your hand under mine, brother," he orders firmly. "You're gonna help her deliver this baby."

I let him direct me and only moments later, Carmi's slick little body slides right into my hands.

My eyes sting and Pippa is a little blurry when I look up at her. Gorgeous: a strand of hair stuck to her damp, flushed cheek, a sheen of tears in her eyes, and the most beautiful smile on her face.

"You blow me away," I tell her as I lift our daughter on her chest.

"Didn't do half bad yourself, brother." Bo grins when I look over at him. "Even though you were a little late to the game."

The next moment the door opens and two EMTs walk in.

～

"Started without me I see?"

The scent of cigar smoke lured me over to the porch of the main house.

I'd stepped outside to get some fresh air and process what was a day I won't forget as long as I live. It all still feels a bit unreal, and if not for the baby I left sleeping in her bassinet beside Pippa in our bed, I would think it was all a dream.

The medics checked Carmi and Pippa at the farmhouse, before loading them both in the back of the ambulance. I was able to hitch a ride and Jonas followed us to the hospital. Bo and Lucy showed up later, giving me a chance to make sure they both knew how grateful I was they'd been around to help. Bo brushed me off, but I had to promise Lucy a replacement of her choice for the old couch.

"We weren't sure if you'd show," Jonas says, offering me a cigar. "It's tradition," he encourages me.

I accept the cigar but I pass on the scotch, I want to have a clear head so I can watch over my girls as they sleep.

"Best moments of my life to this day," Thomas pipes up. "Hard to believe now, but Jonas was the prettiest baby I'd ever seen. Mary had a hard time delivering him—he was damn near twelve pounds—and needed to rest so I got to carry him around that first day. Bottle fed him, burped him, changed him." The old man shakes his head as he reminisces. "Was unheard of at the time and the nurses kept wanting to steal him, but I wouldn't let them."

I smile at Thomas. Only yesterday I might've cracked a

joke, maybe teased him a little, but today I completely understand what he's talking about. This experience has had the most immediate impact on my life, even more than falling in love with Pippa.

Which makes what the old man says next all the more terrifying.

"Of course, by the time he was fifteen and working his way through every girl in the county, I'd have gladly handed him back."

Jesus.

I'm going to have to tell Pippa we're homeschooling.

THE END

Keep reading for a sample of the next book in the series:

High Impact

High Impact

COMING DECEMBER 5, 2022

Manager for Hart's Horse Rescue, Lucy Lenoir, finally feels she has a handle on life after having worked hard to leave her old one behind. So hard, there are times she almost forgets what she escaped. Memories which suddenly come flooding back when she catches a glimpse of a familiar horseman in town.

What's worse, he's in the company of the unlikely cowboy she's only just beginning to trust.

High Mountain Tracker, Bo Rivera, tries hard never to repeat his mistakes. A huge one changed the course of his life and made him particularly cautious, especially around women. So much so, he almost passed up on the best thing to ever walk into his life; the compact, blonde ballbuster in need of a gentle hand.

However, the more he learns about her, the more he realizes a soft touch alone won't keep her demons at bay. Those will need a firmer hand...to keep the gun steady.

~

Lucy

Look at those poor babies.

They can't be more than a week old but won't last much longer if I don't intervene. Their mother isn't looking any better.

I got the call earlier this afternoon and wish I'd been able to wait for deputy to follow me, but potential cases of animal abuse aren't very high on their list of priorities. The woman who called insisted the situation was dire and she's right.

"Hey! You!"

Oh shit.

A rough-looking, burly guy is coming around the corner of the dilapidated farmhouse about fifty yards from where I'm crouched next to the pen. He has a shotgun in his hands and it's aimed at me.

"You've got two seconds to get off my property," he yells, looking pissed.

The kind of rescue work isn't without its occasional challenges and dangers. It isn't the first time I've looked down the barrel of a gun held by some disgruntled farmer or rancher when they didn't appreciate my rescue of their abused animal. Still, it never fails to scare the crap out of me.

I don't like guns. I've never been comfortable around them, although I will say I won't hesitate to grab the shotgun we have by front door at the rescue when facing anyone who threatens our safety or the safety of the animals.

Too much has happened here over the past two years since we moved here from Billings.

We, being Alexandra Hart and myself. I've worked for Alex for over eight years now. I joined her when Hart's Horse Rescue was on a much, much smaller property, just outside Billings, Montana. Then, two years ago, she purchased the property near Libby and I happily followed her here. Of course, since then, she's met and moved in with Jonas Harvey at the High Meadow Ranch, just down the road.

At the rescue we don't only provide a safe haven for the animals, but also rehabilitate injured and or traumatized animals. Alex is something of a horse-whisperer and has a special affinity with the animals I lack. Don't get me wrong, I'm good with the horses—all the animals—but they certainly don't respond to me the way they do to Alex.

Anyway, these days it's just me and the animals at the rescue, where I look after the day-to-day operations. Not a bad gig, not at all. I have a job I love; I have a roof over my head, and I live in what has to be one of the most beautiful places in the world.

Not that I've traveled much. I'm about the farthest away from where I grew up right now, although staring down a barrel is familiar.

According to Lester Franklin's neighbor, he leaves for work every day at the same time and doesn't return home until late afternoon. I'd parked on the neighbor's property and was supposed to wait for a sheriff's deputy to show, when I saw him drive off and came to investigate. I didn't want to miss the opportunity so I went in without backup. Hindsight being twenty-twenty, that had not been my smartest move.

Today being the exception to the rule, he obviously returned early and isn't happy finding me here.

I lift my hands up to show him I'm not armed.

"Your kid goats need to be supplement-fed or they're gonna die," I yell back.

"None 'a your goddamn business what I do with my goats. Yer trespassing!"

He racks his shotgun and repositions it against his shoulder, lining me up in his sights. The sound of it is a bit unnerving, but I know that's what he intends; to scare me off.

"Look, if you're happy to let them die, why not just give them to me to look after?"

The shotgun blast is loud as the dirt in front of me sprays up. I'm down on my face the next second. Guess he wasn't just trying to scare me. I vaguely notice a stinging burn on my shin but my eyes are locked on Lester Franklin, who appears to be cocking his gun, readying it for another shot.

"Hey! Lincoln County Sheriff's Department. Put that dam shotgun down!"

I turn my head slightly to where a fresh-faced sheriff's deputy is standing, legs spread wide and her hand on the butt of her service weapon. Sloane Eckhart. She's the niece of my friend Pippa's husband, Sully, and brand-new to the department. So new, I can still see the creases on her uniform shirt.

"I have every right to defend my property! She's an intruder."

"That's where you're wrong, Mr. Franklin," Sloane fires back right away. "She's at worst a trespasser and if you shoot at her you're the one who's gonna be going to jail! Now, I'm gonna ask you one more time; put the shotgun down!"

Despite my rather precarious position, I grin at the girl's attitude. Hell, she's probably early twenties, looks more like a child playing dress-up than an actual sheriff's deputy, but she's sure not easily intimidated.

"What are you gonna do about it?" Franklin challenges her.

Slow and easy, she slips her weapon in her hand, widens her stance, and aims straight at him.

"I outshot the entire department in an accuracy test two weeks ago," she says calmly. "Want to test me?"

For a few seconds, it looks like we might have a shootout when the guy pans his aim toward Sloane, but at the last moment lowers the barrel.

I get to my feet and notice my lower leg still burning. The front of my jeans on the left side is wet and stained dark. Wonderful.

"Were you hit?"

Sloane walks over, her eyes zoomed in on my leg.

"Just some rock spray hitting me, I think. Just a scratch."

I don't want her distracted, I want her to control Lester while I collect these poor goats.

"Right," she says, giving me a hard look before she walks to her cruiser, the driver's side door still open. "Gonna call some backup. Looks like we need Animal Control out here too."

While Sloane puts in her calls, I pull up the leg of my jeans as I try to keep an eye on Franklin, who continues to hover in front of his house. My leg is a mess. It's difficult to see anything but I look to be bleeding from more than one source.

"Yikes," Sloane comments, walking up. "Maybe I should've called the EMTs as well. That doesn't look good."

*****

Bo

"Can you hand me the wrench?"

I dig through the toolbox and give James the requested tool.

We're out behind the ranch house, in the shed where the pump running the automated watering system is housed. The system provides water to the horses out in the fields closest to the house. There are only a few of the back meadows left to cart water to, but if we can't get this damn pump to work we're gonna be back to hauling it everywhere.

It's a time suck and a general pain-in-the-ass job no one wants to do, which is why we're back here trying to fix it, even though neither James nor I are particularly talented in mechanics.

"Why don't I go ask Pippa to come have a look?" I suggest when James releases a few juicy curse words.

Pippa is married to Sully, another member of our team, and she's a mechanic. They live in one of the cabins on the other side of the ranch house and just welcomed a new baby two weeks ago, so she's home.

"I'm sure she's got other things going on," James mutters.

"Are you kidding? If it was up to her, she would've strapped that baby to her body and already be back at the garage working."

It's true, I walked in on an argument about exactly that topic between her and Sully just yesterday. Pippa is itching to do something with her hands, while her husband feels she needs more time to recover.

He's just worried about her, being protective, and she's afraid to lose autonomy over her life with the new baby and relatively new husband. The fear-driven dynamics are clear to see from an observer's point of view, but I guess even a couple of weeks of sleepless nights, constant feedings, and endless diapers can make you lose perspective.

Pippa is a rock and I have no doubt she'll jump at the opportunity to get out of the house for a bit. Sully's back to work and manning the breeding barn with Fletch today, but there are many at the ranch who'd drop anything to keep an eye on that baby girl for a few minutes.

Poor kid was born into one of the strangest families I've ever known, with a whole bunch of uncles, aunts, an honorary grandfather, and a handful of cousins, of which only one aunt and one cousin are actually blood related. The ranch, High Meadow, is at the center of this haphazard family. Its owner, Jonas Harvey, was my commander in the armed forces. Jonas, Sully, Fletch, James, and I were part of a special ops tracking unit. Like me, Jonas came from a ranching background. When he aged out of the unit, he bought this place, pulling us in one by one as we each aged out.

High Meadow is a stud farm, but in recent years we've been developing our own breeding program as well. In addition to that, the ranch is also the base for High Mountain Trackers. We may all have been too old for Uncle Sam, but we're still able to put our skills to good use with HMT, which is a search and rescue—or recovery—unit on horseback. We get a variety of calls, anywhere from missing children to hunting down criminals, and often work together with local and state law enforcement.

The ranch is our home, even though I've never lived here like most of my brothers. I have my reasons for choosing an old apartment in town over one of the staff cabins on the ranch, although there've been many times I wished things were different. That's life though, you've just got to roll with it. I'm sure there'll come a day I can wake up to beautiful views and sweet mountain air instead of the parking lot at the rear of the restaurant next door, but that day isn't here yet.

There's no one at the cabin, but I find Pippa and the baby in the kitchen at the main house. Carmi is being burped by Alex, Jonas's woman, with his old man, Thomas, looking on. I bend down and give that little downy blond head a kiss.

"How's my little girl?"

"She sure don't look like yours," Thomas pipes up, unable to resist a tease.

There were too many years I would've taken that the wrong way, especially coming from an old, white, Southern boy, but I know he would've said the same thing to Fletch, who is white but dark-haired. This isn't about the color of my skin but the blond hair the baby inherited from her father.

"Hush, after her daddy, Bo gets dibs. He delivered her," Pippa reminds the old man with a grin.

I did. Two weeks ago at the horse rescue.

It wasn't my first baby—before I joined the military I worked as a nurse in different departments—but it had been a few years, maybe even decades, since the last one. Luckily, the basic mechanics of childbirth stay the same and, other than the baby was coming fast, there were no complications.

"Hey, you got a minute?" I ask Pippa. "We can't get the motor on the water pump to—"

352

I don't even get a chance to finish my sentence before she jumps in.

"Yes. You don't mind, do you, Alex?"

Alex makes a face as she snuggles the baby closer. "Like you need to ask."

Pippa follows me outside where we almost bump into Sloane, Sully's niece, who moved here over the summer. She's a sheriff's deputy.

"I was looking for you" she addresses Pippa. "Where's the baby?"

"Kitchen." Pippa cocks her thumb over her shoulder. "I swear," she continues when Sloane rushes up the porch steps. "I've ceased to exist since she was born. Don't get me wrong, I love my baby beyond measure, but it's a little unsettling when I'm being treated like an extension of that little human instead of my own person."

I hear her. Fuck, I'm guilty of it too, heading straight for Cami without even a hello for her mother.

Throwing my arm around her shoulder, I give her a little squeeze.

"Good thing we have a busted water pump to remind us you're not just good at making babies," I tease.

"Haha," she grumbles, elbowing me in the gut.

"Oh, Bo?" I hear Sloane call.

"Yeah, what up?" I ask, turning around.

She's hanging over the porch railing.

"You may wanna swing by Lucy's, when you have a minute."

As always when I hear her name, my attention is piqued. "Why?"

"She had a run-in with a rancher north of town. She didn't want me calling EMTs, but I think she got hit with some buckshot."

I don't realize I'm already moving until I hear Pippa yell out behind me.

"Go!"

~

Also by Freya Barker

High Mountain Trackers:

HIGH MEADOW

HIGH STAKES

HIGH GROUND

HIGH IMPACT (*Dec 2022*)

Arrow's Edge MC Series:

EDGE OF REASON

EDGE OF DARKNESS

EDGE OF TOMORROW

EDGE OF FEAR

EDGE OF REALITY

PASS Series:

HIT & RUN

LIFE & LIMB

LOCK & LOAD

LOST & FOUND

On Call Series:

BURNING FOR AUTUMN

COVERING OLLIE

TRACKING TAHLULA

ABSOLVING BLUE

REVEALING ANNIE

DISSECTING MEREDITH

WATCHING TRIN

Rock Point Series:

KEEPING 6

CABIN 12

HWY 550

10-CODE

Northern Lights Collection:

A CHANGE OF TIDE

A CHANGE OF VIEW

A CHANGE OF PACE

SnapShot Series:

SHUTTER SPEED

FREEZE FRAME

IDEAL IMAGE

Portland, ME, Series:

FROM DUST

CRUEL WATER

THROUGH FIRE

STILL AIR

LuLLaY (a Christmas novella)

About the Author

USA Today bestselling author Freya Barker loves writing about ordinary people with extraordinary stories.

Driven to make her books about 'real' people; she creates characters who are perhaps less than perfect, each struggling to find their own slice of happy, but just as deserving of romance, thrills and chills in their lives.

Recipient of the ReadFREE.ly 2019 Best Book We've Read All Year Award for "Covering Ollie, the 2015 RomCon "Reader's Choice" Award for Best First Book, "Slim To None", Finalist for the 2017 Kindle Book Award with "From Dust", and Finalist for the 2020 Kindle Book Award with "When Hope Ends", Freya spins story after story with an endless supply of bruised and dented characters, vying for attention!

www.freyabarker.com

9 781988 733760